THE
KELP
ISLAND

HE FOREST →

AG

HECK

the
SEAL
ISLANDS

CHRONICLES OF ANCIENT DARKNESS

SPIRIT WALKER

PRAISE FOR
WOLF BROTHER
the first book in the
CHRONICLES OF ANCIENT DARKNESS
SERIES

"Set 6,000 years ago, this fast-paced adventure delves into a world of spirits and mysticism not often seen in children's literature."
—*School Library Journal*

"Torak's coming-of-age tale will keep the pages turning." —*Publishers Weekly*

"The story, told from both Torak's and Wolf's points of view, glides on lines of smooth prose, with concrete, multisensory descriptions establishing the reality of the setting and the complexity of the social networks Torak must negotiate in order to gain the freedom and the help he needs to finish his quest."
—*The Bulletin of the Center for Children's Books*

"*Wolf Brother* is the kind of story you dream of reading and all too rarely find. The descriptions of the ancient world are wonderful. The vivid prose leaps off the page." —*The Times of London*

"Like other great children's books, *Wolf Brother* conjures up an utterly believable yet original world where the story grips you to the very last page."   —Sir Ian McKellen

"The stark, primitive setting provides an innovative contrast to most fantasies. This fast-moving story with engaging characters will appeal."
—*VOYA*

"This invigorating book will thrill a young reader's inner wild child, while the kid's rational self will likely wonder, Just what did Torak's father do to so anger those shamans? And what is the mystery in Torak's past that Renn's father knows of but will not tell? The story's not over! Next book in the series, anyone?"
—*Time Out New York Kids*

ALSO IN THE
Chronicles of Ancient Darkness series

WOLF BROTHER

CHRONICLES OF ANCIENT DARKNESS

SPIRIT WALKER

MICHELLE PAVER

BOOK TWO

KATHERINE TEGEN BOOKS
An Imprint of HarperCollins*Publishers*

Chronicles of Ancient Darkness #2: Spirit Walker
Copyright © 2006 by Michelle Paver
www.harperchildrens.com

Library of Congress Cataloging-in-Publication Data
Paver, Michelle.
    Spirit Walker / Michelle Paver.— 1st ed.
        p.   cm. (The chronicles of ancient darkness ; bk. 2)
    Summary: When a deadly illness begins to afflict the clans, twelve-year-
old Torak, with help from Renn and Wolf, embarks on a journey to find a
cure.
    ISBN-10: 0-06-072828-0 (trade bdg.)
    ISBN-13: 978-0-06-072828-1 (trade bdg.)
    ISBN-10: 0-06-072829-9 (lib. bdg.)
    ISBN-13: 978-0-06-072829-8 (lib. bdg.)
    [1. Voyages and travels—Fiction. 2. Wolves—Fiction. 3. Demoniac pos-
session—Fiction. 4. Prehistoric peoples—Fiction.] I. Title.
PZ7.P2853Spi 2006
[Fic]—dc22   2005014653
                                                                         CIP
                                                                          AC
Book design by Amy Ryan
1 2 3 4 5 6 7 8 9 10
❖
First American Edition

CHRONICLES OF ANCIENT DARKNESS

SPIRIT WALKER

ONE

The auroch appeared quite suddenly from the trees on the other side of the stream.

One moment Torak was gazing at sun-dappled willows—the next, there she was. She stood taller than the tallest man, and her great curving horns could have skewered a bear. If she charged, he was in trouble.

By bad luck, he was upwind of her. He held his breath as he watched her twitch her blunt black muzzle to taste his scent. She snorted. Pawed the earth with one massive hoof.

Then he saw the calf peering from the bracken, and his belly turned over. Aurochs are gentle creatures—

except when they have calves.

Without a sound, Torak drew back into the shade. If he didn't startle her, maybe she wouldn't charge.

Again the auroch snorted, and raked the ferns with her horns. At last she seemed to decide that he wasn't hunting her after all, and slumped down in the mud to have a wallow.

Torak blew out a long breath.

The calf wobbled toward its mother, slipped, bleated, and fell over. The cow auroch raised her head and nosed it to its feet, then lay back to enjoy herself.

Crouching behind a juniper bush, Torak wondered what to do. Fin-Kedinn, the Clan Leader, had sent him to retrieve a bundle of willow bark that had been soaking in the stream; he didn't want to return to camp without it. Neither did he want to get trampled by an auroch.

He decided to wait for her to leave.

It was a hot day at the beginning of the Moon of No Dark, and the Forest was drowsy with sun. The trees echoed with birdsong; a warm southeasterly breeze carried the sweetness of lime blossom. After a while, Torak's heartbeats slowed. He heard a clutch of young greenfinches squealing for food in a hazel thicket. He watched a viper basking on a rock. He tried to fix his thoughts on that, but as so often happened, they drifted to Wolf.

Wolf would be nearly full-grown by now, but he'd

been a cub when Torak had known him: falling over his paws, and pestering Torak for lingonberries. . . .

Don't think about Wolf, Torak told himself fiercely. He's gone. He's never coming back, never. Think about the auroch, or the viper, or—

That was when he saw the hunter.

He was on this side of the water, twenty paces downstream, but downwind of the auroch. The shade was too deep to make out his face, but Torak saw that like him, he wore a sleeveless buckskin jerkin and knee-length leggings, with light rawhide boots. Unlike Torak, he wore a boar tusk on a thong around his neck. Boar Clan.

Ordinarily, Torak would have been reassured. The Boars were fairly friendly with the Raven Clan, with whom he'd been living for the past six moons. But there was something very wrong about this hunter. He moved with an awkward, lurching gait, his head lolling from side to side. *And he was stalking the auroch.* Two slate throwing axes were stuck in his belt—and as Torak watched in disbelief, he pulled one out and hefted it in his hand.

Was he insane? No man hunts an auroch on his own. An auroch is the biggest, strongest prey in the Forest. To attack one on your own is asking to be killed.

The auroch, happily unaware, grunted and rubbed deeper into the mud, relishing the relief from the troublesome midges. Her calf nosed a clump of willowherb, waiting for her to finish.

Torak rose to his feet and warned the hunter with urgent slicing motions of his palm: *Danger! Go back!*

The hunter didn't see him. Flexing his brawny arm, he took aim—and hurled the axe.

It whistled through the air and thudded into the ground a hand's breadth from the calf.

The calf fled. Its mother gave an outraged bellow and lumbered to her feet, casting about for the attacker. But the hunter was still downwind; she didn't catch his scent.

Incredibly, he was reaching for his second axe.

"*No!*" Torak whispered hoarsely. "You'll only hurt her and get us both killed!"

The hunter wrenched the axe from his belt.

Torak thought swiftly. If the axe found its mark, the auroch would be unstoppable. But if she was startled instead of wounded, maybe she would merely make a mock charge, and flee with her calf. He had to get her out of range of that axe, fast.

Taking a deep breath, he jumped up and down, waving his arms and yelling, "Over here! Over here!"

It worked—in a way. The auroch gave a furious bellow and charged at Torak—and the axe hit the mud where she'd stood a heartbeat before. As she splashed toward Torak, he threw himself behind an oak tree.

No time to climb it—she was almost upon him. He

heard her grunt as she heaved herself up the bank—he felt her heat on the other side of the tree trunk. . . .

At the last moment she swerved, flicking up her tail and blundering off into the Forest, her calf galloping after her.

The silence when she'd gone was deafening.

Sweat poured down Torak's face as he leaned against the oak.

The hunter stood with his head down, rocking from side to side.

"What were you *doing*?" panted Torak. "We could've been killed!"

The hunter did not reply. Lurching across the stream, he retrieved his axes and stuck them in his belt, then shambled back again. Torak still couldn't see his face, but he took in the hunter's muscled limbs and jagged slate knife. If it came to a fight, he'd lose. He was just a boy, not even thirteen summers old.

Suddenly the hunter stumbled against a beech tree and began to retch.

Torak forgot his alarm and ran to help him.

The hunter was on hands and knees, spewing up yellow slime. His back arched—he gave a convulsive heave—and he spat out something slippery and dark, the size of a child's fist. It looked . . . it looked like *hair*.

A gust of wind stirred the branches, and in a shaft of sunlight Torak saw him clearly for the first time.

The sick man had yanked handfuls of hair from his scalp and beard, leaving patches of raw, oozing flesh. His face was crusted with thick honey-colored scabs like birch canker. Slime bubbled in his throat as he spat out the last of the hair—then sat back on his heels, and began scratching a rash of blisters on his forearm.

Torak edged backward, his hand moving to his clan-creature skin: the strip of wolf fur sewn to his jerkin. What *was* this?

Renn would know. "Fevers," she'd once told him, "are most common around Midsummer, because that's when the worms of sickness have longest to work: creeping out of the swamps during the white nights when the sun never sleeps." But if this was a fever, it was unlike any Torak had ever seen.

He wondered what he could do. All he had was some coltsfoot in his medicine pouch. "Let me help you," he said shakily. "I have some . . . Ah no, stop! You're hurting yourself!"

The man was still scratching, baring his teeth as people do when the itching is so unbearable that they'd rather turn it into outright pain. All at once, he dug in his fingernails and savaged the blisters, leaving a swathe of bloody flesh.

"Don't!" cried Torak.

With a snarl, the man sprang at him, pinning him down.

Torak stared up into a mass of crusted sores; into two dull eyes filmed with pus. "Don't—hurt me!" he gasped. "My name—is Torak! I'm—Wolf Clan, I—"

The man leaned closer. *"It—is—coming,"* he hissed in a blast of putrid breath.

Torak tried to swallow. "What—is?"

The cankered face twisted in terror. "Can't you see?" he whispered, flecking Torak with yellow spit. *"It is coming!* It will take us all!"

He staggered to his feet, swaying and squinting at the sun. Then he crashed through the trees as if all the demons of the Otherworld were after him.

Torak raised himself on one elbow, breathing hard.

The birds had fallen silent.

The Forest looked on, appalled.

Slowly, Torak stood up. He felt the wind veering around to the east, turning chill. A shiver ran through the trees. They began to murmur to one another. Torak wished he knew what they were saying. But he knew what they were feeling, because he felt it too: something rising and blowing through the Forest.

It is coming.

Sickness.

Torak ran to fetch his quiver and bow. No time to retrieve the willow bark. He had to get back to camp, and warn the Ravens.

TWO

"Where's Fin-Kedinn?" cried Torak when he reached the Raven camp.

"In the next valley," said a man gutting salmon, "gathering dogwood for arrowshafts."

"What about Saeunn? Where's the Mage?"

"Casting the bones," said a girl threading fish heads on sinew. "She's on the Rock; you'd better wait till she comes down."

Torak ground his teeth in frustration. There was the Raven Mage perched high on the Guardian Rock: a small, birdlike figure scowling at the bones, while beside her the clan guardian folded its stiff black wings and uttered a harsh *cark!*

Who else could he tell?

Renn was out hunting. Oslak, whose shelter he shared, was nowhere in sight. By the smoking-racks he spotted Sialot and Poi, the Raven boys closest to him in age—but they were the last ones he'd approach; they didn't like him because he was an outsider. Everyone else was too busy getting in the salmon to listen to some wild tale about a sick man in the Forest. And as Torak looked about, he almost began to doubt it himself. Everything seemed so normal.

The Ravens had built their camp where the Widewater crashes out of a shadowy gorge and thunders past the Rock, then over the rapids. It was up these rapids that the salmon fought their way each summer on their mysterious journey from the Sea to the Mountains. Always they were driven back by the fury of the river, and always they tried again, hurtling through the foaming chaos in twisting, shining leaps—until they died of exhaustion, or reached the calmer waters beyond the gorge, or were speared by the Ravens.

To catch them, the clan sank poles in the riverbed, and spanned the Widewater with a wicker walkway just strong enough to support a few fishermen with spears. It was skilled work, and anyone falling in risked crippling injury or worse, for the river was relentless, the rocks jutting from the rapids as sharp as broken teeth. But the prize was great.

The Ravens' shelters stood empty; everybody was at the smoking-racks, getting in the day's haul before it spoiled. Men, women and children scraped off scales and gutted fish, while others sliced strips of orange flesh from the bones, leaving them joined at the tail for easy hanging on the racks. Sialot and Poi pounded juniper berries, which would be mixed with the dried, shredded meat to keep it sweet—or mask its taste if it was not.

Nothing was wasted. The skins would be cured and fashioned into waterproof tinder pouches; the eyes and bones would make glue; the livers and roe would provide a delicacy at nightmeal, and an offering for the guardian and the spirits of the salmon.

Elsewhere in the Forest, other clans camped by other rivers to take part in the bounty. Boar Clan, Willow, Otter, Viper. And where the people did not camp, other hunters came: bears, lynx, eagles, wolves. All celebrating the running of the salmon, which gave them new strength after the rigors of winter.

This was how it had always been since the Beginning. Surely, thought Torak, one sick man couldn't change all that.

Then he remembered the cankered face and the pus-filmed eyes.

At that moment, Oslak emerged from their shelter, and Torak's heart leaped. Oslak would know what to do.

But to his astonishment, Oslak hardly listened as he blurted out his story, seeming more engrossed in retying the binding on his fishing spear. "You say the man was Boar Clan," he said, frowning and scratching the back of his hand. "Well then, his Mage will take care of him. Here." He tossed Torak the spear. "Get down to the stepping-stones and let me see you take a salmon."

Torak was bewildered. "But Oslak—"

"Go on, go!" snapped Oslak.

Torak gave a start. It was unlike Oslak to get cross. In fact, it never happened. He was a huge, gentle man with a tangled beard and a slightly alarming face, having lost one ear and a chunk of cheek in a misunderstanding with a wolverine. It was just like him not to blame the wolverine. "My fault," he'd say if anyone asked. "I gave her a fright."

That was Oslak. He and his mate Vedna had been the first to offer Torak a place in their shelter when he came to live with the Ravens, and they'd always been kind to him. But Oslak was also the strongest man in the clan, so Torak made no further protest, and took the spear.

As he did, he saw something that stopped him dead.

The back of Oslak's hand was covered in blisters.

"What's—that on your hand?" he said.

"Midge bites," said Oslak, scratching harder. "Worst I've ever had. Kept me awake all night."

"They don't look like midge bites," said Torak. "Do they—hurt?"

Oslak was still scratching. "Strange. Feels as if my name-soul's leaking out. But that can't be, can it?" He peered at Torak as if the light hurt, and his face was fearful and childlike.

Torak swallowed. "I don't think you can lose your name-soul through a cut; only through your mouth, if you're dreaming, or—sick." He paused. "Are you sick?"

"Sick? Why would I be sick?" A shiver shook Oslak's whole body. "But I can't hold on to my souls."

Torak's hand tightened on the spear. "I'll fetch Saeunn."

Oslak scowled. "I don't need Saeunn! Now go!" Suddenly he wasn't Oslak anymore. He was a big man looming over Torak, clenching his fists.

Then he seemed to come to himself. "Just—leave me be, eh? Go on. Thull's waiting."

"All right, Oslak," said Torak as levelly as he could.

He was halfway to the river's edge when he turned and looked back.

Oslak was still scratching. "Leaking *out*," he muttered. Then he went inside the shelter—and Torak saw the raw patch behind his remaining ear where the hair had been yanked out: the thick honey-colored scab, like birch canker.

Torak felt a coldness settle inside him.

He raced down to the stepping-stones, where Oslak's younger brother squatted to clean his knife. "Thull!" he cried. "I think Oslak's sick!"

His tale came out in a breathless jumble, and Thull wasn't impressed. "Torak, those are midge bites. It happens every summer, they drive him mad."

"It isn't midges," said Torak.

"Well, he's fine now," said Thull, pointing at the walkway.

Sure enough, there was Oslak, crouching with a spear—and on the end of it, a wriggling salmon.

Biting his lip, Torak glanced about. It all seemed so *normal*. Children played with glittering handfuls of fish scales. Reckless young ravens teased the dogs by pecking their tails. Thull's son Dari, five summers old, splashed in the shallows with the pine-cone auroch that Oslak had made for him.

Filled with misgiving, Torak clutched his spear and waded in.

The stepping-stones were four boulders between

the walkway and the rapids where beginners learned to keep their balance. Thull pointed to the first stone, but Torak made his way precariously to the fourth, placing himself midriver, and downstream from Oslak. He didn't know what he expected; only that he had to keep watch.

"Keep your eyes on the salmon," shouted Thull from the bank, "not on the water!"

Torak found that impossible. The rocks were slippery with lichen, and around him the green water boiled, with now and then a silver flash of salmon. The fishing spear was long and heavy, making it hard to balance. It had two barbed antler prongs for gripping and holding the fish—*if* Torak caught any, which he hadn't in all previous attempts. When he'd lived with his father, he'd only fished with a hook and line. With a spear, as Sialot never tired of remarking, he was as clumsy as a child of seven summers.

He forced himself to concentrate. Stabbed with his spear. Missed. Nearly toppled in.

"Let them get *past* you before taking aim!" yelled Thull. "Catch them on their way down, when they're tired!"

Torak tried again. Again he missed.

From the smoking-racks came a hoot of laughter. Torak's face flamed. Sialot was enjoying this.

"Better!" called Thull with more kindness than truth. "Keep at it! I'll come back later." He went off to feed the fires, leaving Dari in the shallows, crooning to his auroch.

For a while Torak forgot everything as he strove to catch a fish without either dropping the spear or falling in. Soon he was soaked in spray. And the river was *angry*. Every so often it hurled a huge wave against his rock.

Suddenly he heard a shout from the walkway. He jerked up his head—then breathed out in relief.

Oslak had speared another salmon. With one blow he killed it, then knelt to pull it off the spear.

He's all right, Torak told himself.

As he watched, Oslak scratched his hand. Then he reached behind his ear and clawed at the scab.

The salmon slithered off the walkway. Oslak bared his teeth, wrenched off the scab—and ate it.

Torak recoiled and nearly fell in.

The sun went behind a cloud. The water turned black. The discarded salmon slid past, glaring at him with a dull dead eye.

He shot a glance at the shallows.

Dari was gone.

Another cry from upriver.

He turned.

Dari was on the walkway, tottering toward his uncle—who wasn't warning him back, but *beckoning*.

"Come to me, Dari!" he shouted, his face distorted by a horrible eagerness. "Come to me! I won't let them take our souls!"

THREE

On the banks, none of the Ravens had seen what was happening. Torak had to do something.

As he stood on the stepping-stone gripping his spear, he saw two people emerge from different parts of the Forest.

From the east came Renn, her beloved bow in one hand, a brace of wood pigeons in the other.

From downriver came Fin-Kedinn, limping slightly and leaning on his staff, with a bundle of dogwood sticks over one shoulder.

In a heartbeat both grasped what was happening, and quietly set down their loads.

To stop Oslak noticing them, Torak called out to him. "Oslak, what's wrong? Tell me. Maybe I can help."

"Nobody can *help*!" shouted Oslak. "My souls are leaking out! Being *eaten*!"

Now people turned to stare. Dari's mother leaped forward with a cry. Thull held her back. Oslak's mate Vedna jammed her knuckles in her mouth. On the Rock, Saeunn stood motionless.

Renn had reached the walkway—but despite his limp, Fin-Kedinn was there before her. Silently he handed her his staff.

"Who's eating your souls?" Torak called to Oslak.

"The *fish*!" Yellow froth flew from Oslak's lips. "*Teeth!* Sharp teeth!" He pointed to where the thrashing salmon endlessly broke and remade his name-soul.

Torak felt a twinge of fear. That happened to everyone's name-soul if you leaned over the river, and it didn't do any harm—*unless* you were sick, when it could make you so dizzy that you fell in.

"Soon it will be gone," moaned Oslak, "and I will be nothing but a ghost! Come, Dari! The river wants us!"

The child hesitated—then moved toward him, clutching the pine-cone auroch to his chest.

Torak risked a glance at Fin-Kedinn.

The Raven Leader's face was still as carved sandstone. Putting a forefinger to his lips, he caught Torak's eye. *You're between them and the rapids. Catch them.*

Torak nodded, bracing himself on the rock. His feet were numb with cold. His arms were beginning to shake.

At last Dari reached Oslak, who tossed away his spear and snatched him up. The wicker sagged dangerously.

"Oslak," called Fin-Kedinn. His voice was low, but somehow he made himself heard above the rapids. "Come back to the bank."

"Get *away*!" screamed Oslak.

Torak saw to his horror that Oslak had tied a woven-bark rope to the poles supporting the end of the walkway: one hard pull, and the whole structure would go crashing down, taking him and Dari with it.

Torak couldn't bear it. "Oslak, this is me, Torak! Don't—"

Oslak turned on him. "Who are you to tell me what to do? You're not one of us! You're a cuckoo! Eating our food, taking our shelter! I've heard you sneaking into the Forest to howl for your wolf! We've all heard you! Why don't you give up? He's never coming back!"

Renn flinched in sympathy, but Torak didn't move. He'd seen what Oslak had not: Fin-Kedinn limping onto the walkway.

At that moment Oslak swayed, and the wicker rocked.

Dari's mouth went square, and he began to howl.

Fin-Kedinn stood firm. "Oslak," he called.

Oslak lurched backward. "Stay *away!*"

Fin-Kedinn raised his hands to reassure him that he wasn't coming any closer. Then, as the clan watched in taut silence, he sat cross-legged on the wicker. He was six paces from the bank, and if Oslak pulled the rope, the walkway would collapse; but he looked as calm as if he were sitting by the fire. "Oslak," he said, "the clan chose me for Leader to keep it safe. You know that."

Oslak licked his lips.

"And I will," said Fin-Kedinn. "I will keep you safe. But put Dari down. Let him come to me. Let me take him to his mother."

Oslak's face went slack.

"Put him down," repeated Fin-Kedinn. "It's time for his nightmeal. . . ."

The power of his voice began to work. Slowly Oslak unwound the boy's arms from his neck and lowered him onto the wicker.

Dari gazed up at him as if seeking permission, then turned and crawled toward Fin-Kedinn.

Fin-Kedinn shifted onto one knee and reached for him.

The pine-cone auroch slipped from Dari's fist and into the water. With a squeal Dari grabbed for it. Fin-Kedinn caught him by the jerkin and swept him into his arms.

On the bank, the Ravens breathed out.

Torak's knees sagged. He watched the Raven Leader rise and edge sideways toward the bank. When he drew near, Thull grabbed Dari and held him tight.

On the walkway, Oslak stood like a stunned auroch. The rope slipped from his hand as he gazed at the churning water. Silently Fin-Kedinn went back for him and took him by the shoulders, speaking in words no one else could hear.

Oslak's body slumped, and he let Fin-Kedinn lead him to the bank—where men seized him and forced him down. He seemed puzzled, as if unsure how he'd got there.

Torak found his way to the shallows, dropped his spear in the sand, and began to shake.

"Are you all right?" said Renn. Her dark-red hair was wet with spray, her face so pale that her clan-tattoos were three dark stripes on her cheeks.

He nodded. But he knew she wasn't fooled.

Farther up the bank, Fin-Kedinn was speaking to Saeunn, who'd climbed down from the Rock. "What's wrong with him?" he said as the clan gathered around them.

The Raven Mage shook her head. "His souls are fighting within him."

"So it's some kind of madness," said Fin-Kedinn.

"Maybe," replied Saeunn. "But not a kind I've ever seen."

"I have," said Torak. Quickly he told them about the Boar Clan hunter.

As the Mage listened, her face grew grim. She was the oldest in the clan by many winters. Age had blasted her, polishing her scalp to the color of old bone, sharpening her features to something more raven than woman. "I saw it in the bones," she rasped. "A message. 'It is coming.'"

"There's something else," said Renn. "When I was hunting, I met a party of Willow Clan. One of them was sick. Sores. Madness. Terrible fear." Her eyes were dark as peat pools as she turned to Saeunn. "The Willow Clan Mage sends you word. He too has been reading the bones, and for three days they've told him one thing, over and over. 'It is coming.'"

People made the sign of the hand to ward off evil. Others touched their clan-creature skins: the strips of glossy black feathers sewn to their jerkins.

Etan, an eager young hunter, stepped forward, his face perplexed. "I left Bera on the hill, checking the deadfalls. She had blisters on her hands. Like Oslak's. I did wrong to leave her, didn't I?"

Fin-Kedinn shook his head. His face was unreadable as he stroked his dark-red beard, but Torak sensed that his thoughts were racing.

Swiftly the Raven Leader gave orders. "Thull, Etan. Get some men and build a shelter in the lime wood, out of sight of camp. Take Oslak there and keep him under guard. Vedna, you're not to go near him. I'm sorry, but there's no other way." He turned to Saeunn, and his blue eyes blazed. "Middle-night. A healing rite. Find out what's causing this."

FOUR

The Mage's apprentice took an auroch-horn ladle and scooped hot ash from the fire. She poured it, still smoking, into her naked palm.

Torak gasped.

The apprentice didn't even wince.

At her feet, Oslak clawed the dust, but the bindings held fast. He was strapped to a horse-hide litter, awaiting the final charm. Bera had already undergone it, and was back in the sickness shelter: screaming, sicker than ever.

The Raven Mage and her apprentice had tried everything. The Mage had daubed the sick ones' tongues with earthblood to draw out the madness. She had tied fishhooks to her fingers and gone into a trance to snare their drifting souls. She'd shrouded them in juniper smoke to chase away the worms of sickness. Nothing had worked.

Now a hush fell on the Ravens as she prepared for this final charm. Firelight flickered on their anxious faces.

It was a hot, clear night, with a gibbous moon riding high above the Forest. The wind had dropped, but the air was full of noises. The creak of the smoking-racks. The caws of the ravens in the gorge. The roar of the rapids.

The Mage stepped toward the litter, her bony arms reaching to the moon. In one hand she gripped her amulet; in the other, a red flint arrow.

Torak darted a glance at the Mage's apprentice, but her face was a blank mask of river clay. She didn't look like Renn anymore.

"Fire to cleanse the name-soul," chanted Saeunn, circling the litter.

Renn squatted beside Oslak and trickled hot ash onto his naked feet. He moaned, and bit his lips till they bled.

"Fire to cleanse the clan-soul. . . ."

Renn poured ash over his heart.

"Fire to cleanse the world-soul. . . ."

Renn smeared ash on his forehead.

"Burn, sickness, burn. . . ."

Oslak screamed with fury, and spattered the Mage with bloody foam.

A ripple of dismay ran through the clan. The charm wasn't working.

Torak held his breath. Behind him the Forest stilled. Even the alders had ceased their fluttering to await the outcome.

He watched Saeunn touch the arrow to Oslak's chest, tracing a spiral. *"Come, sickness,"* she croaked. *"Out of the marrow—into the bone. Out of the bone—into the flesh. . . ."*

Suddenly Torak clutched his belly in pain. As the Mage chanted the words, something sharp had twisted inside him.

Slowly she drew the spiral over Oslak's heart. *"Out of the flesh—into the skin. Out of the skin—into the arrow. . . ."*

Again that pain, as if her words were tugging at his insides . . . Is this the sickness? he thought. Is this how it starts?

A firm hand gripped his shoulder. Fin-Kedinn stood beside him, watching the Mage.

"Out of the arrow—" cried Saeunn, rising to her feet, *"and into the fire!"* She plunged the arrow into the embers.

Green flames shot skyward.

Oslak screamed.

The Ravens hissed.

Saeunn's arms dropped to her sides.

The spell had failed.

Torak clutched his belly and fought waves of blackness.

Suddenly, a dark shape flew into the firelight. It was the clan guardian, heading straight for him. He tried to duck, but Fin-Kedinn held him steady. Just in time, the raven swerved. It was angry: its clan was under attack. Torak had no idea why it had flown at him.

He tried to catch Renn's eye, but she was kneeling by Oslak, peering at the marks he'd clawed in the dust.

Twisting out of Fin-Kedinn's grip, Torak ran— between the watchers, out of the camp, and into the Forest.

He reached a moonlit glade and collapsed against an ash tree. The giddiness came again. He doubled up and began to retch.

An owl hooted.

Torak raised his head and stared at the cold stars glinting through the black leaves of the ash tree. He slid to the ground with his head in his hands.

The dizziness had subsided, but he was still shaking. He felt frightened and alone. He couldn't even tell Renn about this. She was his friend, but she was also the Mage's apprentice. She mustn't know. No one must know. If he was sick, he'd rather die alone in the Forest than strapped to a litter.

Then a terrible suspicion took hold of him. *They are eating my souls,* Oslak had said. Was that the rambling of a madman, or did it hide a kernel of truth?

Shutting his eyes, he tried to lose himself in the night sounds. The warble of a blackbird. The wheezy cries of the fledgling robins in the undergrowth.

All his life, Torak had roamed the hills and valleys with his father, keeping separate from the clans. The creatures of the Forest had been his companions. He hadn't missed people. It was hard, living with the Ravens. So many faces. So little time alone. He didn't belong. Their ways were too different from how he'd lived with Fa.

And he missed Wolf so much.

It had been after Fa was killed that he'd found the cub. For two moons, they'd hunted together in the Forest, and faced terrible dangers. At times Wolf had been like any other cub, getting in the way, and poking his muzzle into everything. At others he was the guide, with a mysterious certainty in his amber eyes. But always he was a pack-brother. Being without him hurt.

Often, Torak had thought about going in search of him, but deep down he knew he'd never find the Mountain again. As Renn had said with her usual bluntness, "Last winter was different. But now? No, Torak, I don't think so."

"I know that," he'd replied, "but if I keep howling, maybe Wolf will find me."

In six moons, Wolf had not found him. Torak had tried telling himself that that was a *good* sign: it meant Wolf must be happy with his new pack. But somehow, that hurt most of all. Had Wolf forgotten him?

Faint and far away, voices floated on the wind.

Torak sat up.

It was a wolf pack. Howling to celebrate a kill.

Torak forgot his dizziness—forgot everything—as the wolf song flowed over him like a river.

He made out the deep, strong voices of the lead wolves; the lighter howls of the rest of the pack, weaving respectfully around them; the cubs' wobbly yowls as they tried to join in. But the one voice that he longed to hear was not among them.

He had known that it would not be. Wolf—*his* Wolf—ran with a pack far to the north. The wolves he heard now were in the east, in the hills bordering the Deep Forest.

But he still had to try. Shutting his eyes, he cupped his hands to his mouth and howled a greeting.

Instantly the wolves' voices tightened.

Where do you hunt, lone wolf? howled the lead female. Sharp. Commanding.

Many lopes from you, Torak replied. *Tell me. Is there—sickness in your range?*

He wasn't certain he'd got that right, and sure enough, the wolves didn't seem to understand.

Our range is a good range! they howled, offended. *The best range in the Forest!*

He hadn't really expected them to grasp his meaning. His knowledge of wolf talk was not precise, his ability to express himself even less so. And yet, he thought with a pang, Wolf would have understood.

Abruptly the wolf song ceased.

Torak opened his eyes. He was back in the moonlit glade among the dark ferns and the ghostly meadowsweet. He felt as if he'd woken from a dream.

A shallow thrumming of wingbeats, and he turned to see a cuckoo on a snag, staring at him with a yellow-ringed eye.

He remembered Oslak's sneer. *You're not one of us! You're a cuckoo!* The rambling of a madman, but with a kernel of truth. The cuckoo gave a squawk and flew off. Something had startled it.

Noiselessly Torak rose to his feet. His hand crept to his knife.

In the bright moonlight, the glade seemed empty.

A short way to the east, a stream flowed into the Widewater. Quietly he searched the bank for tracks. He found none; nor any hairs caught on twigs, or subtly displaced branches.

But someone was here. He could feel it.

He raised his head and stared into the beech tree above him.

A creature glared down at him. Small. Malevolent. Hair like dead grass, and a face of leaves.

He saw it for an instant. Then a gust of wind stirred the branches and it was gone.

That was how Renn found him: standing rigid with his knife in his hand, staring upward.

"What's wrong?" she said. "Why did you run away? Are you—did you eat something bad?" She didn't want to voice her fear that he might have the sickness.

"I'm all right," he replied—which clearly wasn't true. His hand shook as he sheathed his knife.

"Your lips have gone gray," said Renn.

"I'm all right," he said again.

As he sat beneath the beech tree, she glanced at his hands, but couldn't see any blisters. She tried not to show her relief. "Maybe a bad mushroom?" she suggested.

"The Hidden People," he cut in. "What do they look like?"

"What? But you know as well as I do. They look like

us, except when they turn their backs, they're rotten—"

"Their faces, what about their faces?"

"I told you, like us! Why? What's this about?"

He shook his head. "I thought I saw something. I thought—maybe it's the Hidden People who are causing the sickness."

"No," said Renn. "I don't think it is." She dreaded having to tell him what she'd learned at the healing rite. It wasn't fair. After everything he'd done last winter . . .

To put it off, she went to the stream and washed the clay from her face, then chipped away the thick layer on her palms, which had allowed her to carry the hot ash without getting burned. Then she grabbed a clump of wet moss and took it back for Torak. "Put this to your forehead. It'll make you feel better."

Sitting in the ferns beside him, she shook some hazelnuts from her food pouch and began cracking them on a stone. She offered one to Torak, but he declined. She sensed that neither of them wanted to talk about the sickness, but both were thinking of it.

Torak asked how she'd found him.

She snorted. "I may not speak wolf talk, but I'd know your howl anywhere." She paused. "Still no word of him?"

"No," he said shortly.

She ate another nut.

Torak said, "The healing rite. It didn't help, did it?"

"If anything, it made things worse. Oslak and Bera seem to think the whole clan's against them." She frowned. "Saeunn says she's heard of sicknesses like this in the deep past, after the Great Wave. Whole clans died out. The Roe Deer. The Beaver Clan. She says there may have been a cure long ago, but it was lost. She says—it's a sickness rooted in fear. That it *grows* fear. As trees grow leaves."

"Like leaves on a tree," murmured Torak. He reached for a stick and began peeling off the bark. "Where does it come from?"

She couldn't put it off any longer. She had to tell him. "Do you remember," she began reluctantly, "what Oslak said on the walkway?"

His fingers tightened on the stick. "I've been thinking that too. 'Eating my souls . . .'" He swallowed. "Soul-Eaters."

The birds stopped singing. The dark trees tensed.

"Is that what you mean?" said Torak. "Do you think the Soul-Eaters have something to do with the sickness?"

Renn hesitated. "Maybe. Don't you?"

He leaped to his feet and paced, dragging the stick over the bracken. "I don't know. I don't even know who they are."

"Torak—"

"All I *know*," he said with sudden fierceness, "is that they were Mages who went bad. All I *know* is that my father was their enemy—although he never told me anything." He slashed at the bracken. "All I *know* is that something happened that broke their power, and people thought they were gone, but they weren't. And last summer . . ." He faltered. "Last summer, a crippled Soul-Eater made the bear that killed Fa."

Savagely he stabbed the earth. Then he threw away the stick. "But maybe you're wrong, Renn, maybe they didn't—"

"Torak—no. Listen to me. Oslak scratched a sign in the dust. A three-pronged fork for snaring souls. The mark of the Soul-Eaters."

FIVE

The Soul-Eaters.

They were woven into his destiny, and yet he knew so little about them. All he knew was that there were seven: each from a different clan, each warped by his hunger for power.

Down by the river, a vixen screamed. In the shelter, Vedna tossed and turned, worrying about her mate. Torak lay in his sleeping-sack, thinking of the evil that could send a sickness to ravage the clans.

To rule the Forest . . .

But no one could do that. No one could conquer the trees, or stop the prey from following the ancient rhythms of the moon. No one could tell the hunters where to hunt.

When at last he slept, his dreams were haunted. He crouched on a dark hillside, frozen in horror as a faceless Soul-Eater crawled toward him. He scrambled back. His hand met a scaly softness that wriggled and bit. He tried to run. Tree roots coiled clammily about his ankles. A winged shadow swooped with a leathery *thwap*. The Soul-Eaters were upon him, and their malice beat at him like flame. . . .

He woke.

It was dawn. The breath of the Forest misted the trees. He knew what he had to do.

"Is Oslak any better?" he asked Vedna as he left the shelter.

"The same," she said. Her eyes were red, but the glare she gave him warded off sympathy.

He said, "I need to talk to Fin-Kedinn. Have you seen him?"

"He's downriver. But you leave him be."

He ignored her.

Already the camp was busy. Men and women crouched on the walkway with spears, while others woke the fires for daymeal. In the distance came the *tock! tock!* of hammer on stone. Everyone was trying not to think about Oslak and Bera, tied up in the sickness shelter.

Torak followed the path downstream: past the rapids, and around a bend that took him out of sight of the camp. Here the Widewater flowed less turbulently, and the salmon were fleeting silver darts in the deep green water.

Fin-Kedinn sat on a boulder by the river's edge, making a knife. His tools lay beside him: hammerstones, shapers, beaker of black, boiled pine-blood. Already a small pile of needle-sharp stone flakes nestled in moss at his feet.

As Torak approached, his heart began to pound. He admired the Raven Leader, but was scared of him too. Fin-Kedinn had taken him in after Fa was killed, but he'd never offered to foster him. There was a remoteness about him, as if he'd decided not to let Torak get too close.

Clenching his fists, Torak stood on the bank. "I need to talk to you," he said.

"Then talk," said Fin-Kedinn without looking up.

Torak swallowed. "The Soul-Eaters. They sent the sickness. It's my destiny to fight them. So that's what I'm going to do."

Fin-Kedinn went on studying a round, buff-colored stone the size of his fist. It was a Sea egg: a rarity in the Forest. The Ravens used mostly slate, antler or bone for their weapons, because flint—in the form of Sea eggs—was found only on the coast, where the Sea clans traded them for horn and salmon-skins.

Frustrated, Torak tried again. "I have to stop them. To put an end to this!"

"How?" said Fin-Kedinn. "You don't know where they are. None of us does." With his hammer-stone he tapped the Sea egg, checking from the sound that the flint was free from flaws.

Torak flinched. That *tock! tock!* brought back painful memories. He'd grown up to the sound of Fa knapping stone by the fire. It had made him feel safe. How wrong he had been.

He said, "Renn told me there have been powerful sicknesses like this in the past—but also a cure. So maybe—"

"That's what I've spent all night trying to find out," said Fin-Kedinn. "There's a rumor that one of the Deep Forest Mages knows a cure."

"Where?" cried Torak. "How do we get it?"

Fin-Kedinn struck the Sea egg a hard blow that took the top clean off. Inside, the flint was the color of dark honey, threaded with scarlet. "Not so fast," he told Torak. "Think first. Impatience can get you killed."

Torak threw himself down on the bank, and tore at the grass.

Using a small antler club, Fin-Kedinn struck flakes off the core, deftly controlling their size by the speed and slant of the blow. *Tock! tock!* went the hammer, telling Torak to wait.

Eventually, Fin-Kedinn spoke. "In the night, an Otter woman came in a canoe. Two of them have fallen sick."

Torak went cold. The Otter Clan lived far in the east, on the shores of Lake Axehead. "Then it's every-where," he said. "I have to get to the Deep Forest. If there's even a chance . . ."

Fin-Kedinn sighed.

"Who else could you send?" said Torak. "You're needed here. Saeunn's too old for the journey. Everyone else has to guard the sick, or hunt, or catch salmon."

Fin-Kedinn chose a thumb-length antler shaper, and sharpened a flint flake with delicate grinding motions. "The people of the Deep Forest rarely concern them-selves with us. Why do you think they'd help?"

"That's why it should be me!" insisted Torak. "My mother was Red Deer Clan! I'm their bone kin, they'd have to listen to me!" But he'd never known his mother, who had died when he was born, and he spoke with more assurance than he felt.

A muscle worked in Fin-Kedinn's jaw as he took up the haft of the knife: a length of reindeer shinbone with a groove in it to take the flint. Dipping a sharpened flake in pine-blood, he slotted it into the bone. "Has it not occurred to you," he said, "that this might be exactly what the Soul-Eaters want?" He raised his head, and his blue eyes burned with such intensity that Torak dropped his gaze. "Last winter after you fought the bear, I forbade anyone to speak of it outside the clan. You know this."

Torak nodded.

"Because of that, the only thing the Soul-Eaters know is that someone in the Forest has power. *They do not know who.*" He paused. "They don't know who, Torak. Nor do they know the nature of that power. None of us does."

Torak caught his breath. Fin-Kedinn's words echoed what Fa had said as he lay dying. *All my life I've kept you apart. . . . Stay away from men! If they find out— what you can do . . .*

But *what* could he do? For a time he'd thought Fa had meant his ability to speak wolf; but from what Fin-Kedinn had said, there had to be more.

"This sickness," said the Raven Leader, "it could be a trick: the Soul-Eaters' way of forcing you into the open."

"But even if it is, I can't just do nothing. I have to help Oslak. I can't stand seeing him like this!"

The hard face softened. "I know. Neither can I."

There was silence while Fin-Kedinn slotted in more flint, and Torak stared across the river. The sun had risen above the trees, and the water was dazzling.

Squinting, he made out a heron on the far bank; a raven wading after scraps of salmon.

The blade was complete: about a hand long, and as jagged and sharp as a wolverine's jaw. To finish it, Fin-Kedinn wound finely split pine root around the haft to make a warm, sure grip. "Now," he said. "Show me your knife."

Torak frowned. "What?"

"You heard. Show it to me."

Puzzled, Torak unsheathed the knife that had been his father's, and handed it over.

It had a beautiful leaf-shaped blade of blue slate, and an antler haft bound with elk sinew. Fa had told him that the blade was of Seal Clan making. Fa's mother had been a Seal, and she'd given it to him when he'd reached manhood; he'd fitted the hilt himself. As he lay dying, he had given the knife to Torak. Torak was very proud of it.

But as the Raven Leader handled it, he shook his head. "Too heavy for a boy. A Mage's knife, made for ceremony." He handed it back. "He was always too casual about such things."

Torak longed for him to say more, but he didn't. Instead he set the new knife across his forefinger, appraising it with a critical eye. It lay level, perfectly balanced.

Beautiful, thought Torak.

The Raven Leader flipped it around, caught it by the blade, and held it out. "Take it. I made it for you."

After a moment's astonishment, Torak took it.

Fin-Kedinn cut short his thanks. "From now on," he said, rising to his feet with the aid of his staff, "keep your father's knife hidden. Your mother's medicine horn, too. If anyone asks about your parents, don't speak of them."

"I don't understand," said Torak.

But Fin-Kedinn wasn't listening. He'd gone still, staring at the river.

Torak shaded his eyes with his hand, but couldn't see much for the glare. Only the heron on the far bank, and a log in midstream, sliding downriver.

In the camp, a woman began to keen: a tearing sound that rose above the rapids and chilled Torak's blood.

Men and women came running down the trail.

Torak gasped.

That wasn't a log floating downriver.

It was Oslak.

SIX

Oslak had taken no chances. He'd gnawed through his bindings, slipped out of the sickness shelter, and climbed the Guardian Rock. Then he'd thrown himself off.

The fall had probably killed him. At least—Torak hoped so. He couldn't bear to think of him being alive when he'd hit the rapids.

The Raven camp was stunned into silence when he reached it. Vedna had stopped keening and stood stony faced, watching the men bring the body on a litter. They took great care not to touch it with their bare hands. No one wanted to risk angering the dead man's souls, which were still in the camp.

As they set down the litter by Oslak's shelter, Saeunn crouched beside it, and—with her finger protected by a leather guard—daubed the Death Marks in red ochre on the body, to help the souls stay together on their journey. Soon the Ravens would carry him into the Forest. It was vital that this be done swiftly, so that his souls would not be tempted to stay in camp.

Fin-Kedinn stood a little apart, his face a mask of granite. He betrayed no grief as he gave orders to double the watch on Bera, and to empty Oslak's shelter of all but his belongings, which would be burned when it was put to the fire. But Torak could tell that he was taking it hard. The Raven Leader had told Oslak that he would keep him safe. He would not easily forgive himself for having failed.

Guilt.

Torak felt it too, weighing him down.

Well, the time for doing nothing was over. When the Ravens took the body into the Forest, he would stay behind, not being part of the clan—and that would be his chance to slip away: to make for the Deep Forest, and seek the cure.

But first there was something he had to do.

As the rites began and women fetched clay for the mourning marks, he made his way quietly to the foot of the Guardian Rock. If his suspicion was right—if the creature with the face of leaves had had anything to do with Oslak's death—then it might have left tracks.

The Guardian Rock was almost sheer on the side that faced the river, but on its eastern side it was more like a steep hill, which could be climbed if one was careful. Many feet had trampled the mud at its base, and some had tracked mud up this eastern flank.

The message in the mud was confused, but Torak made out a faint line of narrow, day-old prints: that was Saeunn, climbing to the top. He saw paw marks criss-crossed by sharp little four-toed prints: that was a dog scampering up, and being teased by a raven. And over there, a man's prints. Torak saw only the toes and the balls of the feet. Oslak had been running as fast as he could.

A lump rose in Torak's throat. He forced it down. Grieve later, when you're on your way.

Slowly he followed Oslak's tracks up the rock.

Oslak had dislodged pebbles and moss as he ran. At one point he'd slipped, grazing himself: here was a tiny smear of blood. Then he'd run on.

He was running as fast as he could, thought Torak. As if all the demons of the Otherworld were after him.

At the top, Torak found what he'd been dreading. Another set of prints: much smaller than Oslak's. They were faint, but he saw enough to know that whatever had made them had not been running—but standing:

standing quite still, a short way back from the edge. Watching Oslak leap to his death.

The footprints were small, like those of a child of maybe eight or nine summers.

Except that this print had claws.

The clan was getting ready to leave when Torak found Renn by the long-fire, grinding earthblood for the burial rites.

Her face was streaked with river clay—the Raven way of mourning—but tears had cut runnels down her cheeks. Torak had never seen her cry. As he approached, she blinked hard.

"Renn," he said, squatting beside her and speaking softly so as not to be overheard, "there's something I've got to tell you. I went up the Guardian Rock. I—"

"What were you doing up there?"

"I found tracks."

Saeunn called to Renn from across the clearing. "Come! We're leaving!"

"There's something in the camp," Torak said urgently. "I saw it!"

Again the Raven Mage summoned Renn.

"Torak, I've got to go!" she said. Pouring the ground ochre into her medicine pouch, she got to her feet. "We won't be gone long. Tell me when I get back. Show me the tracks."

Torak nodded, but didn't meet her eyes. He wouldn't be here when she got back. And he couldn't tell her he was going, because she'd try to stop him, or insist on coming too. He couldn't let her do that. If Fin-Kedinn was right, if there was even a chance that he was walking into a Soul-Eater trap, he wasn't going to risk her life as well as his own.

"I'm sorry you can't come too," said Renn, making him feel worse. Then she ran to take her place at the head of the clan beside her uncle, Fin-Kedinn.

The Ravens moved off, and Torak watched them go. He knew that they would carry Oslak's body a good distance from the camp before building the Death Platform: a low rack of rowan branches on which they would lay the corpse, facing upriver. Like the salmon, Oslak's souls would make their final journey upstream, toward the High Mountains.

The rites at the Death Platform would be brief, and after saying farewell, the clan would leave his body to the Forest. As he'd fed on its creatures in life, so they would feed on him in death. Three moons later, Vedna would gather his bones and take them to the Raven bone-ground. But for the next five summers, neither she nor anyone else would speak his name out loud. This was strict clan law: to prevent the dead man's souls from troubling the living.

Standing in the clearing, Torak watched till they

were gone. When the last Raven had been swallowed by the Forest, the camp felt eerily lonely. Only the dogs remained to guard the salmon.

Quickly, Torak ran to fetch his things. He crammed his light wicker pack with his few belongings: cooking-skin; medicine pouch; tinder pouch; fishhooks; his quiver and bow; his rolled-up sleeping-sack; Fa's knife, wrapped in rawhide; his mother's medicine horn. As he stuck his small basalt axe in his belt, he tried not to think of the last time he'd been forced to pack in a hurry. It had been last autumn, as Fa lay dying.

Torak's hand tightened on the hilt of the knife Fin-Kedinn had made for him. It was lighter and easier to use than his father's; but nothing would ever replace Fa's knife.

Don't think about that now, he told himself. Just get out of here before they come back. And this time, don't forget food.

After what had happened to Oslak, he couldn't face salmon: not the smoked meat, nor the Ravens' flat cakes of dried flesh pounded with juniper berries. Instead, he cut some strips of elk meat hanging from the rafters in Thull's shelter. They'd keep him going till he reached the Deep Forest.

But how long would that take? Three days? Five? He didn't know. He'd never been near it, and had only encountered two Deep Forest people: a silent Red

Deer woman with earthblood in her hair, and a wild-eyed Auroch girl, her scalp weirdly caked in yellow clay. Neither had shown any interest in him, and despite what he'd told Fin-Kedinn, he didn't expect much of a welcome.

On his way out of camp, he passed the Leader's shelter—and that was when it hit him. He was leaving the Ravens, perhaps for good.

First you lost Fa, then Wolf. Now Oslak, and Fin-Kedinn and Renn . . .

It was dark inside the shelter. Fin-Kedinn's corner was neat and spare, but Renn's was a mess: her sleeping-sack crumpled and littered with arrows she hadn't finished fletching. She would be furious that he'd gone without her, and there was no way of saying good-bye.

He had an idea. Outside the shelter he found a flat white pebble. Running to the nearest alder tree, he muttered a thanks to its spirit, cut off a strip of bark, and chewed. Spitting the red mix of saliva and tree-blood into his palm, he painted his clan-tattoo on the stone: two dotted lines, one with a break in the middle. The break wasn't part of the tattoo, it was a small scar on his cheek, but when Renn saw it she would know it was from him.

As he finished making the sign, he stopped. His finger was stained red with alder juice: the same juice he'd used last autumn, in Wolf's naming rite. He'd daubed it on the cub's paws, and been exasperated when Wolf kept licking it off.

"*Don't* think about Wolf!" he cried aloud. "Don't think about any of them!"

The empty camp mocked him silently. *You're on your own now, Torak.*

Hurriedly he shoved the pebble under Renn's sleeping-sack, then ran into the sunlight.

The Forest was full of birdsong, and achingly beautiful. He could take no joy in it.

Shouldering his bow, he turned east, and started for the Deep Forest.

SEVEN

Sorrow ran with Wolf like an unseen pack-brother. He missed Tall Tailless. He longed for his odd, furless face and his wavering howl; for the strange, breathless yip-and-yowl that was his way of laughing.

Many times Wolf had loped off alone to howl for him. Many times he'd run in circles, wondering what to do. He was caught between the Pull of the Mountain, and the Pull of his pack-brother.

The other wolves—the wolves of his new pack—were puzzled. *You have us now! And you're not yet full-grown, you have much to learn! You don't know how to hunt the great prey—how would you survive on your own? Stay here with us!*

They were a strong, close pack, and there had been times when he'd been happy on the Thunderer's Mountain. They'd played uproarious games of hunt-the-lemming; they'd leaped into lakes to frighten ducks. But the other wolves did not understand.

Wolf was thinking of this as he raced to his favorite ridge to catch the smells wafting from the Forest.

The Forest was many lopes away, but he caught the muzzle-watering scent of a newborn fawn, and the sharp smell of tree-blood oozing from a wind-snapped spruce. He heard the slow sucking sound of a boar turning over in its wallow, and the squeak of an otter cub falling off a branch. He longed to be in the Forest with Tall Tailless.

But how could he ever go back?

It wasn't only the thought of leaving his pack that stopped him. It was the Thunderer. The Thunderer would never let him go.

The Thunderer could attack at any time: even now, when the Up was bright and clear, and there was no sign of its angry breath. It could flatten the Forest with storms, and send down the Bright Beast-That-Bites-Hot to blast trees, rocks, wolves. It was all-powerful. Wolf knew that better than most, because it had taken his pack when he was a cub.

He'd gone off to explore, and when he'd come back, the Den had been gone. His whole pack—mother, father, pack-brothers—had lain wet and cold and Not-Breath in the mud. The Thunderer hadn't needed to come close to destroy them. It had sent the Fast Wet roaring down from the Mountains.

Wolf had been lonely and frightened, and *very* hungry. Then Tall Tailless had come. Tall Tailless had shared his kills with him, and let him curl up on top of him to sleep. He had howled with him, and played tag with bits of hide. Tall Tailless had become his pack-brother.

Tall Tailless was a wolf, of course—anyone could smell that—but he wasn't a normal wolf. The fur on his head was long and dark, but the rest of him was without fur, and instead had a loose overpelt—*which he could take off*. His face was flat, and his poor little teeth were hopelessly blunt; and strangest of all, he had no tail.

But he *sounded* wolf, even if he never hit the high yips. And his eyes were true wolf eyes: pale gray, and full of light. Above all, he had the heart and spirit of a wolf.

As Wolf stood on the ridge, sadness filled his chest. He put up his muzzle and howled.

That was when the new smell hit his nose.

Not hunter or prey; not tree or earth or Fast Wet or

stone. This was bad. Something bad, blowing through the Forest.

Wolf whimpered with anxiety. His pack-brother was down there in the badness.

Suddenly everything was clear. The Thunderer might come after him, but Wolf couldn't let that stop him any longer. Tall Tailless needed him.

Wolf leaped down from the ridge, and started for the Forest.

He ran for two Darks and Lights, keeping the Mountains at his tail, and heading for where the Hot Bright Eye sinks down to sleep.

Fear snapped at his hindpaws.

He feared the anger of the stranger wolves whose ranges he crossed; if they caught him, they might tear him to pieces.

He feared the wrath of the Thunderer.

But worse than that, he feared for his pack-brother.

As he ran, the smell grew stronger. Something stalked the Forest.

Tirelessly Wolf wove between the trees, seeking the taillesses. Some of their packs smelled like boar, some like otter, but the one he sought smelled like raven. That was the pack Tall Tailless had joined.

At last he found it, on the banks of a furious Fast Wet.

As he'd expected, nobody knew he was here. That was one of the odd things about taillesses. Although in many ways they were like true wolves—being clever and brave, with a fondness for talking and playing, and a fierce love for their pack—they couldn't smell *at all*, and they were practically deaf. So Wolf went unobserved as he roamed the edge of the Den, seeking his pack-brother.

He couldn't find him.

It had rained the previous Light, and many scents had been washed away; but if Tall Tailless had been here, Wolf would have smelled him.

Then he caught the scent of the lead wolf, who sat by the Bright Beast-That-Bites-Hot, as taillesses love to do. Beside him crouched the half-grown female who was pack-sister to Tall Tailless. She was speaking to the lead wolf in the yip-and-yowl of tailless talk, and she sounded both angry and sad.

Wolf sensed that the female was worried about Tall Tailless.

Running up and down, Wolf sought his pack-brother. He found a big bare patch that smelled of new ash; and some strange, straight trees from which hung many fish. He paused only to gulp down a few before heading back into the Forest to seek Tall Tailless.

Maybe his pack-brother had gone hunting. Yes, that must be it. And he couldn't have gone far, because like all taillesses, he ran on his hind legs, which made him slow.

But though Wolf searched and searched, he found nothing.

The awful truth crashed down on him like a falling tree.

Tall Tailless was gone.

EIGHT

To avoid meeting the Ravens, Torak stayed off the clan paths and kept to the hidden deer trails that wound up the Widewater valley.

The prey soon sensed that he wasn't hunting them, and relaxed. An elk munched willowherb as he passed. Forest horses flicked up their tails and cantered into the trees, then turned to stare till he was gone. Two boar sows and their fat, fluffy piglets raised their snouts to watch him go by.

The new leaves were still crinkled from the bud, and letting in plenty of sunlight. He made good speed. Like all Forest people he traveled light, carrying only what he needed for hunting, fire making and sleep.

All his life he'd wandered the Forest with Fa, pitching camp for a night or so, then moving on. Always moving on. That had been the hardest part about living with the Ravens. They only broke camp every three or four moons.

And there were so many of them! Twenty-eight men, women, and children. And babies. Until last winter, Torak had never even seen one of those. "Why can't it walk?" he'd asked Renn. "What does it *do* all day?" She'd laughed so much she'd fallen over.

At the time, that had made him cross. Now it made him miss them all the more.

He left the valley of the Widewater south of the Thunder Falls, and headed east into the next valley. There he had a brief encounter with two Willow Clan hunters in dugout canoes. To his relief they were in a hurry, and didn't ask where he was going, pausing only to give him a warning before heading downriver.

"A sick man escaped from our camp last night," said one. "If you hear howling, run. He doesn't know he's a man anymore."

The other shook his head grimly. "This sickness. Where did it come from? It's as if the very breath of summer is poisoned."

As midafternoon wore on, Torak began to feel watched.

Many times he stopped to listen, but he never heard anyone, and whenever he doubled back, he found nothing. And yet—the Follower was there. He could sense it. As the shadows lengthened, he pictured madmen roaming the Forest; small, malevolent creatures with sharp claws and faces of leaves.

He pitched camp near a noisy river where the damselflies were blue darts of light, and the midges nearly ate him alive until he rubbed himself with wormwood juice.

It was the first time in six moons that he'd slept on his own in the Forest, and he took care to choose the right spot. Flat ground, high enough above the river to avoid flash floods, and away from ant nests and obvious prey trails; and no overhanging deadwood or storm-weakened trees to fall on him in the night.

After the Ravens' reindeer-hide shelters, he was keen to get back to the way he'd lived with Fa, so he built a shelter of living trees. He found three beech saplings and bent them inward, lashing them together with pine root to make a snug sleeping space. This he thatched with fallen branches, and covered with leaf mold, weighing that down with more branches. In the morning he would untie the saplings, and they would spring back unharmed.

After making a mattress of last autumn's crunchy beech mast, he dragged his gear inside. The shelter had a rich, earthy tang. "A good smell," he said out loud. His voice sounded uneasy and forced.

It was a warm night with a southerly breeze, so he made only a small fire, walling it in with stones to stop it escaping into the Forest, and waking it up with his strike-fire and a handful of birch-bark tinder.

He remembered nights with Fa when they'd sat over the embers, wondering about this mysterious, life-giving creature who was such a good friend to the clans. What did the fire dream of as it slept inside the trees? Where did it go when it died?

For the first time, too, he thought of the bone kin he might soon encounter. Maybe with the Red Deer Clan he would feel that he belonged. After all, if things had been different, he could have *been* Red Deer. When he was born, his mother could have named him for her own clan, rather than Fa's; and then he would have grown up in the Deep Forest, and Fa might not have been killed, and he would never have met Wolf. . . .

It was too much to think about. He went off to find food.

He dug up some sweet orchid roots and baked them in the embers, and made a hot mash of goosefoot leaves flavored with crow garlic. It tasted good, but he wasn't hungry. He decided to keep it for daymeal.

He was hanging his cooking-skin in a tree out of the way of foragers, when a cry echoed through the Forest.

He froze.

It was not the yowl of a vixen, or a lynx seeking a mate. It was a man. Or something that had once been a man. Far in the west, by the sound of it.

With a creeping sense of dread, Torak watched the light between the trees begin to fail. Midsummer was not far off, so the night would be brief. Just long enough for his spirits to falter.

Dusk deepened, and still the Forest rang with the chatter of thrushes and the raucous laughter of wood-peckers. The birds would sing all night. He was glad of the company.

He thought of the Ravens sitting around their long-fire. The smell of woodsmoke and baked salmon; Oslak's rumbling laugh . . .

The very breath of summer is poisoned.

Quickly he unrolled his sleeping-sack, crawled in and laid his weapons by his side. A moment ago he'd been wide awake. Now he was exhausted.

He slept.

Shrill laughter tore through his dreams. Hazily he became aware of a loud groaning—both familiar and deadly. . . .

He was alert in an instant. It was the sound of a falling tree—*and it was falling his way.*

His sleeping-sack was twisted around his legs, he couldn't get free. Wriggling like a caterpillar, he squirmed through the entrance hole. Struggled to his feet—hopped—fell—narrowly missed the fire—and threw himself sideways into the ferns just as the tree crashed onto the shelter.

Sparks shot upward. Dark branches swayed and came to rest.

Torak lay among the ferns: heart pounding, sweat chilling his skin. He'd checked for storm-weakened trees, he knew he had. Besides, there was hardly any wind.

That laughter. Malevolent, yet horribly childlike. It hadn't been only in his dreams.

Not daring to move, he waited till he was sure that nothing else was coming down. Then he went to inspect the ruins of the shelter.

A young ash had fallen across it, killing the three saplings and trapping his gear inside. With luck he could salvage the gear, which—by firelight at least—appeared undamaged. But if he hadn't woken when he had, he would have been killed.

And yet—if the Follower had wanted to kill him, why warn him by laughing? It was as if it was playing with him. Putting him in danger, to see what he would do.

The fire was still burning. With a glowing brand in one hand and his knife in the other, he took a look at the ash tree.

He found axe-marks. Small, crude blows. But effective.

This was odd, though. No tracks on the ground. No sign that someone had braced himself to hack at the tree.

Again he swept the ground with firelight. Nothing. Maybe he'd missed something, but he didn't think so. The one thing he knew about was tracking.

With his finger he touched the oozing tree-blood. It was thickening. That meant the tree trunk had been cut some time before, then pushed over while he slept.

He frowned. It's impossible to fell a tree in silence. Why hadn't he heard anything?

Then it came to him. He'd filled his waterskin at the river—which had drowned out other sounds.

As he stood there amid the dark and dying trees, he wished Wolf were with him. Nothing would get past Wolf. His ears were so keen that he could hear the clouds pass. His nose was so sharp that he could smell the breath of a fish.

But Wolf isn't here, Torak told himself savagely. *He's far away on the Mountain.*

For the first time in six moons, he couldn't howl for his lost friend. He didn't like to think of who—or what—might answer his call.

It was past middle-night by the time he'd salvaged his gear and built another shelter, and he was numb with fatigue. He was also uneasily aware that he'd caused the deaths of three saplings. He could feel their souls hanging in the air around him: wistful, bewildered; unable to understand why they'd been robbed of their chance of becoming trees.

It's your fault, the older trees seemed to whisper. *You bring evil with you. . . .*

This time, he didn't risk getting into his sleeping-sack. Instead he woke the fire, and sat in his new shelter with the reindeer hide around his shoulders and his axe on his knees. He didn't want sleep. He just wanted dawn to come. . . .

He awoke with a start. Again he had that feeling of being watched—but this time it was different. There was a smell in the air: hot, strong and familiar, a little like hedge mustard, although his sleep-fuddled mind couldn't place it.

Then he saw the gleam of eyes on the other side of the fire. His hand tightened on his axe. "Who are you?" he said hoarsely.

The creature grunted.

"Who are you?" Torak repeated.

It moved into the light.

Torak tensed.

A boar. An enormous male, fully two paces from snout to tail, and heavier than three sturdy men. Its large, furry brown ears were pricked, and its small clever eyes met Torak's warily.

Torak forced himself to stay calm. Boars don't usually attack unless they're wounded or defending their young; but an angry boar can move as fast as a deer, and is invincible.

"I mean you no harm," he told the boar, knowing it wouldn't understand but hoping his tone would carry his meaning.

The large ears twitched. Firelight gleamed on its yellow tusks. Then the boar gave an irritable grunt, lowered its massive head, and started rooting around in the wreck of the shelter.

All it wanted to do was eat. Summer is a lean time for boars, with last autumn's berries and acorns long gone. No wonder it was busy grubbing up roots, beetles, worms; anything it could find.

The boar took no more notice of Torak, and after a while, he got into his sleeping-sack and curled up, listening to the comforting sound of snuffling. His new companion was gruff and none too friendly, but welcome all the same. Boars have keen senses. While it stayed close, no sick man or malevolent Follower could get near him.

But soon it would be gone.

As Torak stared into the red heart of the embers, he wondered if Fin-Kedinn had been right; if he'd let himself be tricked into leaving the Ravens. Maybe whoever—whatever—was after him had got him exactly where it wanted. Alone in the Forest.

Whoever it was, they'd been busy in the night.

It was raining when Torak crawled out of the shelter. The boar had gone, the fire was cold, and someone had rolled away the stones and smoothed out the ashes. Someone had taken Torak's arrows—had crept inside the shelter while he slept, withdrawn them from the quiver by his head, and planted them in the ash to make a pattern.

Torak recognized it at once. The three-pronged mark of the Soul-Eaters.

He went down on one knee and yanked out an arrow.

"All right," he said aloud as he got to his feet. "I know you're clever, and I know you're good at sneaking up on me. But you're a coward if you don't come out and face me right now!"

No one emerged from the dripping undergrowth.

"Coward!" shouted Torak.

The Forest waited.

His voice echoed through the trees.

"What do you want? Come out and face me! *What do you want?*"

Rain pattered on the leaves and ran silently down

his face. His only answer was the rattle of a wood-pecker far away.

The morning passed, and still it rained. Torak liked the rain: it kept him cool, and the midges away. His spirits rose as he crossed two more valleys. The feeling of being watched lessened. He heard no more demented howls.

Maybe that was because the boar was keeping him company. He didn't see it, but he kept finding traces of its presence. Big patches of churned-up earth where it had rooted for food. A muddy wallow beside a much-rubbed oak tree, where it had had a good scratch after taking a bath.

Torak found this reassuring. He had a new friend. He wondered how old the boar was, and if it was the father of the piglets he'd seen the previous day.

As the afternoon wore on, their paths crossed. They drank at the same stream, and rested in the same drowsy glade. Once, as they were both searching for wood mushrooms, the boar gave a tetchy grunt and chased Torak away, then stamped on the mushroom he'd been about to eat. When Torak went to look, he saw why. It wasn't a wood mushroom at all, but a poisonous look-alike, as its bruised red flesh showed. In the boar's bad-tempered way, it had been warning him to be more careful.

Next morning it was still raining, and the Forest slumbered beneath a mantle of cloud. But as Torak trudged farther east, he realized that it wasn't only the clouds that were shutting out the light. The Forest itself was growing darker.

He was used to the Open Forest, where the trees let in plenty of sun, and the undergrowth is usually fairly light; but now he had reached the hills that guarded the Deep Forest. Towering oaks reared before him with mighty limbs spread wide to ward him back. The undergrowth was taller than he was: dense stands of black yew and poisonous hemlock. The sky was hidden by an impenetrable canopy of leaves.

There had been no sign of the boar all day, and Torak missed him. He began to fear not only what followed him, but what lay ahead.

He thought of the tales his father had told him. *In the Deep Forest, Torak, things are different. The trees are more watchful; the clans more suspicious. If you ever venture in, be careful. And remember that in summer, the World Spirit walks in the deep valleys, as a tall man with the antlers of a deer. . . .*

In the late afternoon, with the rain still falling, Torak paused at a stream to rest. Hanging his gear on a holly tree, he went to refill his waterskin.

In the mud he found fresh tracks. The boar had been here before him, and recently: the tracks were sharp, their dewclaws deeply indented. It was good to know that his friend was close. As he knelt to fill the waterskin, he caught the familiar mustardy scent, and grinned. "I was wondering where you'd gone."

On the other side of the stream, the bracken parted—and there was the boar.

Something was wrong. The coarse brown fur was matted with sweat. The small eyes were dull, and rimmed with red.

Torak let fall the waterskin and backed away.

The boar gave a squeal of rage.

And charged.

NINE

Torak leaped for the nearest tree as the boar crashed toward him.

Panic lent him strength. He caught at a branch and hauled himself up, swinging his legs out of reach as the tusks gouged the trunk where his foot had been.

The tree shuddered. Torak clawed bark.

Hooking his leg over the branch, he hoisted himself into the fork. He wasn't even two paces above the boar, but he couldn't go any higher, the tree was too spindly. He'd lost his boots, and his feet were slippery with mud; he clutched branches to steady himself. One broke with a crack. The boar threw up its head and glared.

The brown eyes that had been so steady and wise were bulging and bloodshot. Something had happened to turn it into a monster. That reminded him horribly of Oslak.

"But I'm your *friend*," he whispered.

The boar gave a wheezy roar and thundered off into the Forest.

When it did not come back, Torak blew out a shaky breath. But he knew it was too soon to climb down. Boars are cunning; they know how to lie low. This one could be anywhere.

His legs were cramped, and as he shifted position, pain shot through his right calf. Glancing down, he was startled to see that it wasn't mud that had made him slip, but blood. The boar's tusk had caught him on the calf, but in the shock of the attack he hadn't felt it. Nothing he could do about it now.

The rain eased, and the sun came out. Around him he saw holly and oak trees, with an undergrowth of bracken and foamy meadowsweet. It all looked so peaceful.

The boar's mustardy scent hung in the air. It could be five paces away and he'd never know it. Not till it was too late.

Below him a redstart alighted on a clump of burdock, scattering raindrops. He thought, *It wouldn't have come if the boar were near.*

To make sure, he drew his knife and, with a quick apology to the willow's spirit, lopped off a small branch and tossed it down.

The redstart flew off. The bracken exploded.

Clasping the tree, Torak watched the boar savage the branch he'd let fall: tusking and trampling it to a mess of pulped fibers. If he'd jumped down, that would have been him.

The boar tossed the shredded stick into the bracken, wheeled around, and lowered its head. Then it threw itself against the tree.

Its shoulder hit the trunk like a boulder thudding to earth. Willow leaves fell like rain. Grimly, Torak clung on.

Again the boar struck.

And again.

And again.

In a flood of panic, Torak saw what it was doing. It was trying to knock down the tree.

And it could do it, too, because—he realized with mounting horror—he'd climbed the wrong tree. Instead of the sturdy oaks and hollies that could have withstood a rampaging boar, he'd chosen a slender willow with a trunk only slightly thicker than he was.

Oh, very clever, Torak, he snarled inside his head.

Another thud—and this time, a loud splintering. Below him, a wound gaped in the bark. He saw pinkish-brown wood, and glistening tree-blood. . . .

Do something. Fast.

The nearest oak was *maybe* within reach, if he edged along this branch—

He jerked back. Don't even try. The branch might look strong, but it'd take never his weight. This tree was a crack willow, and its wood was notoriously brittle. So not only had he picked the *smallest* tree within reach, but also the most fragile.

With startling suddenness, the boar stopped. Torak found its silence almost more terrifying than its rage.

He knew that this would be a fight to the death—and that he would probably lose. His axe, bow and arrows hung neatly on the holly, two paces out of reach.

Hope drained out of him like water into sand. There was no way out. He was going to die.

Without knowing what he was doing, he put his hands to his lips and howled. *Wolf! Where are you? Help me!*

No answer came to him on the wind. Wolf was far away on the Mountain.

And this part of the Forest seemed empty of people. No one would hear his cry and come to his aid.

Howling made him feel vulnerable, but in a strange way it also gave him strength. You are a member of the

Wolf Clan, he told himself. You are not going to die like a squirrel up a tree.

Swiftly, before doubts set in, he cut a switch of willow a bit longer than his arm, and stripped it of side branches. He squared off the tip, then split its end lengthways to make a tight, springy fork. The distance to his weapons was about two paces. Maybe—*maybe*—he could use the forked stick to hook the thong at the end of his axe, and lift it off the holly.

Beneath him, steam rose from the boar's sweat-blackened hide as it followed his every move.

Luckily, the willow branch that extended closest to the holly was also the sturdiest. Torak edged along it as far as he dared, holding the forked stick at full stretch.

It didn't reach far enough.

He edged back again. Whipping off his rawhide belt, he looped it around the willow trunk, knotted it, and grasped its free end. That let him lean out farther.

This time—yes! He hooked the forked stick through the axe-handle loop, and slowly lifted it off the holly branch.

The axe was heavy. The forked stick bent—and Torak watched helplessly as the axe slid off the end and thudded into the mud.

The boar squealed, hooked its tusks under the shaft, and tossed it into the bracken.

Torak could not allow himself to be disheartened.

Still at full stretch, he moved the forked stick toward his bow. Gently, *gently* he eased it under the bowstring. The bow was much lighter than the axe—merely a strip of yew wood strung with sinew—and he lifted it easily off the branch.

As soon as he had the bow slung over his shoulder, hope surged through him. "You see that?" he shouted at the boar. "You didn't think I could do it, did you?"

Now for the arrows. Still gripping his belt, Torak strained to reach his quiver with the forked stick. He hooked it. It was light, a wovengrass cone, but as he drew it toward him it tilted, and arrows spilled into the mud. He jerked the quiver toward him—just in time to save the last three.

For a moment he felt ridiculously pleased. "Three arrows!" he yelled.

Three arrows. To kill a full-grown boar. That would be like trying to fell a bull elk with a bunch of flowers.

The boar snorted and resumed its attack on the trunk. The willow didn't have long to go.

Crouching in the shivering tree, Torak struggled to take aim. Branches hampered his draw arm—he couldn't get a clear shot. . . .

He loosed an arrow. It thudded into one shoulder. The boar roared, but went on tusking the roots. That arrow had done as much damage as a gnat bite.

Clenching his teeth, Torak loosed another. It

glanced harmlessly off the thick skull.

Use your wits, Torak. Hit a boar on the skull or the shoulder bone and you won't do any damage. Hit *behind* the shoulder, and you've got a chance at the heart.

Another splintering crunch—and the willow lurched wildly. Now Torak was barely out of reach.

The boar wheeled around for another attack. Just before it charged, Torak glimpsed paler fur behind its foreleg—took aim—and let fly.

The arrow stuck deep. The boar squealed—and crashed onto its side.

Silence.

All Torak could hear was his own gasping breath, and the rain pattering in the bracken.

The boar lay still.

Torak waited as long as he could bear. When it didn't move, he lowered himself down to the ground.

Standing on the torn earth with the willow dying behind him, he felt exposed. He had no arrows and no axe; only his knife.

It *must* be dead. Its foam-flecked sides weren't moving.

But he would take no chances. The carcass was three paces away. He wouldn't go near it till he was better armed.

Stealthily, he made his way behind the wreck of the willow, searching the bracken for his axe.

Behind him the boar staggered to its feet.

Desperately Torak scanned the bracken. It had to be somewhere. . . .

The boar threw itself into a charge.

Torak saw his axe—lunged for it—whirled around, and sank it into the massive neck.

The boar fell dead.

Torak stood, his legs braced, his chest heaving; both hands clutching his axe.

Rain streamed down his cheeks like tears, and fell sadly on the leaves. He felt sick. Never in his life had he killed prey when he didn't need meat. Never had he killed a friend.

Letting go of the axe, he knelt and put a shaky hand on the hot, bristly pelt. "I'm sorry, my friend," he told the boar. "But I had to do it. May your souls . . . be at peace."

The glazed eye met his sightlessly. The boar's souls had already left. Torak could feel them. Close. Angry.

"I will treat you with respect," he said, caressing the sweat-soaked flank. "I promise."

In the matted fur, his hand touched something hard.

He parted the hairs—and gasped. It was a dart of some kind, buried deep in the boar's ribs.

With his knife he dug it out, and washed it in the stream. He'd never seen anything like it. It was shaped like a leaf, but viciously barbed, and made of fire-hardened wood.

Behind him among the trees, he heard laughter. He spun around. The laughter faded into the Forest.

The meaning of what he'd found sank in. This was why the boar had attacked. It had not been sick. It had been wounded. Terribly wounded by someone so cruel, so evil, that they had not gone after it and finished it off, as they were bound to do by all the sacred laws of the hunt, but had left it mad with pain, to savage anyone it found.

And since Torak seemed to be the only one in this part of the Forest, whoever had shot the boar must have intended its first victim to be him.

TEN

Torak wrapped the slab of boar's liver in burdock leaves and tucked it into the fork of an oak tree.

"My thanks to the clan guardian for this meat," he muttered, as he'd done countless times before. For the first time in his life, he didn't feel thankful. All he could think about was the wise old boar snuffling in the leaf mold, and keeping him company for the night. The fat, fluffy piglets who had lost a father.

He limped back to the carcass. It was enormous. After a struggle, he'd managed to roll it over and slit the belly to get at the innards, but that was as far as he'd got.

Until now, the biggest prey he'd ever killed had been a roe buck, and that had taken two exhausting days to deal with. The boar was many times bigger. It would take him a whole half-moon.

He didn't have a whole half-moon. He had to reach the Deep Forest and find the cure.

But he had no choice. It was the oldest law of all that when you made a kill, you had to treat the prey with respect, and use every part of it. That was the Pact that had been made long ago between the clans and the World Spirit. Torak had to honor it or risk untold bad luck.

He also had to tend to the wound in his calf. It was burning. Not even the rain cooled it down.

By the stream he found a clump of soapwort. Mashing some of the wet leaves to make a slippery froth, he washed his leg. The pain was so bad that it made his eyes water.

Now to sew up the wound. He found some bone needles in his pack—which hung unharmed on the holly tree—and chose the thinnest, and a length of deer-sinew thread. The thread he'd made from the roe buck had been lumpy and thick, and when Vedna had seen it she'd pursed her lips and given him some of hers. It was as fine as spider's gossamer, and he thanked her under his breath.

The first stab of the needle was agonizing. Drawing

the thread through his skin made him moan, and he had
to hop in circles with the needle sticking out of his calf
before he could work up the courage to make another
stitch. When he'd finished, tears were streaming down
his face.

Next, the dressing. He used some chewed green
willow bark—at least there was plenty of that—
although dabbing it on stung like fury. Then a soft pad
peeled from the inside of a horsehoof mushroom, with
a birch-bast binding to keep everything in place.

When it was over, he was trembling. The wound
was still throbbing, but the pain had lessened a little.

He found his boots—muddy but undamaged—and
pulled them on. He was glad they were summer ones,
with a rawhide sole and soft buckskin sides, which
wouldn't chafe his calf. Lastly, he stowed the rest of the
horsehoof mushroom in his pack, for changing the
dressing in a few days.

A few days . . .

He would still be here, working on the carcass. If
the Follower didn't get him first.

The rain had stopped. Water dripped off the ruined
willow, and glistened on the carcass of the boar. A pair
of ravens flew down, eyeing it hopefully. Torak shooed
them away.

Black spots darted before his eyes, and he realized
he was faint with hunger. Butchering the carcass would

have to wait. He had to eat.

He'd finished the supplies he'd taken from the Ravens, but with the carcass, he had no shortage of meat. He'd never felt less like eating.

Watched by the ravens, he forced down the rest of the liver. Drinking the blood was harder. Most of it had drained into the mud—a mistake that he couldn't now repair and that, being against the Pact, would bring him bad luck. To make amends he took his birchwood cup from his pack and scooped up what remained in the body cavity. He tried not to think about Oslak whittling the cup for him one long winter's night; or that he was drinking the blood of a friend.

To take away the taste, he crunched up some young burdock stems. Then—at last—he made a start on the carcass.

Skinning it was back-straining, arm-wrenching work, and it was nearly dusk by the time he'd finished. He was covered in blood and shaking with tiredness, and the hide was a muddy, stinking mess. He still hadn't washed it or started scraping off the flesh and fat. After that there would be days spent curing it with wood ash and mashed brains, and drying the meat, and splitting the bones for fishhooks and arrowheads.

Not forgetting, of course, that he still had to build a shelter and a fire before it got dark. . . .

"Wishing won't get it done," said a voice behind him.

Torak gave a start.

He couldn't see anyone. The bracken was man-high, filled with shadow.

"Who are you?" he said. He took a step forward—then realized he'd left his weapons by the carcass.

That was when he saw it. A face in the bracken, staring at him.

A face of leaves.

ELEVEN

The creature with the face of leaves was not alone. Another appeared close by. Then another and another. Torak was surrounded.

As more emerged from the trees, he saw that although their faces resembled that of the Follower, they were full-grown men and women—and they didn't have claws.

They wore their brown hair long, and braided with the tail hairs of forest horses. The men's beards were dyed green, like the moss that hangs from spruce trees. The lips of both men and women were stained a darker green; but most startling of all were the leaves on their faces. Torak saw that these were dense greenish-brown tattoos: oak leaves for the women, holly for the men. The tattoos gave the disquieting impression that they were peering from the trees—even when, as now, they stood in the open.

They went barefoot, with knee-length leggings and sleeveless jerkins of wovenbark, although of a finer, suppler weave than Torak had ever seen. Each carried a magnificent, well-oiled bow; and each bow was nocked with a green slate arrow fletched with wood-pecker feathers. All arrows were trained on him.

Swiftly he put his fists over his heart in a token of friendship.

The arrows didn't move.

"You are—of the Deep Forest?" he said hoarsely. It was a guess. Something about them felt different from the Follower. He sensed wildness and danger—but not evil.

"And you," said the woman who had first addressed him, "you have reached its borders and must turn back."

"I thought the Deep Forest was farther east—"

"You were wrong," said the woman in a voice as chill as a deep Forest pool. She had a narrow, distrustful face with hazel eyes set too close together, and she looked older than the others. Torak wondered if she was the leader.

"You have reached the True Forest," she said. "You may not pass."

The "True Forest"? In spite of himself, Torak was annoyed. What was wrong with the Forest where he'd grown up?

"I come as a friend," he said, trying to sound friendly but not quite succeeding. "My name is Torak. I have bone kin in the Deep Forest. Oak Clan and Red Deer by my mother. What clan are you?"

The woman drew herself up. "Forest Horse," she said haughtily. "As you would know if you were telling the truth."

"I am telling the truth," said Torak.

"Prove it."

Face flaming, Torak went to his pack and brought out his mother's medicine horn. It was made from the hollowed-out tip of a red deer antler, fitted with a black oak base and stopper. Fin-Kedinn had told him to keep it hidden; but he couldn't think of any other proof.

"Here." He held it out.

The Leader recoiled as if he'd threatened her. "Put it down!" she cried. "We never touch strangers! You might be a ghost or a demon!"

"I'm sorry," Torak said hastily. "I'll—put it here."

He set it on the ground, and the Leader leaned forward to inspect it. Torak reflected that the Forest Horses seemed to have more in common with their clan-creatures than merely their horsetails.

"It is of Red Deer making," declared the Leader.

A murmur of surprise rippled through her people.

Taking a step toward Torak, the Leader peered at his face. "You have something of the True Forest in you, despite the evil you did here; but your clan-tattoos are unknown to us. You may not pass."

"*What?*" said Torak. "But I have to!"

"He cannot enter the True Forest!" said one of the clan. "See how he treated the boar!"

"And the willow tree!" said another. "Look at her lying in the mud! Dying with nothing to ease her pain!"

"How do you ease a tree's pain?" said Torak indignantly.

Seven pairs of hazel eyes glared at him through their leaf-tattoos.

"You have used our brother and sister very ill," said the Leader. "That you cannot deny."

Torak glanced at the shattered tree and the muddy carcass. "Take them," he said.

"What?" said the Leader, her eyes narrowing.

"Take the boar and the willow," said Torak.

"There's only one of me, but seven of you. You could deal with them much better than I could. And that way, we'd avoid the bad luck."

The Leader hesitated, as if suspecting a trick. Then she turned to her people. To Torak's surprise, she didn't speak, but made a series of slight, subtle gestures with one hand.

Immediately, four of them stepped forward, whipped out slender knives of green slate, and descended on the carcass. With astonishing speed and skill they cut it up, then packed it with the hide and innards in wovenbark nets drawn from their packs, and slung them over their shoulders.

"We will return for our sister," said one, with a nod at the willow and a scornful glance at Torak. "We will lay her to rest." Then he was gone, melting into the Forest with his three companions.

All trace of the boar had vanished, apart from the tusks, which one of the Forest Horses now set before Torak. "These you must keep," she told him severely, "to mark the great wrong you did to the prey. If you were of the True Forest, you would be forced to wear them forever as a penance."

Torak appealed to the Leader. "I know I did wrong, but I didn't mean it."

"That doesn't matter."

He took a deep breath and tried again. "I came here because we need your help. There's a sickness in the Forest—"

"We know of this," cut in the Leader.

"You do? Has it struck here too?"

The Leader raised her chin. "We have no sickness in the True Forest. We guard our borders well. But the trees tell us many things. They tell of the evil that haunts their sisters in the west. They whisper whence it came."

Torak thought about that. "It's said that one of your Mages has the cure."

"We have no cure," said the Leader.

Torak's jaw dropped. "I know I've angered you," he said carefully, "and I'm sorry. But if your own clan doesn't have the cure, then maybe another—"

"We have no cure!" insisted the Leader. "There is no cure in the Deep Forest! The people of the Otter spoke too hastily! They are always too hasty, just like their clan-creature!"

"Can you really not help at all?" said Torak in disbelief. "Not you or anyone else in the Deep Forest? People are dying."

"I am grieved," said the Leader, not sounding grieved at all, "but I cannot alter the truth. What you seek is by the Sea."

Torak stared at her. *"The Sea?"*

"You must head west. This is the message of the trees. Head west till you can go no farther. There you shall find what you seek."

"Why should I believe you?" said Torak. "You're just trying to get rid of me."

The Leader's green face closed. "The trees never lie. If you had more than a splinter of the True Forest in your souls, you would know this. But you do not—or you would not have done the evil you did here!"

"I didn't want to kill the boar," said Torak, "but I had to. It attacked me. Someone had wounded it and left it to go mad."

The remaining Forest Horses cried out in horror.

"This is a terrible evil!" said the Leader. "Where is your proof? How could we be unaware of this, when not a twig may snap in our Forest that we do not hear?"

Torak stooped and picked up the dart he'd dug from the boar's side. Then he remembered the Forest Horses' reluctance to touch a stranger, and put it back on the ground.

He was unprepared for their reaction. The Leader snarled, revealing shockingly white teeth between her dark-green lips. "You *dare* accuse us?"

"Of course not!" said Torak. Then he saw what he'd missed before: a clutch of dark wooden darts—exactly like the one that had wounded the boar—

dangling from her belt.

"Then whom *do* you accuse?" demanded the Leader. "Some other Deep Forest clan? Speak quickly, or you die!"

"I don't know!" cried Torak. "I mean—I've seen it, but I don't know what it is! I only know that I found this dart in the boar's side!"

To his relief, the Forest Horses lowered their bows.

"I call it the Follower," he said. "It has a face like yours—no, no, I mean—a face tattooed with leaves, but smaller, like a child, and with claws on its hands and feet."

The Leader backed away. Her green lips thinned, and beneath the leaf-tattoos her face went pale. "You must leave at once," she said, breathing hard. "If you take one step into the True Forest, I swear by all the trees who gave me birth that you will not live to take another!"

Torak met her eyes, and saw the fear in them. "You know what it is, don't you?" he said. "The Follower. You know what it is."

The Leader did not reply. She made another sign to her people, and they turned and melted into the trees.

"No!" shouted Torak, running after them. "Tell me what it is! At least tell me that!"

An arrow whipped past his face.

"Tell me what it is!" he yelled.

Just before she vanished, the Leader turned. *"Tokoroth . . ."* she whispered.

"What does that mean?" said Torak.

"Tokoroth . . ."

The green face faded into the leaves.

Long after she had gone, the name hung on the air like an evil thought.

Tokoroth . . .

TWELVE

"A *tokoroth?*" said Renn, nursing her bandaged hand. "What's that?"

"Not here," snapped Saeunn.

Without another word she started through the camp. Though she was bent as an old tree battered by storms, she moved with surprising speed, clearing the way with her staff: past the people working at the smoking-racks, past the Guardian Rock, and into the shadow of the gorge. She did not look around. She simply assumed that Renn would follow.

Biting back her irritation, Renn did. As she went, people cast her the same wary glances they normally reserved for the Mage. More and more, they regarded her as Saeunn's apprentice. Renn hated that.

It was three days since the sickness had struck, and in that time, four more Ravens had fallen ill. To stop them harming others or themselves, Fin-Kedinn had taken drastic action, shutting them in a cave on the other side of the river, and setting a constant guard.

Renn could taste the fear in the air. She could see it in people's eyes. Will I be next? Will you?

She was horribly afraid that the bite on her hand meant it would be her. She needed to talk to someone; to be told she was wrong. But Saeunn had forbidden her to speak of it.

In the past, that wouldn't have stopped Renn; she'd been defying Saeunn all her life, and saw no reason to stop now. But everyone to whom she usually told her secrets was gone. Oslak was dead. Vedna had returned to her birth clan, the Willows. Torak had disappeared.

Torak. It was two days since he'd left, and even thinking about him made her furious. He was no friend of hers. Friends do not run away without a word, leaving only a pebble, a painted pebble.

To work off her feelings, she'd been hunting every day; and since she was a good hunter, Fin-Kedinn had let her go. It was while she was hunting that she'd got bitten. So in a way, that was Torak's fault too.

It had happened that morning. She'd risen at dawn

and started through the misty Forest to the hazel thicket on the southeast side of the valley, where she'd set some snares.

When she'd reached the thicket, she'd thought it was empty. Then, from deep within, had come a rustling of leaves.

That was when she'd forgotten one of the first rules Fin-Kedinn had ever taught her, and stuck in her hand without looking.

The pain was terrible. Her scream shook the Forest and sent wood pigeons bursting from the trees.

Howling, she yanked back her hand—but whatever had bitten her clung on tight. She couldn't see it, the leaves were too dense, and she couldn't shake it off. Pulling out her knife, she plunged in—then jerked back in horror. It wasn't a viper or a weasel, it was a *child*. In a flash she took in a glitter of eyes in a mass of grimy hair, sharp brown teeth sunk deep in her palm.

She raised her knife to ward it off—and the creature shot her a look of pure malevolence, let go of her hand, and hissed at her—*hissed* like an angry wolverine—then fled.

That was when Thull and Fin-Kedinn had come running, axes at the ready.

For some reason Renn did not understand, she didn't tell them what had happened, but hid her hand behind her back and concealed how shaken she was by

a show of embarassment. "Stupid of me not to look
first! Lucky it was only a weasel!"

Thull had been relieved it was nothing worse, and
had headed back for camp. Fin-Kedinn had given her a
measuring look, which she'd returned in silence.

"What *was* it?" she said now as the Raven Mage
halted twenty paces into the gorge. Uneasily, Renn
glanced about. She didn't like the gorge, and seldom
ventured in unless she had to.

Though it was midday, they were in deep shadow.
The gorge was always in shadow, its looming sides
shutting out all but a sliver of sky. The Widewater
didn't like it any more than Renn. Angrily it thundered
over a chaos of boulders.

Renn shivered. In here, a tokoroth could creep up
behind you, and you'd never even hear it. . . .

"Tokoroth," muttered Saeunn, making her jump.

"But what does that mean?"

Saeunn didn't answer. Crouching on a patch of hard
red earth by the river's edge, she tented her tunic over
her bony knees. Her feet were bare, her toenails brown
and hooked.

Once, Torak had told Renn that Saeunn reminded
him of a raven. "An old one, with no kind feelings left."
Renn thought she was more like scorched earth: dried
up and very, very hard. But Torak was right about the
feelings. Renn had known the Raven Mage all her life,

and she'd never seen her smile.

"Why should I tell you about the tokoroth?" said Saeunn in her rasping croak. "You want to know this, yet you refuse to learn Magecraft."

"Because I don't like Magecraft," retorted Renn.

"But you're good at it. You know things before they happen."

"I'm good at hunting too, but you—"

"You lose yourself in the hunt," cut in Saeunn, "to escape your destiny. To escape becoming a Mage."

Renn took a deep breath and held on to her temper. Arguing with Saeunn was like trying to cut flint with a feather. And it didn't help that there might be some truth in what she said.

She resolved to be patient until she'd got what she wanted. "Tell me about the tokoroth," she said.

"A tokoroth," said Saeunn, "is a child raised alone and in darkness, as a host for a demon."

As she spoke, the gloom deepened, and a thin rain began to fall, pocking the red earth.

"A tokoroth," she went on, "knows no good or evil. No right or wrong. It is utterly without mercy, for it has been taught to hate the world. It obeys no one but its creator." She stared at the black, rushing water. "It is one of the most feared creatures in the Forest. I never thought to hear of one in my lifetime."

Renn looked down at her injured hand. Beneath Saeunn's poultice of coltsfoot and cobwebs, the wound throbbed painfully. "You said 'its creator.' What do you mean?"

Saeunn's clawlike hand gripped her staff. "The one who captured the child. The one who caught the demon and trapped it in the body of the host."

Renn shook her head. "Why have I never heard of this before?"

"Few now know about tokoroth," said Saeunn, "and even fewer speak of them. Besides," she added with an edge to her voice, "you don't wish to learn Magecraft. Or had you forgotten?"

Renn flushed. "How are they created?"

To her surprise, the corners of the lipless mouth went down in an approving grimace. "You go to the roots of things, that's good. That's what a Mage does."

Renn stayed silent.

Saeunn drew a mark in the earth that Renn couldn't see. "The dark art of creating tokoroth," she said, "was lost long ago. Or so we thought. It seems that someone has learned it afresh." She took away her hand to reveal the three-pronged fork of the Soul-Eaters.

Renn had half expected that, but it was a shock to have her suspicion confirmed. "But—*how* are they made?" she said, her voice barely audible above the roar of the Widewater.

Saeunn rested her chin on her knees and gazed into the water, and Renn followed her gaze—down, down, to the murky bottom of the river. "First," said the Mage, "a child is taken. Maybe it goes missing when its kin turn away for a moment. They search, thinking it has wandered off into the Forest. They never find it. They grieve, believing it lost, or taken by a lynx or a bear."

Renn nodded. She knew people who'd lost children that way, everyone did, and she always felt a tearing pity for them. She too had lost kin. Her father had been missing for five moons before his body was found. She'd been seven summers old. She remembered the agony of not knowing.

"Better for the child," Saeunn said grimly, "if it *had* fallen prey to a bear. Better than being taken for a tokoroth."

Renn frowned. "Why? At least it's still alive."

"Alive?" One bony hand clenched. "Kept in darkness for moon after moon? No warmth but what will barely keep it alive? No food but rotting bat meat tossed into its own filth? Worst of all, no people. Not till it has forgotten the touch of its mother's hand; forgotten its very name."

Renn felt the chill of evil seeping into her bones.

"Then," said Saeunn, "when it is nothing but an empty husk—only then does its creator summon the demon and trap it in the body of the host."

"You mean—the child," mumbled Renn. "It is still a child."

"It is a host," Saeunn said flatly. "Its souls are in thrall to the demon forever."

"But—"

"Why do you doubt this?" said Saeunn.

"Because it's still a child, maybe it could be rescued—"

"Fool! Never let kindness get in your way! Now tell me. What *is* a demon? Quick! Tell!"

It was Renn's turn to be fierce. "Everyone knows that. Why do you want me to say it?"

"Don't argue, girl, do as I say!"

Renn blew out. "A demon," she said, "comes into being when something dies and its souls are scattered, so that it loses its clan-soul. With only the name-soul and world-soul left, it doesn't have any clan feeling, so it can't know right or wrong. It hates the living." She broke off, remembering the moment last autumn when she'd looked into the eyes of a demon, and seen nothing but hot, churning hatred. "It lives to destroy all living things," she faltered. "Only to destroy."

The Mage struck the ground with her staff and gave a croak almost like laughter. "Good! Good!" She leaned forward, and Renn saw the thick vein throbbing at her temple. "You've just described a tokoroth. It may *look* like a child, but do not be deceived! That's only the body. The demon has won. The child's souls are buried too deep ever to escape."

Renn hugged herself. "How could anyone do that to a child?"

Saeunn lifted her shoulders in a shrug, as if the existence of evil were too obvious to need comment.

"And what is a tokoroth *for*?" said Renn. "Why would you want to make one in the first place?"

"To do your bidding. To slink into shelters. To steal. To maim. To terrify. Why do you think Fin-Kedinn sets a watch every night?"

Renn gasped. "You mean—you knew it was here?"

"Since the sickness came. We just didn't know why."

Renn thought about that. "So—you think the tokoroth is causing it?"

"The tokoroth does the bidding of its creator."

"The Soul-Eaters."

Saeunn nodded. "The tokoroth is causing the sickness at the bidding of its masters—in some way we don't understand."

Again Renn was silent. Then she said, "I think Torak saw it. Before he left, he tried to warn me. But—he didn't know what it was." A new thought struck her. "Is there more than one?"

"Oh, I think we can be sure of that."

Renn struggled to take that in. "So there could be one here, and maybe another went after him?"

Saeunn spread her hands.

Suddenly the Forest Renn had grown up in seemed full of menace. "But *why* are they causing the sickness? What do they *want*?"

"I don't know," said Saeunn.

That frightened Renn more than anything. Saeunn was the Mage. She was supposed to know.

With a shiver, Renn stared at the thundering water. She thought of Torak heading east—maybe trailed by something far worse than he knew. . . .

"You cannot go and warn him," Saeunn said sternly. "It is too late. You would never find him."

"I know," said Renn without turning her head.

To herself she added, But I've still got to try.

THIRTEEN

Wolf couldn't find Tall Tailless, but he knew that he had to keep trying.

Once, he'd caught the scent in a tangle of beech saplings where his pack-brother had dug a Den—but then he'd lost it again. The scent was chewed up with that of boar scat, and with the stink of the badness that haunted the Forest—and a troubling new smell: the smell of demon. Wolf had learned that smell when he was a cub. The memory was very bad.

Once more he cast about, but in vain. And always the fear snapped at his hindpaws.

The Thunderer was angry with him for leaving the Mountain. Wolf felt it in his fur and in the tingling of his pads. It was coming after him. Soon it would attack.

The Up had gone very dark, and the breath of the Thunderer was stirring the trees. Sounds were becoming louder, smells sharper, as they always did when it began to growl.

At last Wolf caught the scent of his pack-brother. He could have howled for joy. Filled with new purpose, he ran on, and the prey ran with him, desperate to escape, and sensing that Wolf wasn't hunting them. A beaver slid off a riverbank and swam for its den. A red deer doe raced with her fawn for the safety of the thickets.

Suddenly the Thunderer vented its fury. The Wet burst upon the Forest, flattening bracken and bending trees like grass. A deafening crash—and down from the Up came the Bright Beast-That-Bites-Hot, missing Wolf by a pounce, and hitting a pine tree instead. The tree screamed. The Bright Beast swallowed it whole. Wolf swerved—but one of the Bright Beast's cubs fell in front of him and bit him on the forepaw. With a yelp he leaped high—then raced away with the stink of dying tree in his nose.

He felt as frightened as a cub. He wanted his mother. He wanted Tall Tailless. He was all alone, and very, very scared.

Renn was all alone in the Forest, and getting scared.

She'd slipped away from the camp two days before, and still hadn't found Torak. Twice she'd heard the demented shrieks of the sick echoing through the trees, and once she'd caught a rustling overhead. It felt as if every bush, every tree, concealed a tokoroth.

And now the storm was coming. The World Spirit was angry.

Through a gap in the branches she saw a heavy bank of wolf-gray cloud, and heard a rumble of thunder. She was already within striking range. She must take cover.

The valley she was crossing had granite crags on its eastern side, and she saw some promising dots of darkness that might be caves. She ran, snatching up sticks of firewood as she went.

The storm burst with appalling suddenness. The World Spirit hammered at the clouds, splitting them open to let loose the rain, hurling dazzling arrows of lightning upon the Forest. Renn caught the flare of a tree going up in flames in the distance. If she wasn't careful, she'd be next.

At last she found a cave—but wet as she was, she hung back. A cave can be a shelter or a death trap, so she checked for signs of bear or boar, and that the roof was high enough: otherwise the lightning might find its way down a crack, and through her head. When she was sure it was safe, she plunged in.

She was shaking with cold and desperate for a fire, but first she saw to her bow. Pulling it out of its salmon-skin wrapping, she hung it on a tree root jutting from the cave wall. After that she propped up her arrows to dry, so that they wouldn't warp. Then she woke up a fire.

Out in the Forest, the storm raged. Renn wondered where Torak was, and if he'd found shelter.

Tracking him from the Raven camp had not been easy, and to begin with she'd had to guess. She'd reasoned that he'd stayed off the main clan trails, which left a number of choices. Bears and other hunters tend to stay down by the rivers where the prey comes to drink, which means that elk and deer trails are higher up the slopes. After what had happened last autumn, Renn had guessed that Torak would want to avoid bears, which meant he'd probably have taken the prey trails.

She'd been proven right when she'd found his shelter, but it had given her a shock to see it crushed beneath an ash tree. A huge relief to find no body inside; and she'd quickly located the remains of the new shelter beside it. She'd known it was his because he made his fires in a star pattern, which wasn't the Raven way.

Next morning she'd lost the trail again. A boar had obliterated the tracks.

The fire spat, jolting her back to the present.

Her wounded hand throbbed. As she huddled closer to the flames, she pictured the tokoroth's sharp brown teeth; heard again that malevolent hiss. . . .

"Something to eat," she said to chase away the thought.

Her pack contained dried elk meat, smoked salmon from the racks, and salmon cakes—although in a fit of mischief she hadn't taken fresh ones, but had raided Saeunn's private store: a neat stack of cakes packed into a length of dried auroch gut.

She took one, broke off a bit for the clan guardian, then ate the rest. It was from last summer's catch but still good. It reminded her sharply of the clan.

Beside her lay the wickerwork quiver that Oslak had taught her to make. On two fingers of her left hand were the leather finger guards that Vedna had sewn. Her right forearm bore the wrist guard of polished green slate that Fin-Kedinn had made for her when he'd taught her to shoot. She rarely took it off, and her brother had often teased her about that. Her brother . . . He had died the previous winter. It hurt to think of him.

To cheer herself up, she took out the little grouse-bone whistle that Torak had given her the previous autumn. It didn't make any sound that she could hear, but she always kept it with her. Wolf seemed to hear it well enough, and once she'd used it to summon him, and it had saved her life.

Now she gave it a tentative blow.

Nothing happened.

Of course, she hadn't expected that it would. Wolf was far away on the Mountain.

Feeling lonely, she unrolled her sleeping-sack and curled up by the fire.

She awoke to the prickling certainty that she was not alone.

The storm had passed, but the rain was still coming down in torrents, gurgling through secret channels in the cave walls. The fire had sunk to a smoldering glow. Beyond it—in the dark at the mouth of the cave— something was watching her.

She struggled upright and groped for her axe.

The thing in the cave mouth was big: too big for a tokoroth. A lynx? *A bear?*

But if it was a bear, she would hear it breathing. And it wouldn't stay outside.

Somehow that didn't make her feel any better.

"Who's there?" she said.

She sensed rather than heard the creature come forward. Whatever it was, it moved as silently as breath.

Then she saw the gleam of eyes.

She cried out.

The creature backed away. Then it edged once more into the light.

Renn gasped.

It was a wolf. A big one, with a heavy coat of sodden gray fur. Its head was lowered to catch her scent, and it didn't look threatening or afraid. Just—wary.

Renn took in the thick mantle of black fur across its shoulders. The great amber eyes.

Those eyes . . .

It couldn't be.

Slowly she put down her axe.

"Wolf?"

FOURTEEN

"Wolf?" Renn said again.

The wolf's tail was down but faintly wagging, his ears rammed forward. He was watching her intently, but not meeting her eyes—and he was shivering, although whether from cold, fear or eagerness, she couldn't tell.

She leaped to her feet. "*Wolf!* It's me, Renn! Oh Wolf, it is you, isn't it?"

At her outburst, the wolf backed away, giving short little grunt-whines that sounded aggrieved.

She couldn't remember how Torak had said "hello"

in wolf talk, so she got down on her hands and knees, grinning and trying to catch the wolf's eye.

That didn't seem right either. The wolf turned his head and backed even farther away.

But was it really Wolf? When she'd known him he'd been a cub—but he'd grown so much! From nose to tail he was almost longer than she was; and if they'd stood side by side, his head would have reached her waist.

When he was a cub, his fur had been a fluffy light gray, with a sprinkling of black across the shoulders. Now it was rich and thick, the gray subtly blended with white, black, silver and foxy red. But he still had that black mantle across the shoulders; and those extra-ordinary amber eyes.

Thunder crashed directly overhead.

Renn ducked.

The wolf yelped and shot to the back of the cave. His ears were flattened, and he was trembling violently.

Whoever he is, thought Renn, he's not yet full-grown, even if he looks it. Inside, he's still part cub.

Out loud she said gently, "It's all right. You're safe here."

The wolf's ears flicked forward to listen.

"Wolf? It is you, isn't it?"

He put his head on one side.

She had an idea. From her food pouch she shook a handful of dried lingonberries into her palm. As a cub, Wolf had adored lingonberries.

The wolf drew close to her outstretched hand, and his black nose twitched. Then he delicately snuffled up the berries.

"Oh, *Wolf*," cried Renn, "it *is* you!"

He darted back into the shadows. She'd startled him.

She shook more lingonberries into her palm; and after some cajoling, he came forward and snuffled them up. Then he tried to nibble her finger guards. To distract him, she put a salmon cake on the ground. Wolf patted it with one forepaw in a gesture she remembered— then gulped it down without even chewing.

Four more went the same way, and now Renn was sure. The Wolf she'd known had loved salmon cakes.

On hands and knees, she crawled toward him. "It's me," she said, reaching out and stroking the pale fur on his throat.

Wolf leaped up and raced to the mouth of the cave, where he ran in circles, whining. She'd done something wrong. Again.

In dismay she retreated to the fire and sat down. "Wolf, why are you here?" she said, although she knew he wouldn't understand. "Are you trying to find Torak, too?"

Wolf licked crumbs of salmon off his chops, then trotted to the back of the cave and lay down with his muzzle between his paws.

Outside, the thunder faded into the north as the World Spirit strode back to its Mountain. The cave filled with the gurgle of rain, and the pungent smell of wet wolf.

Renn longed to tell Wolf how glad she was to see him, to ask if he'd found Torak; but she didn't know how. She'd never paid much attention when Torak spoke wolf, because she'd found it disturbing; it had made her feel as if she didn't really know him. Now she searched her memory.

Wolves, Torak had said once, *don't talk with their voices as much as we do, but more with their paws and tails, and ears and fur, and—um, with their whole bodies.*

But you haven't got a tail, Renn had pointed out. *Or fur. And you can't move your ears. So how do you do it?*

I leave bits out. It's not easy, but we get by.

If it was hard for Torak, how was she going to manage? How was Wolf going to help her find Torak if they couldn't even talk to each other?

Wolf did not *at all* understand the female tailless.

Her yip-and-yowls told him she was being friendly, but the rest of her was all chewed up: sometimes threatening, sometimes saying sorry, and sometimes just—unsure.

At first she'd seemed glad to see him, although he'd sensed a lot of mistrust. Then she'd stared at him rudely, and made it worse by rearing on her hind legs. Then she'd tried to apologize. Then she'd given him lingonberries and the flat fish without eyes that smelled of juniper. Then she'd apologized *again* by scratching his throat. Wolf had been so confused that he'd run in circles.

Now the Dark was over, and he was bored with waiting for her to wake up, so he pounced on her and asked her to play.

She pushed him off, saying something in tailless talk that sounded like "Way! Way!" Wolf remembered Tall Tailless doing that. It seemed to be tailless for a growl.

Leaving the female to get up and stumble out into the Light, he bounded off to explore the Den, and was soon digging a hole, enjoying the power of his paws and the feel of the earth against his pads.

He heard a mouse scurrying in a tunnel. He stomped on the earth and seized the mouse in his jaws, tossed it high, then crunched it in two. He ate some beetles and a worm, then trotted out to find the female.

The Hot Bright Eye was shining in the Up, and

he smelled that the Thunderer was gone. Greatly relieved, he raced through the ferns, relishing their wetness on his fur. He heard a fledgling magpie exploring its nest, and a forest horse in the next valley, scratching its belly on a fallen spruce. He smelled the female down by the Fast Wet, and found her standing with the Long-Claw-That-Flies in her forepaws, pointing it at the ducks.

Scaring ducks was one of Wolf's favorite games. It was how he'd learned to swim, when he'd leaped into what he'd *thought* was a little Wet covered in leaves, and gone under instead. Now he longed to crash into the Wet and send the ducks hurtling into the Up. Not to hunt them; only for fun.

First, though, he must check with the female.

Politely he waited, asking her with a flick of his ears if she was hunting the ducks.

She ignored him.

Wolf waited some more, knowing that taillesses hear and smell so poorly that you can be right in front of them and they don't know you're there.

At length he decided it must be all right, and crept through the ferns to where the ducks paddled, unaware.

He pounced. The ducks shot into the Up in a satisfying spray of indignant squawks.

To Wolf's astonishment, the female yowled at him angrily. "Woof! Woof!" she howled, waving the Long-Claw at him.

Offended, Wolf trotted away. She should have *told* him she was hunting. He had asked.

But he wasn't offended for long. And as he ran off to explore, he reflected that in some strange way, he needed the female to help him find Tall Tailless.

Wolf didn't know how he knew this; it was simply the sureness that came to him sometimes. And now it was telling him that he needed to stay close to the female.

The Hot Bright Eye rose in the Up, and at last she started along a deer trail to seek Tall Tailless. Being the leader, she went ahead and Wolf trotted behind—which was an effort, because she was as slow as a new-born cub.

After a while, they stopped at a little Wet, and the female shared some of the juniper fish. But when Wolf licked her muzzle and whined for more, she laughed and pushed him away.

He was still wondering why she'd laughed, when the wind curled around, and the scent hit him full on the nose.

He stopped. He raised his muzzle and took long, deep sniffs. *Yes!* The best scent in the Forest! The scent of Tall Tailless!

Wolf turned and ran back to follow the scent trail, all the way to a pine tree where, some Lights before, Tall Tailless had rested his forepaw. Wolf raised his head to smell where the scent trail led.

Back there! *They were going the wrong way!* Tall Tailless *wasn't* heading for the deep Forest—he was heading *back*, to where the Hot Bright Eye sinks down to sleep!

The female was too far off for Wolf to see, but he could hear her crashing through the bracken, heading the wrong way.

He barked at her. *Wrong way! Back back back!*

He was frantic to follow his pack-brother, for he felt in his fur that Tall Tailless was many lopes away. But still the female refused to understand.

Snarling with frustration, Wolf ran to fetch her.

She stared at him.

He leaped at her, knocking her to the ground and standing on her chest, barking.

She was frightened. And she seemed to be finding it hard to breathe.

Leave her, then.

Wolf spun around on one forepaw and raced off to find Tall Tailless.

🐾 🐾 🐾

Winded, Renn got up and brushed herself off.

The Forest felt empty after Wolf had gone, but she was too proud to use the grouse-bone whistle to call for him. He had left her. That was that.

In low spirits, she reached a fork in the trail, and stopped. She searched for some sign that Torak had come this way. Nothing. Just impenetrable holly trees and dripping bracken.

Wolf had been so excited. And he'd been heading *west*. . . . West? But that would lead to the Sea. Why would Torak have turned away from the Deep Forest and headed for the Sea?

Suddenly, Wolf appeared on the trail before her.

Joy surged through her—but she repressed a cry of welcome. She'd made mistakes before. She wasn't going to repeat them.

Squatting on her haunches, she told him in a soft voice how pleased she was to see him: keeping her eyes averted, and only now and then letting her gaze graze his.

Wolf trotted up to her, wagging his tail. He nosed her cheek and gave her a ticklish grooming-nibble, followed by a lick.

Gently she scratched behind his ears, and he licked her hand, this time refraining from trying to eat her finger guards.

Then he turned and trotted west.

"West," she said. "You're sure?"

Wolf glanced back at her, and she saw the certainty in his amber eyes.

"West," she said again.

Wolf started along the trail, and Renn followed him at a run.

FIFTEEN

Torak caught a tang of salt on the air and came to a halt.

That smell brought back memories. He'd been to the seashore once, five summers ago. Once had been enough.

Above him the pines soughed in the breeze. North through the trees, the Widewater surged over boulders, eager to reach the Sea. Torak wasn't so eager. But the Forest Horse Leader had told him that what he sought was by the Sea. He wondered if he'd been a fool to believe her. He was bitterly aware that he was no nearer to finding the cure than when he'd left the Ravens. First he'd gone east, and now west. It was as if someone were playing with him; pushing him about like a bone on a gaming-stone.

It was two days since he'd left the edge of the Deep Forest. Two days and nights on the alert for the Follower. But though he sensed that it was still with him, it hadn't shown itself, or played one of its lethal tricks.

Then last night things had got abruptly worse—but for reasons that had nothing to do with the Follower.

Torak had been sitting by the fire, struggling to stay awake while he listened to a storm growling away in the eastern hills. Twice he heard a snatch of cruel laughter on the wind. Twice he ran out of the shelter—to find nothing but tossing branches and glinting stars.

Then—very far off—he heard the wolf.

Heart racing, he strained to catch the meaning of the howls. But they were too far away, the pines too loud. He couldn't make them out. . . .

Desperate, he dropped to the ground and pressed both hands flat, trying to pick up the faint tremors which wolf howls sometimes send through the earth.

Nothing.

Had he really heard it? Or had he only heard what he'd wanted to hear?

He'd stayed up most of the night, but he didn't hear

it again. It was if he'd dreamed it. But he knew that he hadn't.

The scream of a seabird wrenched him back to the present.

To his right the trees thinned, and he went to investigate—and nearly fell over a cliff. It wasn't high, but it was steep. He saw crumbly earth and tree roots; heard a clamor of seabirds. They seemed to be nesting in it.

More cautiously, he continued west with the cliff to his right. Pine needles deadened his footfalls. His breath sounded loud. The ground sloped down, and suddenly there were no more trees, and the sunlight blinded him. He had reached the edge of the Forest.

Before him the Widewater flowed into what appeared to be a very long, narrow lake—except that the lake had no end. To the west he saw a distant clutch of pine-covered islands. Maybe those were the Seal Islands, where his father's mother had been born. Beyond them lay the glittering haze of the open Sea.

As soon as he saw the Sea, memories flooded back.

He was seven summers old, and brimming with excitement. Until now, Fa had kept him away from people, but today they were going to the great gathering of the clans.

Fa didn't tell Torak *why* they were going, or why they had to disguise themselves by painting their faces with bearberry juice. He made a game of it, saying it was best if nobody knew their names.

Torak had thought it was fun. In his ignorance, he'd thought the people at the clan meet would think so, too.

By the time they got there, the shore at the mouth of the Fastwater was dotted with a bewildering number of shelters. Torak had never seen so many different kinds: of wood and bark, turf and hide. Or so many people . . .

His excitement didn't last long. The other children scented an outsider, and closed in for the attack.

A girl threw the first stone: a Viper with cheeks as plump as a squirrel's. "Your Fa's *mad*!" she sneered. "That's why he ran away from his clan, because he swallowed the breath of a ghost!" Willow and Salmon Clan children joined in. "Mad! Mad!" they jeered. "Painted faces! Addled souls!"

If Torak had been older, he would have realized that he couldn't win against so many, and beaten a retreat. Instead the red mist had descended. No one insulted his father.

He'd snatched up a fistful of pebbles, and was on the point of letting fly when Fa had come along and hauled him off. To Torak's astonishment, Fa didn't seem to care about the insults. He was laughing as he swung Torak high in his arms and started back for the Forest.

He'd been laughing the night he'd died. Laughing at a joke Torak had made as they were pitching camp. That was when the bear had come.

It was nine moons since Fa had been killed, but there were still times when Torak couldn't believe that he was really gone. Some mornings when he'd just woken up, he would lie in his sleeping-sack and think, *There's so much I've got to tell him. About Wolf and Renn and Fin-Kedinn* . . .

Then it would hit him all over again. He was never going to tell Fa anything.

Don't think about it, he told himself.

But that hadn't worked in the past, and it didn't now.

Leaving the trees, he found himself on a narrow, curving beach of gray sand. At his feet, purple mounds of seaweed gave off a salty stink. To his left, great slabs of rock lay in chaos, as if shattered by a giant hammer. To his right, the Widewater flowed into the shimmering Sea.

Torak's spirits quailed. He didn't know this world. Seagulls screamed overhead, utterly unlike the tuneful singing of Forest birds. He saw unfamiliar tracks in the sand: a broad furrow flanked by five-clawed prints like half-eaten moons. He guessed they'd been made by some large, heavy creature dragging itself toward the water. But he didn't even know if it was hunter or prey.

He climbed onto the rocks, and tiny white shells crunched under his boots. They looked like some kind of snail, but he didn't know their name, or the name of the fleshy plants that grew in the cracks, their yellow flowers trembling in the breeze.

A few paces away, a black-and-white bird like a magpie, but with a long red beak, pecked at a shell stuck to the rock. The bird struck suddenly and hard, prized off the shell, and ate the innards. Then it flew off with a loud, piping call.

Torak watched it go. Then he knelt at the water's edge and peered into a strange, swaying world. He saw golden-brown fronds and threadlike green weeds. When he put in his hand, the fronds felt slimy as wet buckskin, and the weeds clung to his fingers like hair. A creature with a warty orange shell felt his shadow, and slid beneath a stone.

The salt stink was making his head throb, and the glare hurt his eyes. He was gripped by an overpowering urge to run back into the Forest: to hide, and never come out.

Then he thought of the clans battling the sickness. If he didn't find the cure . . .

He forced himself to stay—and went in search of food.

He didn't know what was good to eat on the shore, but to his relief he found a clump of goosefoot at the edge of the Forest, and picked handfuls of the succulent shoots. He made a driftwood fire, and heated some large pebbles in the embers. Then he half filled his cooking-skin with seawater, hung it from a tripod of driftwood, and with a forked stick added the hot pebbles—followed by the goosefoot, and the remains of a hare he'd snared the night before. Soon he had a tasty, if very salty, stew.

He was tired, although too on edge to sleep. Instead he took off his clothes and had a wash. The seawater left him clean, but a bit sticky. He pulled on his leggings, and laid his boots and jerkin to air on the rocks.

At the bottom of his pack he found the boar's tusks.

Maybe the Forest Horse Leader had been right. Maybe he should make an amulet of the tusks, in memory of the friend he'd had to kill.

Taking them to a rock pool, he cleaned them, scraping the flesh from the insides with a stick. Then he put them on the rocks to dry.

Next he strung a line of bramble-thorn fishing hooks across an inlet where he guessed the fish might come to feed among the weeds. For bait he used the flesh from the tusks; but to keep the hooks below the surface, he would need sink-stones.

There were pebbles on the beach, but no more rawhide cords in his pack for tying them to the lines.

He didn't like the idea of cutting strips from the slimy brown seaweed. There might be Hidden People in the water: maybe those weeds belonged to them.

A couple of split pine roots would do. Which meant going back into the Forest.

He felt safer among the trees, and he wanted a reason to stay. Maybe he should cut more pine roots; always useful to have some to spare. And that meant going farther in, because you must never cut more than two roots from the same tree.

The sun was getting low by the time he got back to the Sea. His things lay on the rocks where he'd left them.

Almost.

Whoever had searched his gear had gone to some lengths to replace it, but Torak knew instantly that it had been moved. A patch of yellow flowers by his pack was slightly crushed: that was where he'd set down the pack in the first place. The boar tusks, too, had been rearranged: he made out the faint crescents of damp where they'd originally lain.

Noiselessly he slipped back into the Forest. Crouched low. Wished the undergrowth were higher.

Voices on the sand, thirty paces away. Two boys were climbing out from behind the rocks. Walking slowly, searching for tracks.

Both were bigger than Torak, and looked about a summer older than him. They had sun-darkened faces and long yellow hair beaded with shells. Bands of slitted gray hide tied across their eyes gave them a blank, masklike look.

Torak didn't need to see their eyes to know that they meant him harm. Their weapons told him that: sturdy harpoons with barbed bone heads, and knives of blue flint. The smaller one carried a slingshot stuck in his belt.

They were barefoot, in knee-length breeches of some kind of supple gray hide, and sleeveless jerkins that revealed wavy blue clan-tattoos all over their arms. Their jerkins bore a strip of clan-creature skin: glossy gray fur marked with small dark rings. Whale? Seal? Torak didn't know.

But the oddest thing about them was that he could see their tattoos and their clan-creature skins at all, because over their jerkins each boy wore a long-sleeved parka of very light, yellowish hide: so light that Torak could see right through it. He wondered what kind of creature had skin that you could see through.

"He can't have gone far," said the shorter of the two, his voice carrying in the evening air.

"He must have slunk back into the trees," said the other. "Like one of those—what d'you call them? Horses?"

His companion sniggered. "Detlan, I don't think horses slink."

"How would you know, Asrif?" said Detlan. "You've never seen one either."

"I've heard about them," said Asrif. "Come on, let's go. He's not coming back."

"He'd better not," said Detlan. "Tainting the Sea with his filthy Forest gear . . ."

Holding his breath, Torak watched them make their way down to the rocks.

From beneath an overhang they pulled two long, slender hide canoes. The canoes were utterly different from those Torak was used to: extremely shallow in the draft, and covered at prow and stern with tight-stretched gray hide. And they must be extraordinarily light, because each boy hoisted his boat on his head without difficulty, and carried it down to the water.

Torak watched them set the canoes in the shallows, then leap aboard. With narrow double-bladed paddles they began to row, and soon disappeared, gliding silently out of sight beyond the rocks.

But he knew that it was too soon to feel relieved. This felt like a trap. He would wait them out. And like all hunters, he knew how to wait.

The breeze fell to nothing, and the water became as smooth as polished slate. The only sounds were the suck and slap of wavelets, and a duck nibbling seaweed in the shallows.

The sun sank lower. The duck spread its wings and

flew off. Dusk came on—although as it was the middle of the Moon of No Dark, night would be merely a brief interval of deep blue twilight.

Still Torak waited.

It was nearly dawn when he judged it safe to go out. Stiff from crouching so long, he made his way onto the rocks.

The dew had dampened his pack, but when he checked its contents, he found to his relief that nothing had been taken.

Hungry, he went to check the fishhooks. Stooping to draw in the line, he brushed away piles of seaweed that the wind had blown across it.

Except—there had been no wind. So how had that seaweed got there?

He leaped back just as the rope snapped taut around his ankle and yanked him off his feet.

SIXTEEN

Torak fell, knocking his head on a rock. A tall figure blotted out the sun.

Against the glare, Torak glimpsed a dark face and a blaze of yellow hair; a knife in one hand and a rope in the other, pulled tight on the noose around his ankle.

"I've got him," said his captor to someone Torak couldn't see. Then to Torak, "Come quietly or I'll hurt you." He spoke without malice, but clearly meant what he said.

Torak, however, was not about to come quietly. He didn't know many fighting tricks, but he knew about feints. As his captor leaned down to tie his hands, he whipped out his knife. His captor's head jerked to follow the blade—and with his free foot Torak kicked the boy's shin as hard as he could. With a howl of pain the boy crashed onto the rocks.

Torak cut the rope at his ankle and raced off into the Forest—keeping low, and zigzagging through the willow-herb so that they wouldn't get a chance to take aim.

"You can't get away from us, Forest Boy!" called a voice some way behind him—and he recognized the small boy with the slingshot, the one named Asrif.

About sixty paces in, Torak threw himself beneath a fallen pine, biting his lips to keep his breath from betraying him. The Forest was deathly quiet. There was nothing to cover the noise of his escape.

"We've got you surrounded," yelled another boy somewhere to his right; he recognized the big one, Detlan.

"Better come out," urged the third boy, the tall one from the rocks.

Make me, Torak told him silently.

A stone smacked into the tree trunk above his head.

"Oh, you're in trouble, Forest Boy!" taunted Asrif. By the sound of it, he was making no attempt at stealth.

"How could you do it?" cried Detlan.

"*Why* did you do it?" shouted the tall boy.

Why did I do what? wondered Torak. Then he

realized what they were doing: talking to distract him while they closed in.

Quickly he looked about. Before him the ground sloped down into a long, lush hollow. He made out alders and willows; pale-green moss and fluffy white haregrass. If you knew the Forest, that told you one thing: a bog. But from what they'd said about horses, they didn't seem to know the Forest at all.

Staying low, Torak crept to the edge of the bog. It was big—about twenty paces long and fifteen wide— and by the smell of it, deep. No way around it. He'd have to get across, and noiselessly. Only when he was on the other side would he lure them in.

It might work. If he didn't fall in himself.

Quietly he climbed a willow overhanging the bog— first making sure that it wasn't a crack willow. Then he made his way out onto a branch. There was an alder on the other side, if he could reach it. . . .

He jumped, landing half in the alder, with his feet trailing in cold, stinking mud. A branch snapped as he hauled himself up, and he breathed an apology to the tree.

Shouts behind him. "Down there!"

They crashed toward him, noisier than a herd of aurochs, and he fled up the slope, junipers scratching his shins.

Below him his pursuers bellowed with rage. Good.

They'd blundered into the bog.

"Filthy Forest tricks!" yelled one.

"You're not getting away with this!" howled another.

But it sounded as if only two of them were down there. Where was the third one, the tall boy from the rocks?

No time to think about that. He reached the top of the slope—and would have tumbled off the cliff if he hadn't grabbed a sapling just in time.

He stifled a cry of frustration. He hadn't come nearly as far as he'd thought.

The bog wouldn't slow his pursuers for long; and even if he could scramble down the cliff, the river was too wide to swim, and in those canoes they'd easily catch him. He'd have to follow the Widewater upstream, and hope he could lose them in the Forest. Which would mean leaving his gear behind on the rocks; although at least he still had his knife. . . .

His knife . . .

What he held in his hand was the knife Fin-Kedinn had made for him, but Fa's knife—his most precious possession—was in his pack.

Above him there was a tearing sound—and he glanced up to see a large branch rushing toward him. He leaped aside—but not far enough. The branch caught him painfully on the elbow, and he cried out.

"Up there!" bayed his pursuers.

He heard a ripple of laughter—and looked up to see a face of leaves disappearing into the trees.

A stone struck him on the cheekbone, and he fell against the sapling.

"We've got him," said a voice close by.

Through a blur of pain, Torak saw the tall boy from the rocks moving calmly toward him through the pines. "Asrif," he said to his companion, "I've told you before, not the head. You could have killed him."

Asrif tucked his slingshot in his belt and grinned. "And then wouldn't I have been sorry."

They were back on the rocks: Torak with his hands bound behind him, his captors prowling up and down. They no longer wore the strips of hide across their eyes, but it wasn't an improvement. He could see the violence in them; their fingers flexing on the hilts of their knives. Strange knives, with hilts made of something that was neither wood, antler nor bone.

The tall boy who'd caught him on the rocks came close. He had a clever, watchful face, and eyes as cold as blue flint. "You shouldn't have run," he said quietly. "That's what a coward does."

"I'm not a coward," said Torak, meeting his gaze. His cheek was throbbing, his feet and shins burning with scratches.

Asrif gave a gleeful laugh. "Oh, you're in trouble, Forest Boy!" He had a weaselly look, and kept baring his teeth in an edgy grin. "He is, isn't he, Bale?" he said to the tall boy.

The boy called Bale did not reply.

"I don't understand," said Detlan, shaking his head. "To taint the Sea with the Forest! Why would he do it?" His heavy brows made a deep crease on the bridge of his nose, and Torak guessed that he wasn't too bright, but very good at following orders.

Torak turned to Bale, who seemed to be the leader. "I don't know what you think I've done, but I never—"

"Deerskin," spat Bale, pacing up and down. "Reindeer hide. Forest wood. Have you no respect?"

"For *what?*" said Torak.

Detlan's jaw dropped.

Asrif tapped his forehead. "He's mad. He must be."

Bale narrowed his eyes. "No. He knew what he was doing." Then to Torak, "Bringing your unclean Forest skins right onto the shore! Setting your cowardly traps to snare our skinboats—trailing them in the Sea herself!"

"I was fishing," said Torak.

"You broke the law!" roared Bale. "*You tainted the Sea with the Forest!*"

Torak took a breath. "My name is Torak," he said. "I'm Wolf Clan. What clan are you?"

"Seal, of course." Bale tapped the strip of gray fur on

his chest. "Don't you know sealskin when you see it?"

Torak shook his head. "No, I've never seen one."

"*Never seen a seal?*" said Detlan, aghast.

Asrif hooted. "Told you he was mad!"

Torak's face grew hot. "I'm Wolf Clan," he said again. "But I'm also—"

"Is that what this is?" sneered Asrif. With a piece of driftwood he jabbed at the strip of wolfskin on Torak's jerkin.

Bale's lip curled in scorn. "So that's wolf hide. Looks a poor sort of creature to me."

"You wouldn't say that if you'd ever seen one," Torak said heatedly. Then to Asrif, "Leave that alone!" Fa had prepared that skin for him last spring, from the carcass of a lone wolf they'd found in a cave. Since then it had been unpicked and sewn to his winter parka, and now to his summer jerkin. He was dreading the time when it would be worn to shreds.

Bale flicked Asrif a glance, and the smaller boy shrugged, and threw away the stick.

"I may be Wolf Clan," Torak told Bale, "but my father's mother was Seal. So whether you like it or not, we're bone kin."

"That's a lie!" spat Bale. "If you were kin, you'd know the law of the Sea."

"Bale," broke in Detlan, "we should start back. She's getting restless."

Bale glanced at the Sea. The waves had turned choppy. "This is your doing," he told Torak. "Angering the Sea Mother. Tainting her waters with the Forest."

Asrif snickered. "Oh, Forest Boy, it'll be the Rock for you!"

"The Rock," Torak said blankly.

Asrif's grin widened. "A skerry near our island. You know what a skerry is, don't you?"

"It's a rock in the Sea," put in Detlan, who seemed to be struggling to grasp the depths of Torak's ignorance.

"They give you a skin of water," said Asrif, "but no food, then they leave you on the Rock for a whole moon. Sometimes the Sea Mother lets you live; sometimes she washes you off." His grin faltered, and in his pale-blue eyes Torak saw fear. "Washes you off," he repeated, "into the jaws of the Hunters."

"Asrif, that's enough," said Bale. "We'll have to take him with us, and let the Leader decide."

"*No!*" protested Torak.

Bale wasn't listening. "Asrif, load up the trade goods. Detlan, we need a fire to purify us, especially him. I'm going to repair my boat." With that he jumped off the rocks and onto the beach.

Detlan seemed glad of something to do, and set about gathering armfuls of dried seaweed and drift-wood. Soon he had a big fire blazing, giving off plumes of thick gray smoke.

"What are you going to do to me?" said Torak.

"Give you a taste of the Sea," said Asrif with his weaselly grin.

"You can hardly go near our skinboats stinking of the Forest," said Detlan, as if that were too obvious to need pointing out.

Before Torak could protest, Detlan had stripped him naked and pushed him into the fire.

He managed to leap clear of the flames—but Asrif was waiting on the other side, and forced him back with his harpoon—back through the acrid, choking smoke.

Again they pushed him through it until his eyes were streaming and his throat raw. Then they tossed him into the Sea.

The cold hit him like a punch in the chest, and he swallowed salt water. Kicking with all his might, he struggled to the surface, but couldn't break the bindings around his wrists.

Rough hands hauled him out and dragged him coughing onto the rocks. Then they cut the bindings at his wrists and bundled him into a gray hide jerkin and breeches that Asrif fetched from his boat. Torak felt naked without his knife and his clan-creature skin, and he hated having to wear someone else's clothes. "Give me—back—my things!" he spluttered.

"Lucky for you the Salmon Clan didn't want to trade," snorted Asrif, "or you wouldn't have anything to wear!"

"He's so skinny!" said Detlan as he yanked Torak to his feet. "Don't they have enough prey in the Forest?"

Half pushing, half pulling, they led him down to the sand. Swiftly Asrif loaded his canoe at prow and stern with large, lumpy bundles wrapped in hide. A short distance away, Bale crouched by his boat, smearing a patch on its side with what looked like fat from a small hide pouch. His hands moved tenderly, but when he saw Torak, he glowered. "Take him with you, Detlan," he growled. "I don't want him near my boat."

"In you go," said Detlan, pushing Torak toward his craft. Like Asrif's, it was laden with bundles—including Torak's gear—but only at the prow end.

Torak hesitated. "Your friend. Bale. Why is he so angry with me?"

It was Asrif who answered. "One of your fishhooks snagged his skinboat. It's as well for you that he can repair it."

Torak was puzzled. "But it's only a boat."

Asrif and Detlan gaped.

"A skinboat is not just a *boat*!" said Detlan. "It's a hunting partner! Don't ever let Bale hear you say that!"

Torak swallowed. "I didn't mean to—"

"Just get in," muttered Detlan. "Sit in the stern,

keep your feet on the crossbar, and *don't move.* If you put your foot through the hide, we'll both go down."

The skinboat was so shallow that it rocked with Torak's every move, and he had to grip the sides to keep from falling out. Detlan, although much heavier, leaped in without a wobble. Torak noticed that he braced his thighs against the sides of the craft for balance.

Bale led the way, skimming across the waves at amazing speed. With the wind at their backs they sped like seabirds over the water, and when Torak twisted around, he was dismayed to see how quickly the Forest was falling away.

Soon they reached the islands he'd seen from the shore—but to his alarm, they kept going. "But—I thought we were going to your islands!"

"Oh, we are!" grinned Asrif.

"Then why have we gone past them?"

Detlan threw back his head and laughed. "Not those islands! Much farther! A whole day's rowing!"

"*What?*" cried Torak.

They cleared the last island, and suddenly there was no more land to right or left. There was nothing but Sea.

Torak clutched the sides and stared down into the murky water. "I can't see the bottom," he said.

"Of course you can't!" said Detlan. "This is the Sea!"

Torak twisted around and saw the Forest sinking beneath the waves—and with it, all hope of finding the cure.

Suddenly on the wind he caught the howl of a wolf. It wasn't just any wolf. It was *Wolf.*

Where are you? I am here! Where are you!

Wildly Torak staggered to his feet. *"Wolf!"*

"Get down!" bellowed Detlan.

"Too late to go back now!" mocked Asrif. "And don't even think about jumping in, because then we'd have to shoot you!"

Too late . . .

Too late, Torak heard Wolf howling for him as the Forest disappeared into the Sea.

"Wolf!" he yelled.

Wolf had heard his plea—had braved the wrath of the World Spirit to seek his pack-brother—but Torak had put himself utterly beyond his reach.

SEVENTEEN

The three skinboats flew over the waves as the sun sank toward the Sea, and hope died in Torak's heart.

In his mind he saw Wolf running up and down the shore: howling, unable to comprehend why his pack-brother had forsaken him.

Torak couldn't bear it. If only he'd howled a reply. But he'd been too stunned. And by the time it had occurred to him, he was far away, and Wolf's howls were nothing but memory.

Bitterly he berated himself for breaking the law of the Sea. If Renn had been with him this would never have happened; the Seals would never have got angry, and he'd be back there now with Wolf.

A gust of wind drenched him with spray, stinging his eyes and making the wound on his calf smart. He lurched and nearly went overboard.

"Keep still!" said Detlan over his shoulder. "If you fall in, I'm not hauling you out."

"Hear that, Forest boy?" shouted Asrif from his skinboat.

"Save your breath, Asrif," cried Bale. "Still a long way to go."

Torak clutched the skinboat with numb fingers. Wherever he turned, he saw nothing but waves. The Sea had swallowed everything. Forest, Mountain, Raven, Wolf. He felt as insignificant as dust on the watery hide of this vast, endlessly heaving creature.

Peering over the edge, he stared into impenetrable dark. If he fell in, when would he reach the bottom? Or would he keep sinking down and down forever?

A bird flew past. At first Torak thought it was a goose, but then he saw that it was black all over, and flying so low that its wing tips almost touched the Sea.

Some time later, they passed a flock of small, plump seabirds sitting on the water, talking to one another in mysterious, un-birdlike groans. They had black backs and white bellies, and very bright, triangular red and yellow beaks.

Detlan caught Torak staring at them. "Puffins," he said crossly. "They're puffins. Don't you have puffins in the Forest?"

Torak shook his head. "Are they hunter or prey?"

"Both," said Detlan. "But we never hunt them. Puffins are sacred to the Mages." He paused, reluctant to talk, but unable to tolerate Torak's ignorance. "They're not like other birds," he said at last. "They're the only creature that can fly through the air, *and* dive in the Sea, *and* burrow under the earth. That's why they're sacred. Because they can visit the spirits."

Asrif brought his skinboat alongside theirs. "I bet there's nothing like them in your Forest," he jeered.

There wasn't, but Torak was not about to admit it. He gave Asrif a hostile stare.

The evening wore on, and still the sun hung low in the sky. Soon it would be Midsummer, the time of the white nights, when the sun didn't sleep at all.

Torak would have given a lot to go to sleep. His limbs were cramped, and he kept nodding off, then jolting awake again.

Then, from far beneath the waves, he heard singing.

Of one accord, all three Seals stopped paddling.

Bale whipped off his sun-visor and scanned the waves. Asrif bared his teeth in a grimace. Detlan muttered under his breath and clutched an amulet at his breast.

Torak leaned over the side, listening.

Such a remote, lonely song. Long, wavering cries that made ripples in his mind. Echoing groans as bottomless as the deeps. It was as if the Sea herself were singing a lament.

"The Hunters," breathed Detlan.

"There," Asrif said quietly, pointing to the northwest.

Bale turned his head, then nodded. "They're after capelin. We must be careful not to disturb them."

Torak squinted into the sun, but saw nothing. Then—ten paces away—he made out a large patch of calm water. It reminded him of the smoothness you see where a river flows over a rock just beneath the surface. "What is it?" he whispered.

"A shoal of capelin," murmured Detlan over his shoulder. "They hide far below, and the Hunters chase them to the surface. That's why the gulls are coming."

As if from nowhere, seabirds appeared, mewing excitedly. But according to Detlan, it was below the surface that the Hunters would make their kill. Torak pictured the terror among the fishes as they crowded together, seeking safety, but unable to get away from the Hunters who came at them from the dark. . . .

But what *were* the Hunters?

"Watch the water," whispered Detlan.

Torak shaded his eyes with his palm.

The Sea began to seethe. Bubbles broke the surface. The water turned pale green.

"That's the capelin rising," hissed Detlan. "The Hunters are beneath them, and all around. They've nowhere to go but up. . . ."

More gulls came, till the sky was a screaming tumult. And now Torak saw a dense mass of fish rising to the surface: slender, twisting bodies packed so tight that they turned the Sea to silver and made the water boil. In their panic, some leaped clear of the waves, desperate to escape. But the gulls were waiting for them.

A fish broke the surface right beside Torak: a silver dart no longer than his hand. A huge bird with a wingspan wider than a skinboat swept down, speared it in one sharp talon, and bore it skyward. Craning his neck, Torak recognized the broad, flicked-up wing feathers of an eagle.

A gull flew after it, intent on stealing its prize. The sea-eagle gave a contemptuous twitch of its ash-colored tail and flew away.

Down among the gulls, the fight for fish was savage. Torak saw one gull struggling to fly away with a half-swallowed capelin jutting from its gullet, while two more chased it, tugging at the fish's tail.

Then he saw something that made him forget the seabirds.

A black fin broke the surface.

He gasped.

The fin was as tall as a man, and moving faster than a skinboat.

"Ah," breathed Detlan. "The Hunters are come."

Torak glanced at the Seals. All three were watching with awe—and in Bale's case, admiration.

Another towering fin broke the surface. Then another—this one with a notch bitten out of it just below the tip. It was moving fast and with deadly purpose, circling the capelin.

So that's a Hunter, thought Torak. His father had drawn him pictures of whales in the dust, but until now Torak had never grasped how huge they were. With a shiver he realized how vulnerable he was, bobbing about in a skinboat as fragile as an eggshell. . . .

Suddenly he heard a splash—and turned to see a column of spray shooting high into the air. Then a great black tail lifted clear of the water and thrashed down again. More spray flew. The water became a chaos of flying foam and shattered sunlight. And this time when the Hunter with the notched fin turned to circle the capelin, it had a young one swimming beside it, its small fin just keeping up with the big one.

On and on the Hunters circled—dived—then surfaced again, taking their fill of the prey. Then—suddenly—they vanished.

Holding his breath, Torak scanned the Sea. They could be anywhere. They could be right beneath the skinboat. . . .

A throaty *kwssh!* behind him—and a jet of spray drenched the boat from prow to stern. And there was the one with the notched fin, so close that Torak could have reached out and touched the enormous blunt-nosed head—black on top and white underneath, with an oval patch of white behind the eye. For a moment the huge jaws gaped, and Torak saw sharp white teeth longer than his middle finger. For a moment a dark, shining eye met his. Then the Hunter arched its gleaming back and dived.

He braced himself, but it didn't come again. All that remained of the hunt were the gulls squabbling over scraps, and a glitter of silver fish scales drifting down through the green water.

Bale bowed to the Sea where the Hunters had been, then took up his paddle and moved off. The others followed in silence.

Only after they were well clear of the hunting ground did Detlan turn to Torak. "So now you've seen them," he said.

Torak was silent for a moment. "They hunt in a pack," he said. "Like wolves."

Detlan scowled. "The Hunters are like no Forest creature you've ever seen. They're the fastest creatures

in the Sea. And the cleverest. And the deadliest." He
swallowed. "A single Hunter can make a whirlpool that
can sink the biggest skinboat. One flick of his tail can
snap a man's backbone like a capelin's."

Torak glanced over his shoulder. "Do they hunt
people?"

"Not unless we hunt them."

"And do you?"

Detlan glared at him. "Of course not! The Hunters
are sacred to the Sea Mother! Besides," he added,
"they always avenge harm done to their own." His
heavy face became thoughtful. "There's a story that
once, before the Great Wave, a boy from the
Cormorant Clan caused the death of a young Hunter.
He didn't mean to do it, it was an accident; the
Hunter had become tangled in the boy's seal net, and
he'd harpooned it before he could see what it was." He
shook his head. "The boy was so terrified that he never
went out in a skinboat again. All his life—his whole
life—he stayed on the shore with the women. But many
winters later, when he was an old, old man, he was
seized with such a longing to be once more on the Sea
that he told his son to take him out in his skinboat."
Detlan licked his lips. "The Hunters were waiting for
them. They were never seen again."

Torak thought about that. "But—he hadn't meant to

kill the young one. Was there no way he could have appeased them?"

Again Detlan shook his head, and after that they didn't speak for a long time.

The wind dropped and they entered a fog bank. Bale and Asrif disappeared. Detlan's paddle cut noiselessly through the water.

A barren rock slid by to Torak's right, with a gull perched on top.

"There," said Detlan with a nod. "That's the Rock."

Somewhere in the fog, Asrif sniggered. "Soon that'll be you, Forest boy."

Torak set his teeth, determined not to give them the satisfaction of seeing him flinch; but inside, his spirits quailed. The Rock was scarcely bigger than a skinboat, and even at its highest point it was no taller than he was. One big wave would wash him into the Sea. He couldn't imagine surviving on it for a day, let alone a whole moon.

On they went through the fog. Torak felt it settle on his skin, beading his strange new clothes with damp.

Up ahead, something bobbed in the water.

He blinked.

It was gone.

No—there it was again, bobbing up beside him. A head like a dog's: a gray dog with a blunt, whiskered muzzle and large, inquisitive black eyes.

Detlan saw it and smiled. "Bale! Asrif!" he called. "The guardian has come to show us the way home!"

The seal rolled over, showing a pale, spotted belly. Then it flipped around, scratched its muzzle with one handlike flipper, shut its nostrils tight, and sank below the surface, where it swam alongside the skinboats.

So that's a seal, thought Torak. He thought it an odd blend of ungainliness and sleek beauty.

The guardian led them well, and the fog cleared as abruptly as it had descended. Suddenly they were out in sunlight again.

"We're home," said Detlan. Laughing, he lifted his paddle high, scattering droplets.

Torak gasped. Before him lay an island like none he'd ever seen.

Three jagged peaks reared straight out of the Sea. There was no Forest. Just mountains and Sea. The mountains were almost sheer, their grim flanks speckled with seabirds and veined with waterfalls that cascaded from patches of ice mantling their shoulders. Only at their feet could Torak see a swathe of green— and below that, a wide, curving bay with a slash of sand stained pink by the setting sun.

Smoke rose from a cluster of humped gray shelters on the sand. Beside each shelter stood a rack on which were laid several skinboats. Torak saw that below them on the beach, two saplings had been planted, and lashed together to form an arch. The saplings were bright scarlet. Uneasily he wondered what they were for.

From across the water came the murmur of voices and the clamor of birds. With a shock he saw that the cliffs were alive with seabirds: thousands of them— wheeling, crammed onto ledges. The shelters of the Seals, too, seemed precarious and cramped. He couldn't imagine how people could live like this: caught on a narrow strip of land between mountain and Sea.

"The Seal Islands," said Bale, bringing his skinboat alongside Detlan's. There was no mistaking the pride in his voice.

"How many islands are there?" said Torak. He could only see one.

Bale looked at him suspiciously. "This, and two smaller ones to the north. The Cormorant and the Kelp clans live on those, but this—this is the Seals' home. It's the biggest, which is why the whole group takes its name. The biggest and the best."

Of course, thought Torak sourly. Everything the Seals did had to be the best.

But as they drew nearer, he forgot about that. There seemed to be something very wrong with the bay. Its waters were deep crimson: too deep to be colored only by the setting sun.

Then he caught a familiar, salty-sweet stink, very strong in the windless air. It couldn't be. . . .

It was.

The Bay of Seals was full of blood.

EIGHTEEN

The clamor of seagulls dinned in Torak's ears, and the smell of blood caught at his throat.

He saw children paddling in foaming red shallows, and women washing hide in crimson water. Men moved like shadows before a leaping fire, piling huge slabs of meat beside the sapling arch. Limbs, hands, faces: all were stained scarlet, like people in a dream.

"Someone's made a big kill," said Asrif.

"First of the summer," said Bale, "and we missed it." He made it sound as if that were Torak's fault.

Suddenly Torak realized that all this meat came

from just a single kill. He saw a tail fin longer than a skinboat. What he'd taken for saplings were the jaw-bones of a whale.

At least—he guessed it was a whale, although it wasn't a Hunter. Instead of teeth, its jaws trailed a long fringe of coarse black hair, which a Seal man was chopping off with a knife. He'd cut off his own hair, too. It lay at his feet in the same pile as the whale's.

As Torak waded onto the slippery red pebbles, he saw how happy everyone was. The whole clan was bubbling with celebration. A kill this size would mean food for days to come.

Bale leaped out of his skinboat and told Torak to *stay there*. "Islinn will decide what to do with you after the feast."

Alone on the shingle, Torak was painfully aware of the Seals' stares. Among the Ravens he'd been an out-sider, but this was worse. And these people were his bone kin.

He watched Bale unstrap his bundles and toss them to a weather-beaten man who'd come down to meet him. From the resemblance between them, Torak guessed they were father and son.

He saw Detlan setting his skinboat on a rack, flanked by a beaming woman and a small girl, clearly his sister, who was jumping up and down, clamoring for his attention. Detlan looked embarassed, but pleased to see her.

Asrif, still in the shallows, was being scolded by a shrewish woman even shorter than he was. "You were supposed to bring back *two* bundles of salmonskin!" she said, jabbing her finger in his chest. "How could you leave one behind?"

"I don't *know*," mumbled Asrif. "I packed them both, I know I did. And now it's not there."

Bale was speaking to his father and pointing at Torak. Then he ran up the beach to talk to a man by the fire.

Dusk came on, the Seals went to make ready for the feast, and still Torak waited. His cheek hurt. He was ravenous.

He saw now why nobody had bothered to tie him up. There was nowhere to run to: the mountains walled in the bay. At the south end, a waterfall pounded down from a cliff face. At the north, a track climbed up toward an overhang that jutted over the Sea like an enormous skinboat. Unless the Seals let him go, he'd never get off the island. He would be trapped, while in the Forest the clans sickened and died. . . .

The sky turned deep blue. Food smells wafted down to him. He saw cooking-skins hanging from supports of what looked like whale bones, and fair-haired women chatting as they stirred. Unlike the Seal men, their calves rather than their arms bore the wavy blue lines of their clan-tattoos.

Near them, a group of girls giggled as they dug into a steaming mound from which came the rich smell of baked meat. Torak knew this way of cooking from the Ravens, but he'd never seen it done quite like this. A hunk of meat as big as he was had been wrapped in seaweed, then buried in a pit of fire-heated stones, and covered with more seaweed and sand.

The women began sharing the food into bowls. Torak noticed that only they did the cooking, while the men had cut up the carcass. That struck him as bizarre. Didn't Seal girls hunt? He wondered what Renn would say about that.

Hungrily he watched the clan gather in a circle around the fire. Still no one came to fetch him.

A murmuring began, like the sighing of the Sea, and the whole clan lifted its arms. A figure stepped from the circle, and Torak recognized the man who'd cut off his hair. Bearing a basket of capelin, the man approached the jawbone arch, and set the offering beneath it. Torak guessed he was thanking the whale for giving its life to the clan. But instead of returning to the feast, the man trudged into the gloom, toward a cave at the foot of the overhang.

When Torak had almost lost hope, Detlan came for

him, and they went to sit some distance from the fire, with Asrif and Bale.

A girl handed Torak a bowl. It was so heavy that he nearly dropped it, and to his astonishment he saw that it was made of stone. Why in the name of the Forest would anyone make bowls out of stone? How would you carry them when you moved camp?

A disturbing idea came to him. Perhaps the Seals *never* moved camp.

"Eat," said Detlan, tossing him a spoon.

Torak glanced at his bowl. It contained a hunk of dark-pink meat topped by a thick slab of gray fat, and a smaller piece of purplish flesh. Around it swam a sludgy stew that stank of the Sea, half a capelin, and two long, pale things that looked like fingers.

"What's the matter," said Bale, "not good enough? You're lucky we're feeding you at all."

"Haven't you ever eaten shellworms?" said Asrif.

"What's in it?" asked Torak.

"The red meat's whale," said Detlan, "and that's blubber on top." With his knife, he speared his own chunk of purple meat. "Whale heart. Very special. We all get a piece, to take in its strength and courage." He crammed it into his mouth and chewed.

"Bet you don't have anything this good in the Forest," said Asrif.

Torak ignored him and ate. The whale meat was

stringy, the blubber oily and bland, and the shellworms had no taste at all. But the capelin was good.

"Had you really never seen a seal?" said Detlan.

"Detlan, why waste your time?" said Bale.

But Detlan seemed to have taken Torak's ignorance as a personal affront. "Seals give us *everything*," he said earnestly. "Clothes, shelters, skinboats. Food, harpoons, lamps." He paused, clearly wondering if he'd left anything out.

"What about your parkas?" said Torak, curious despite himself. "That thin hide you can see through. That can't be seal."

"It is," said Asrif. "It's gutskin."

"I told you," said Detlan, "the seals give us everything. We are the people of the seal."

Torak frowned. "But no one's allowed to hunt their clan-creature. So why do you?"

All three of them looked horrified.

"We would *never* do that!" cried Detlan. Angrily he struck the spotted fur on his chest. "*This* is our clan-creature! This is *ring*-seal! What we hunt—what we eat—that's *gray* seal!"

Torak had never heard of such a distinction, and it struck him as slippery and false. Something must have shown in his face, because Detlan's brows lowered ominously.

"Told you it was a waste of time," said Bale, rising to his feet. Then to Torak, "Come on. Time to face the Leader."

Islinn the Seal Clan Leader was old and shrunken. He looked as if the life were being sucked out of him.

His wispy white hair and beard were beaded with tiny blue slate beads, and his ears were pierced with twisted, spearlike shells whose weight had stretched his earlobes to his shoulders.

Bale forced Torak to his knees. Then he named the captive to the Seals, and told them how he'd broken the law.

At that, many people cried out and ran to lay placating hands on the whale's jawbone. The Leader stroked his beard with a shaky hand, but said nothing. His rheumy eyes moved constantly. Torak wondered if they hid intelligence, or the lack of it.

At last Islinn spoke. "You *say* that you're kin," he murmured in a reedy voice that sounded as if he barely had the strength to force it from his chest.

"My father's mother was a Seal," said Torak.

"What was his name?"

"I can't name him. He died last autumn."

The Leader pondered that, then murmured to the man beside him. The man's face was hidden by drifting smoke, but Torak could tell from the thick, sandy hair and the muscled limbs that he was much younger than Islinn. His jerkin and breeches were plain, but his belt was magnificent. Made of braided hide, it was two hands wide, and fringed with the red and yellow beaks of puffins.

Puffins, thought Torak. He must be the Mage.

"Name your father's mother," said the Leader.

Torak did.

The Leader's lipless mouth tightened.

Among the Seals, someone caught their breath.

"I knew the woman," wheezed the Leader. "She mated with a Forest man. I never knew that she'd had a son."

"How do we know that she did?" said the Mage without turning his head. "How do we know that the boy is who he says he is?" He spoke quietly, but all the Seals leaned forward to listen.

It was a remarkable voice: smooth flowing and low pitched, but with an undertow of great power, like the Sea. It was a voice that anyone would want to hear. For a moment, Torak almost forgot that it had called him a liar.

The Leader was nodding. "My thoughts too, Tenris."

The smoke shifted, and Torak saw the Mage for the first time—or at least, he saw one side of his face, for

Tenris was still turned away. He was handsome in a sharp-boned way: with a straight nose, a wide mouth flanked by deep laughter lines, and a dark-gold beard cut close to the strong line of his jaw.

Torak sensed that this was the man who wielded the real power among the Seals; the man who would decide his fate. For a moment, he was reminded of Fin-Kedinn. "I am telling the truth," he said. "I am your bone kin."

"We need more than your word," said the Mage. He turned into the light, and Torak saw that the left side of his face was terribly burned. One gray eye peered from a lashless socket. His scalp had been scorched a mottled pink. Only his mouth was unscathed. He gave Torak a wry smile, as if daring him not to flinch.

Torak put his fists over his heart and bowed. "I admit that I broke your law," he said, "but only because I didn't know. My father never taught me the ways of the Sea."

Tenris the Seal Mage tilted his ruined head. "Then what were you doing on the shore?"

"The Forest Horse Leader told me I'd find what I'm looking for by the Sea."

"And what are you looking for?"

"A cure."

"For what? Are you ill?"

Torak shook his head. Then he told Tenris about the sickness.

The effect on the Seals was startling.

The Leader threw up his wrinkled hands.

Many Seals shouted in alarm.

Bale leaped to his feet, his face thunderous. "Why didn't you warn us?" he cried. "What if you've brought it back?"

Torak stared at him. "You know the sickness? You've seen it before?"

But Bale had turned away, his face etched with pain.

"It came three summers ago," the Leader said grimly. "His younger brother was the first to die. Then three more. My son among them."

"But now you're free of it?" said Torak, biting back his excitement. "You found a cure?"

"For the Seals," snarled Bale. "Not for you."

"But you must give it to me!" cried Torak.

Bale rounded on him. "*Must?* You break our law, you anger the Sea Mother, and now you say we *must?*"

"You don't know what it's like in the Forest!" said Torak. "The Ravens are sick. And the Boars and the Otters and the Willows. Soon there won't be enough people to hunt—"

"Why should we care?" said the Leader.

The Seals murmured agreement.

"Merely because," put in Tenris, "you *say* that you're kin?"

"But I am!" insisted Torak. "I can prove it! Where's my pack?"

At a glance from Tenris, Asrif ran to a shelter, returning moments later with Torak's pack.

Eagerly Torak pulled out the bundle that held his father's knife. "Here," he said, unwrapping it and holding it out to the Mage. "The blade was made by the Seals. My father's mother gave it to him, and he made the hilt."

Tenris went very quiet as he studied the knife. Torak saw that his left hand was a burned and twisted claw, but his right was unharmed. The long brown fingers shook as they touched the blade.

With pounding heart, Torak waited for him to speak.

The Leader, too, was peering at the knife. He didn't seem to like what he saw. "Tenris," he breathed, "how can this be?"

"Yes," murmured Tenris. "The hilt is red deer antler, mated to a blade of Sea slate." He raised his head and fixed Torak with a gaze grown cold. "You say your father made this. Who was he that he dared to mix the Forest with the Sea?"

Torak did not reply.

"My guess," said Tenris, "is that he was some kind of Mage."

Belatedly Torak remembered Fin-Kedinn's warning, and shook his head.

To his surprise, a corner of Tenris's mouth twitched. "Torak, you're not a very good liar."

Torak hesitated. "Fin-Kedinn told me not to talk of him."

"Fin-Kedinn," repeated Tenris. "I've heard the name. Is he a Mage too?"

"No," said Torak.

"But there are Mages among the Ravens."

"Yes. Saeunn."

"And did she teach you Magecraft?"

"No," said Torak. "I'm a hunter, like my father. He taught me hunting and tracking, not Magecraft."

Again Tenris met his eyes—and this time Torak felt the full force of his intelligence, like a shaft of strong sunlight piercing clouds.

Suddenly the Mage's face softened. He spoke to the Leader. "He's telling the truth. He is our bone kin."

The Leader squinted at Torak.

Bale shook his head in disbelief.

"Then you will help me?" said Torak. "You will give me the cure?"

Tenris deferred to Islinn. "It's for you to decide,

Leader." But he leaned over and whispered in the old man's ear.

Aided by Tenris and Bale, the Leader rose to his feet. "Since you are kin," he wheezed, "we will deal with you as one of our own." He paused to catch his breath. "If one of us had broken the law, he would be made to appease the Sea Mother. So must you. Tomorrow you will be taken to the Rock, and left there for a moon."

NINETEEN

Torak is back at the edge of the Forest. The sun is shining, the Sea is a dazzling blue, and he's breathless with laughter as he rolls in the sand with Wolf.

An ecstasy of tail-wagging and flailing paws, of high twisting leaps! Wolf lands full on his chest and knocks him flat, covering his face with nibble-greetings; Torak grabs his scruff and licks his muzzle, telling him in low, fervent yip-and-yowls how much he's missed him.

Wolf has grown so much! His flanks and haunches are solid with muscle, and when he rears up and puts his forepaws on Torak's shoulders, they come head to head. But he's still the same Wolf. The same clear amber eyes and well-loved smell of sweet grass and warm, clean fur. The same mix of puppyish fun and mysterious wisdom.

Wolf gives him a rasping lick on the cheek, then races off across the sand; a moment later he's back, shaking a piece of seaweed in his jaws and daring Torak to snatch it . . .

. . . and now the seaweed is floating in the cold Sea, and they are both struggling to stay alive. Wolf is terrified of deep water. He tilts his muzzle above the waves—his ears flat back, his eyes black with terror. Torak tries to swim closer to reassure him, but his limbs are dream-heavy, and he only drifts farther away.

Then, over Wolf's back, he sees the fin of the Hunter.

Wolf hasn't yet seen it; but he's closer, so it will take him first.

Torak tries to scream a warning—but no sound comes. There is no escape. No land. Just the pitiless Sea, and the Hunter closing in for the kill.

Torak will not let it take Wolf. That is a certainty: as sure as the icy waves buffeting his face; as sure as his own name. There is no hesitation. He knows what he must do.

Taking a deep breath, he dives. He moves with agonizing slowness, but manages to swim beneath Wolf, then up again, putting himself in the path of the Hunter. Now Wolf is behind him. Now Wolf will have a chance.

There is nothing between Torak and the tall black fin. He sees the silver wave curling back. He sees the great blunt head racing toward him through the green water. His heart swells with terror.

The Hunter's jaws open wide to swallow him. . . .

Torak awoke with a shudder.

He was lying in a Seal shelter surrounded by slumbering people. His cheeks were wet with tears. He dashed them away. He longed to be back in the dream with Wolf. But Wolf was far away. And he, Torak, was destined for the Rock.

For a moment he lay staring into the gloom. Above him he saw the arching whale ribs that made the frame of the shelter, their seal-hide covering heaving gently in and out. The whale had swallowed him, after all.

Quietly he got up and made his way between the sleepers. Bale turned on his side and opened a wary eye, but let him pass. They both knew why. Where could he run to?

Torak stumbled out into the gray light. High above him, clouds poured over the peaks and flowed slowly down the cliffs. In the Seal camp nothing stirred, not even a dog.

Thirsty, Torak made his way along the bay to where the waterfall tumbled down the cliff and over a bed of boulders toward the Sea. Here the Bay of Seals was more lush than it had appeared last night. The grass was studded with yellow suncups and purple cranesbill, and the lower slopes of the cliffs were bright with rowan and birch.

Torak thought it cruel that the Seals should allow him the freedom to enjoy all this. He felt like a fish caught in a net: swimming about, but knowing it was trapped.

Kneeling by the stream, he cupped freezing water in his palm.

The Follower crouched on a boulder on the other side of the stream, watching him.

Torak froze. Icy water trickled through his fingers.

"What do you want?" he said hoarsely.

The creature did not stir. Its tangled mane hid all but its claws, and the gleam of its eyes.

"Why are you following me?" cried Torak. "What do you *want*?"

A shadow slid across the rocks toward him—and he glanced up to see a gull swooping low. When he looked again, the Follower was gone.

With a cry he splashed across the stream—but it had vanished among the boulders and juniper scrub.

He had not imagined it. When he stooped to examine the rock where it had been, he found scratch marks in the lichen.

His thoughts raced. It had followed him across the Sea. . . .

"Who were you talking to?" said a voice behind him, and he turned to see Bale staring suspiciously. "You were talking to someone. Who?"

"Nobody," said Torak. "I was . . . talking to myself."

Why had it followed him? And how had it got across the Sea?

Then he remembered Asrif's missing bundle of salmon-skins. That must be it. While the Seal boys had been busy with their captive, the Follower had emptied one of the bundles and hidden inside. Torak hated to think of it so close, curled up in a skinboat. . . .

"I don't believe you," said Bale. "If you were talking to yourself, why are you looking so guilty?"

Torak didn't answer. He looked guilty because he was. *What if you've brought it back?* Bale had said last night. He'd meant the sickness, not the Follower. But was there a difference?

Torak leaped to his feet and waded across the stream. "Where's Tenris?" he said urgently. "I've got to speak to him."

Bale's blue eyes narrowed. "Why? He's not going to help you."

Torak ignored him. He'd had an idea. It was dangerous—dealing with Mages always was—but it might just keep him off the Rock. "Where is he?" he said again.

Bale jerked his head toward the overhang that towered above the north end of the bay. "On the Crag. But he won't want to talk to you."

"Yes he will," said Torak.

The track wound steeply up the flank of the mountain, and in places Torak had to scramble on hands and knees.

Breathless, he reached the top—and found himself on a narrow neck of rock that broadened into a flat, boat-shaped promontory jutting over the Sea. In the middle stood a low slab of granite, roughly shaped in the likeness of a fish. On this lay a pile of Sea eggs. Beside it squatted the Seal Mage, murmuring under his breath.

"Mage," panted Torak, "I must talk to you!"

"Not so loud," warned Tenris without looking up. "And take care not to tread on the lines."

Glancing down, Torak saw that the whole surface of the Crag was webbed with fine silver lines: not hammer-etched, but polished into the gray rock, and so smooth that neither lichen nor weather could take hold. Torak saw Hunters and fishes, eagles and seals: some chasing each other, some overlaid, as if eating one another; all dancing the endless dance of hunter and prey.

The Seal Mage rose with three Sea eggs cradled in

his burned hand, and began laying them out on the Crag. "You've come to bargain for your life," he said.

"Yes," said Torak.

"But you've offended the Sea Mother."

"I didn't mean to—"

"She doesn't care," said Tenris, setting down a stone. Without turning around he said, "Here, help me with this. Hand me the Sea eggs one by one."

Torak opened his mouth to protest, then shut it again. Together they moved about the Crag, Torak handing over the stones when the Mage held out his hand. Once, as they neared the edge, Torak caught a dizzying glimpse of the Sea far below.

"She looks calm today, doesn't she?" said Tenris, following his gaze. "But do you have any idea how powerful she is?"

Torak shook his head.

With easy grace the Mage set down another stone, and at his belt the puffin beaks clinked softly. "The man who killed the whale we feasted on last night had to cut off his hair to make amends for taking one of her children. He must live alone for three days without eating, or touching his mate. Only when the whale's souls have returned to the Mother can he come back." He gestured at the Sea eggs at his feet. "That's what I'm doing with these. Making a path to guide the souls." He paused. "What you need to understand,

Torak, is that the ways of the Mother are far harsher, less predictable, than the ways of your Forest."

From down below came the distant sound of voices. Glancing over the edge, Torak saw that the Seal camp was waking up. Bale was talking to two men, and pointing up at the Crag.

"Mage," said Torak, "there's something I have to—"

Tenris silenced him with a raised hand. "She lives in the very deep of the Sea," he murmured, "and she is stronger than the sun. If she is pleased, she sends the seals and the fishes and the seabirds to be hunted. If she is angry she keeps them with her, and thrashes her tail to make storms. When she breathes in, the Sea sinks. When she breathes out, the tide comes in."

He paused, gazing at the figures moving on the beach. "She kills without warning, malice or mercy. Many winters ago, the Great Wave came out of the west. Only those who climbed to this Crag survived." He turned to Torak. "The power of the wind is very great, Torak; but the power of the Sea is unimaginable."

Torak wondered why Tenris was telling him all this.

"Because knowledge is power," said the Mage as if he'd heard his thoughts.

Torak glanced about him. "Is this where you made the cure?"

To his surprise, Tenris gave a wry smile. "I was wondering when you'd bring that up."

Moving back to the altar rock, he took up a crab claw that had been lying on top, put it to his lips, and blew out a thin stream of aromatic blue smoke. "With the cure," said Tenris between puffs, "it isn't where, but *when*. It can only be made on one night of the year. The most potent night of all. Can you guess which one?"

Torak hesitated. "Midsummer?"

Tenris shot him a keen glance. "I thought you didn't know Magecraft."

"I don't. But Midsummer's my birthnight, so it was in my mind. And it's also the night of greatest change, and everyone knows that Magecraft—"

"Is about change," said Tenris. Again he smiled. "As indeed is life. Wood into leaf. Prey into hunter. Boy into man. You have a quick mind, Torak. I could have taught you much. It's a pity you're for the Rock."

Torak seized his chance. "That's what I need to tell you. I'm not—I'm not going to the Rock."

Tenris went still. In the bright morning light his burns were stark. "What did you say?"

Torak caught his breath. "I'm not going to the Rock. You're going to make the cure. And I'm going to take it back to—"

"*I* am going to make the cure?" repeated Tenris. The chill in his voice was like the sun going in. "And why would I do that?"

"Because if you don't," said Torak, "your people will get sick too."

He told Tenris about the Follower, and how it had reached the island. He told him of his belief that the Follower was a Soul-Eater spy, sent to cause the sickness. Tenris listened without saying a word, smoking his crab-claw pipe. It was impossible to tell what he felt, but Torak sensed the rapid current of his thoughts.

Apprehensively he watched the Mage circle the altar rock, then take up the final Sea egg and move toward him.

"Did you plan this?" said Tenris.

Torak was horrified. "Of course not!"

"Because there's something you should know, Torak. I don't like tricks."

"It wasn't a trick! I had no idea the Follower had crossed the Sea. Tenris, I'm only asking you to make the cure because—"

"'Only'?" Tenris cut in. "This is not some potion I can simply ladle out of a pail! It took me three moons to perfect! I had to scale the Eagle Heights to find the selik root that grows nowhere else. I had to weave a spell on Midsummer night that no one had attempted since the coming of the Wave!"

Torak licked his lips. "Midsummer is only four days away."

Tenris stared at him. "You don't give up, do you?"

"I can't," said Torak. "The clans are sick."

Tenris turned the Sea egg in his hand, and his eyes glinted dangerously. "What's to stop me putting you on the Rock, and keeping the cure for the Seals?"

Torak opened his mouth, then shut it again. He hadn't thought of that.

"Learn from this, Torak," warned Tenris. "Never try to lock wills with a Mage. Especially not with me."

Torak raised his chin. "I thought Mages were supposed to help people."

"What do you know about Mages? You're only a hunter."

"The Ravens *need* you! So do the Otters and the Willows and the Boars, and for all I know, the other clans too! If you put me on the Rock, who will take the cure to the Forest?"

Tenris set down the final Sea egg at his feet. "*If* I made the cure, you'd have to help."

Torak held his breath.

"Each summer," said Tenris, "the Sea clans celebrate the Midsummer rites on a different island. This time it's the turn of the Cormorants. Many of us leave today; more will follow. Soon the camp will be empty."

"I'll do whatever it takes," said Torak.

To his surprise, Tenris laughed. "So hasty! You don't even know what it involves!"

"I'll do what it takes," Torak said again.

Tenris stood looking down at him, and for a moment his ruined face contracted with pity. "Poor little Torak," he murmured. "You don't know what you're agreeing to. You don't even know where you are."

Torak glanced down, and at last he saw the pattern that Tenris had been making with the Sea eggs.

It was an enormous spiral, and they were standing at its center, like two flies caught in a web.

TWENTY

Renn had searched the shore, but she was no closer to discovering where Torak had gone.

Wolf had followed the scent for a day and a night, weaving tirelessly through the trees, but always running back for her so that she didn't get left behind.

When he'd reached the mouth of the Widewater, his eagerness had turned to agitation. Whimpering, he'd raced up and down the sand. Then he'd put back his head and howled. Such a terrible, wrenching howl.

Her search had revealed the remains of two fires: a big, messy one on the rocks, and a smaller one that was definitely Torak's, as well as a line of his double-barbed fishhooks. But of Torak himself, she could find no trace. It was as if he'd vanished into the Sea.

That night she huddled in her sleeping-sack, listening to the sighing of the waves, wondering what had happened to him. The Sea Mother could have sent a storm to drown him within arrowshot of land. Her Hidden People could have dragged him under in their long green hair. . . .

She fell into a troubled sleep. But all night long, Wolf ran up and down the shore.

He was still there in the morning. He wouldn't eat, wouldn't hunt, and showed only a fleeting interest in the fulmars nesting on the cliff—which was probably just as well, as fulmar chicks spit a foul-smelling oil, and Renn had no way of warning him. Now it was noon, and she knew she couldn't stay any longer. "I have to find help," she told Wolf, knowing he wouldn't understand, but needing to talk for her own sake. "Are you coming?"

Wolf flicked his ears in her direction, but stayed where he was.

"Somebody may have seen him," said Renn. "A hunting party, or—someone. Come on, let's go!"

Wolf leaped onto the rocks and gazed out to Sea.

"Wolf. *Please*. I don't want to go without you."

Wolf did not even turn his head.

She had her answer. She would be going alone. With

a pang she shouldered her pack and headed toward the Forest.

Behind her, Wolf put up his muzzle and howled.

Wolf didn't know what to do.

He needed to stay in this terrible place and wait for his pack-brother; but he also needed to follow the female into the Forest.

He hated it here. The pale earth stung his eyes, the hot rocks bit his paws, and the fish-birds cawed at him to go away. But most of all he feared the huge, moaning creature who slumbered before him. She had a cold and ancient smell that he knew without ever having learned. And if she woke up . . .

Wolf did not understand why Tall Tailless had gone where his pack-brother couldn't follow, or why his scent was so chewed up with that of three other tail-lesses. Wolf smelled that they were half-grown males, and angry, and not of the Forest—that they belonged to the Great Wet.

And now the female had gone too, blundering through the trees in the noisy way of the taillesses. Wolf didn't want her to go. At times she could be cross, but she could also be clever and kind. Should he follow her? But what if Tall Tailless came back and found nobody here?

Wolf ran in circles, wondering what to do.

🐾 🐾 🐾

Renn hadn't expected to miss Wolf quite so much.

She missed his warmth as he leaned against her, and his impatient little whine when he wanted a salmon cake. She even missed his enthusiasm for chasing ducks.

It hurt that he'd chosen not to follow her, and she felt lonely as she crossed the stepping-stones over the Widewater, into the birchwood on the other side. Not for the first time, she asked herself what she was doing so far from her clan, in a Forest haunted by sickness. If Torak had wanted her with him, he would have asked. She was chasing a friend who didn't want her.

As she went deeper, the stillness began to trouble her. Not a thrush sang. Not a leaf stirred.

There should be people here, too. She knew this part of the Forest. When she was nine, Fin-Kedinn had put her to foster with the Whale Clan, to learn the ways of the Sea. She knew that many other clans hunted along the coast: Sea Eagle, Salmon, Willow. They came for the cod in spring and the salmon in summer, and for the seals and the herring that sheltered here from the winter gales. But now the Forest felt eerily quiet.

Ahead, the trees thinned, and she glimpsed several large, untidy shelters made of branches. They resembled the eyries of eagles, and her spirits rose. The Sea Eagles were one of the more approachable

Sea clans. They could be proud, but they always welcomed strangers; and they were fairly relaxed about mixing the Forest and the Sea, taking their lead from their clan-creature, who took its prey from both.

But the camp was deserted. The fires had been stamped out, leaving a bitter tang of woodsmoke. Renn knelt to touch the ashes. Still warm. She moved to the midden pile. Some of the mussel shells were wet. The Sea Eagles had only just left.

Behind her, something breathed.

She wheeled around.

It was coming from that shelter over there.

Drawing her knife, she moved toward it. "Is anyone there?"

From the dark within came a guttural snarl.

She froze.

The darkness exploded.

With a cry she jumped back.

The creature sprang at her—then jerked to a halt. In a daze she saw that it was tethered at the wrists by sturdy bindings of braided rawhide.

"What are you *doing*?" shouted a voice behind her, and strong hands dragged her away. "Are you sick too?" cried her captor, spinning her around. "Answer! Are you sick? What's this on your hand?"

"A b–bite," she stammered. "It's a bite, I'm not sick. . . ."

Ignoring her, he turned her head roughly to examine her face and scalp. Only when he found no sores did he release her.

"I'm not sick!" she repeated. "What's *happened* here?"

"Same as everywhere," he muttered.

"The sickness," said Renn.

At the mouth of the shelter, the creature who had once been a man rocked back and forth, snarling and slobbering. Patches of his scalp glistened where he'd yanked out handfuls of hair. His eyes were gluey with pus.

The other man glanced at him, and pain tightened his face. "He was my friend," he said. "I couldn't bring myself to kill him. It would've been better if I had." He turned to Renn. "Who are you? What are you doing here?"

"I'm Renn," she said. "Raven Clan. Who are you?"

"Tiu." He held up his left hand, and on the back she saw his clan-tattoo: the four-clawed mark of the Sea Eagle.

"What will happen to your friend?" asked Renn.

Tiu went to retrieve a fishing spear propped against a tree. "In a couple of days he'll chew through the ropes. He'll have as much chance as any of us."

"But—he'll hurt someone."

Tiu shook his head. "We'll be long gone."

"You're leaving the Forest?" said Renn.

With a last look at his friend, Tiu left the clearing, heading west.

Renn followed at a run.

"The island of the Cormorants," he told her. "It's their turn for the Midsummer rites; and unlike some, they're not afraid to let us come."

"What about the other clans?" said Renn as they reached a sheltered bay where people hurried to load sturdy hide canoes.

"The Whales and the Salmons headed for the Cormorants a few days ago. The Willows went south." Tiu threw her a sharp glance. "And you? Why aren't you with your clan?"

"I'm looking for my friend. Have you seen him? His name's Torak. Thin, a little taller than me, with black hair and . . . "

"No," said Tiu, turning away to help a woman with a bundle.

"I saw him," called a young man loading rope into a canoe.

"When?" cried Renn. "Where? Is he all right?"

"The Seals took him," came the reply. "You won't be seeing him again."

"Three Seal boys came a few days ago," said the young man, whose name was Kyo. "They had flint and seal-hide clothes, but I was in no mood to trade, so I didn't show myself." He frowned. "The Whales made the trade. They were so desperate for Sea eggs, they didn't tell the Seals about the sickness, in case it scared them off—"

"What about Torak?" broke in Renn. "You said you saw them take him."

"All I saw was a boy in a skinboat," said Kyo. "Dark, like you said. Thin, angry face. Lots of bruises. He didn't go without a fight."

Renn's fists clenched. "Why did they take him?"

Kyo shrugged. "With the Seals, who knows? They're not like us, they've never learned to live in peace with the Forest."

"I've got to get to their island," said Renn.

Tiu snorted. "Not possible."

"But you're going to the Cormorants," she said, "and their island isn't far from the Seals, is it?"

"You don't understand," Tiu said angrily. "We have no quarrel with the Seals, and we want to keep it that way!"

"But my friend is in danger!"

"We're all in danger!" snapped Tiu.

Renn looked at the worried faces around her, and wondered how to persuade them. "There's something you need to know," she said. "My friend—Torak. He can do things that others can't. He might be able to find a cure."

Tiu crossed his arms across his chest. "You're making that up."

"No. Listen to me. I need to tell you who he is." By doing that, she would be going against Fin-Kedinn's orders; but Fin-Kedinn wasn't here. "You all know what happened last winter," she said. "You know about the bear."

People stopped what they were doing and drew nearer to listen.

"It killed some of our people," Renn went on. "It killed people here too, didn't it? Two from the Willow Clan. And we heard that among your clan it took a child."

Tiu flinched. "Why talk of this? What good does it do?"

"Because," said Renn, "my friend is the one who rid the Forest of the bear."

Tiu stared at her. "You said he's just a boy—"

"I said he's more than that. Fin-Kedinn would tell you if he was here. You know Fin-Kedinn?"

Tiu nodded. "He has the respect of many clans."

"He's my uncle. He'd tell you that what I'm saying is true."

Anxiously Renn watched Tiu draw the others aside to talk. Moments later he returned. "I'm sorry. We don't want to quarrel with the Seals."

"Then don't take me to their camp," she said.

"Leave me somewhere on their island, I'll find my own way."

Kyo spoke to Tiu. "There's that little bay to the southwest of their camp. We could put in there, and they'd never know."

"And I could give her seaworthy clothes," said a woman, "and purify her for the journey. Tiu, she's just a girl, we can't leave her here on her own."

Tiu sighed. "You're asking a lot," he told Renn.

"I know," she replied.

She was about to go on, when—behind a juniper bush—she spotted a gleam of eyes. Amber eyes watching her.

Her heart leaped.

Excitedly she turned to Tiu. "And I'm about to ask even more."

"What?"

"There's someone else who needs to come too."

The shore rang with laughter.

The Sea Eagles might be fleeing their camp, having left behind two dead and one mad with sickness, but the sight of a young wolf covered in fulmar spit made everyone smile.

"You won't need to purify him," someone remarked. "It looks as if he's done that by himself!"

Fulmar spit or no, Renn wanted to fling her arms

around Wolf—but she contented herself with greeting him quietly, and scratching his flank.

Feebly, Wolf wagged his tail. He looked miserable. He'd taken a faceful of foul-smelling oil, then made it worse by trying to rub it off in the sand. He'd learned the hard way about not bothering fulmar chicks.

"I thought you *liked* strong smells," Renn told him.

Wolf rubbed his face against her jerkin in a vain attempt to rid himself of the troublesome oil.

Tiu hurried past them with a bundle in his arms. "If you can get him into my canoe," he said over his shoulder, "you can bring him. If not, you'll have to leave him behind."

"I'm not leaving him," said Renn.

"Then be quick! We're leaving!"

"Come on, Wolf," said Renn, running down to the canoe.

Wolf didn't move. He stood with his big paws splayed and his hackles up, eyeing the canoe rocking in the shallows.

Renn's heart sank.

You didn't need to speak wolf talk to know what he was saying.

I am not going in that. Not ever, ever, ever.

TWENTY-ONE

Torak dreamed of Wolf again, but this time Wolf was warning him. *Uff! Uff! Danger! Shadow! Hunted!*

What shadow? asked Torak. Where?

But Wolf was getting farther and farther away—and Torak couldn't run after him, because someone was holding him back.

"Let me *go*!" he shouted, lashing out with his fists.

"Wake up!" said Bale.

"What?" Torak opened his eyes. He was in the Seal shelter, and daylight was streaming in through the door flaps.

A day had passed since he'd spoken to Tenris on the Crag. A whole day of waiting, while the Seal Mage persuaded Islinn not to send him to the Rock, and Midsummer drew nearer, and in the Forest the sickness . . .

"Who's Wolf?" Bale said abruptly.

"What? No one. I don't know what you mean."

Bale wasn't fooled. "You're not even awake and you're telling lies," he said in disgust.

Torak did not reply. The dream lay heavy on him. *Shadow. Hunted.* What did that mean? Was it a warning against the Follower, or something else?

"Get up," said Bale, kicking him in the thigh.

"Why? Are we setting off for the Heights?"

"That's tomorrow. Today I've got to teach you skin-boating."

"*You?* Why you?"

"Ask Tenris, it's his idea." From his tone he didn't like it any more than Torak. "Get some daymeal and meet me on the shore. I'll fetch the boats."

"But why Bale?" Torak asked the Seal Mage when he found him on the rocks, gathering seaweed. "Why can't it be someone else?" Anyone else, he thought.

The Seal Mage gave him a lopsided smile. "And this is the thanks I get for keeping you off the Rock."

"But Bale of all people, he—"

"—happens to be the best at skinboating," said

Tenris. "Here, hold the basket and watch, you might learn something."

"But—"

"This is kelp," said Tenris, grasping a long stem of leathery brown weed. "If you dry it, it goes hard, like this"—he tapped the hilt of his knife. "If you wash it in sweet water, then soak it in seal oil, you can make rope. Did you see how I cut it? Always leave the holdfast on the rock so that it can grow back. That's important."

When Torak stayed stubbornly silent, the Seal Mage paused. "You're going to need Bale," he said. "And you'll need Asrif, too, he's the best at rock climbing. Detlan will go along to lend some muscle."

"All three of them?"

"Torak, you can't do this on your own."

"I know. But I thought you'd be coming. You were the one who found the root before. Why not now?" He liked the Seal Mage. Tenris reminded him of Fin-Kedinn, only kinder and less remote.

With a sigh the Seal Mage touched the scarred side of his face. "The fire that did this didn't only burn me on the outside. It scorched my lungs." He tossed the kelp into the basket. "I'd be no use to you on the Heights."

Torak was abashed. "I didn't know. I'm sorry."

"So am I," Tenris said mildly. "But there's another reason I'm sending them. They're your kin, Torak.

Whether you like it or not, you need to win their trust."

"I don't care about that," said Torak.

"Well you should." The Mage's voice was gentle, but the undertow of strength was unmistakeable. "Concentrate on Bale. If you win him over, the others will follow. And Torak." His mouth twitched. "It'll help if you're a quick learner."

"No, no, *no!*" cried Bale, paddling closer to Torak's skinboat with infuriating ease. "Brace your legs against the sides—you're tilting, shift your weight—no, not that much, you'll capsize!"

Reaching over, he yanked the skinboat upright. "I *told* you! Don't use the paddle to steady yourself; that's not what it's for! You balance with your hips and your thighs, not your hands. If you're out hunting, you might need to drag a seal aboard, and then you'd need both hands free."

"It'd help if it didn't wobble so much," muttered Torak. With its shallow draft and knife-edged hull, his skinboat was in constant danger of capsizing. He felt like a beetle struggling to stay afloat on a twig.

"That's not the boat's fault," said Bale, "it's yours."

"Why does it have to be so shallow?"

"If the sides were any higher, you'd waste your strength fighting the wind. Try again. No! I *told* you!

Don't slap the water, slice it! You need to be silent, completely silent!"

"I'm trying," said Torak between clenched teeth.

"Try harder," snapped Bale. "Don't you have canoes in the Forest?"

"Of course we do!" Torak thought with longing of the dugouts of the Boars, and the Ravens' dependable deer-hide crafts. "But they're good and solid, and we never—"

"Good and solid won't get you far on the Sea," said Bale derisively. "A round-bottomed boat would make bubbles that'd warn the seals you were coming from fifty harpoon throws away; and a hull that couldn't twist would break up in the first heavy swell. No, no, *over* the waves, not through them! You've got to skim the surface like a cormorant. . . ."

A big wave buffeted Torak's prow, drenching him.

On the shore, children laughed. The smallest were playing at skinboats in holes in the sand lined with scraps of seal hide. The bigger ones were splashing about in beginners' crafts. Unlike Torak, they didn't have to worry about rolling over, as their boats were fitted with crossbars that were steadied at either end by gutskin sacks filled with air.

When Bale had threatened Torak with a beginner's boat, he'd been outraged; but now after an exhausting day, he was tempted. Bale was an unforgiving teacher, driving him relentlessly. Clearly he was hoping to be able to tell Tenris that Torak was a failure.

It was beginning to look as if he'd get his wish. Torak was soaking wet, and his head was throbbing with sun-dazzle. His thighs and shoulders were screaming for rest, his arms shaking with fatigue. He could hardly hold his paddle, let alone keep his balance.

It didn't help that Bale handled his own skinboat superbly. He could bring it about with a flick of his wrist, and stand up in it as easily as if he were on dry land. He wasn't even showing off. He was simply so at home on the water that he didn't need to think about it.

Now, as the wind got up and Torak floundered to stay afloat, the older boy came alongside him, deftly steadying his own craft by sticking one end of his paddle in a cross strap, which left the other blade in the Sea, and both hands free. "You'll have to do better than this," he said as he leaned over and started scooping out the water in Torak's boat with a baler.

"Or what?" said Torak. "You'll leave me behind?"

"Yes, that's what I'm hoping."

"Give me a chance. I've only had a day. You've been doing this since you were what, about six?"

"Five." He glanced at the beginners in the shallows, and a shadow of sadness crossed his face. "My brother started even younger."

"Just give me a chance," said Torak.

Bale thought for a moment. "Head off over there," he said. "I'll follow. This time, don't think about each stroke. Just keep your eyes on the Sea, and go as fast as you can."

Torak brought his boat about, and started to paddle.

For a while all he managed was his usual floundering, with the skinboat bucking like a hare in springtime and the waves slapping him stingingly in the face.

Then something happened. Almost without noticing, he seemed to find a rhythm with the paddle. The blades cut the water without splashing, and with each stroke he felt the power of the Sea beneath him—*beneath* him, not against him. Faster and faster he went—and suddenly the skinboat gave a surge, and he was skimming over the waves, as fast and free as a seabird.

"I've got it!" he cried.

Bale came up beside him, watching with unsmiling concentration.

"Beautiful!" shouted Torak. "It's beautiful!"

Bale nodded slowly. Now he was biting back a grin.

A gust of wind caught Torak's skinboat and spun him around, sending him straight toward the older boy.

"Turn away!" yelled Bale. "Hard! Hard! You're going to ram me!"

Fighting the wind, Torak dug in his paddle—but it

gave a jerk that nearly pitched him overboard—and when he brought it out of the water, he saw that the blade had snapped clean off.

"*Watch out!*" shouted Bale as Torak careened toward him.

"I can't turn it!"

Bale dug in his paddle and shot ahead—just in time to avoid a collision—while Torak's boat slewed around and capsized.

His clothes dragged him down, and it was a relief when Bale came about and caught him by the neck of his jerkin.

"What were you *doing*?" he yelled. "You could have sunk us both!"

"It was an accident!" spluttered Torak.

"An accident? You tried to ram me!" Furious, he wrenched Torak's boat upright, then held its prow while Torak scrambled aboard.

"I said it was an accident!" panted Torak. "My paddle broke!"

"That's impossible! They're made of the strongest driftwood—"

"Then what's this?" Torak brandished what remained of his paddle. "If they're so strong, why did mine snap like a piece of kindling?" He fell silent, peering at the broken stem of the paddle. Someone had cut it. They'd only cut halfway through, leaving just enough to make it workable, but liable to snap at any time.

"What is it?" said Bale.

Torak's thoughts flew to the Follower. But it could have been anyone: Bale or Asrif or Detlan—or anyone else among the Seals.

Without a word he held out the broken paddle, and Bale took it. He was observant. Swiftly he spotted the cut edge of the stem. "You think I did this," he said.

"Well did you?"

"No!"

"But you want me to fail. You said so."

"Because you'll slow us down, or get into trouble, and need rescuing."

"No I won't," said Torak with more conviction than he felt. "Bale, we want the same thing. We want the cure."

"And I'm supposed to believe that my clan is threatened," Bale said sarcastically, "just because you managed to talk your way off the Rock?"

Torak stared at him. "What do you mean?"

"I don't know what story you told Tenris on the Crag," said Bale, "but I do know that you're a lying little coward who'd do anything to save your skin." He tossed Torak the broken paddle. "Maybe that's why you were so ready to believe I could play a trick like this. Because it's the sort of thing you'd do in the Forest."

Bale's insults were ringing in Torak's ears as he made his way wearily back to shore. The older boy had gone on ahead, and carried his boat up to the racks. As far as he was concerned, there was nothing left to say.

You can't do this on your own, Tenris had said. *You need to win their trust. . . . Concentrate on Bale . . . the others will follow.*

He was right, and Torak knew it. He had to prove to Bale that he hadn't tricked anyone.

He had an idea. If he could prove that the Follower was on the island, Bale would have to believe him.

Find the tracks, he told himself. Not even Bale could argue with that.

And it should be possible. Torak might not be any good at skinboating, but he knew how to find a trail.

As he reached the south end of the bay, dusk was coming on—or rather, the brief blue glow that counted for dusk this close to Midsummer. Leaving his skinboat on the beach, he crossed the stream, and started working his way along the bank. Terns hovered and dived above him, but he ignored them.

It was a good time for tracking: the low light would sharpen the shadows. He was glad, too, that the Seals were busy waking the fires for nightmeal, so that nobody saw him come ashore. He didn't feel like explaining what he was doing.

No prints in the soft mud. But there, on the grass: the merest hint where something small—the Follower?—had brushed off the damp as it passed.

It was hard to trace—dew trails always are—but Torak used the trick his father had taught him, turning his head to one side and looking at it from the corner of his eye.

After a few false starts, he tracked it to a stretch of limpet-crusted rocks that tilted into the Sea. Beyond the rocks, at the very edge of the bay, stood a clump of birch. To his surprise, the trail didn't lead toward them, but onto the rocks. He found a tiny piece of scuffed lichen, and a scent of rottenness where the Follower had scampered across a pile of dead seaweed.

Finally, in a patch of sand left by a previous tide, he saw it: a perfect, sharp-clawed print. Very fresh. No time for ants or sand midges to blur the edges.

Look at this, Bale, he shouted in his head.

A cackle of laughter to his left—and there it was: a small humped figure shrouded in long hair like moldy seaweed.

Torak was too elated to be scared. Here was the proof he needed. If he could catch it, Bale would have to admit defeat.

The creature turned and scuttled away.

Torak scrambled after it.

The seaweed was slimy under his bare feet, and a voice of caution sounded in his mind. The Follower would like nothing better than if he took a tumble into the Sea.

He reached a cleft in the rocks where the swirling Sea sent up jets of spray. The cleft was too wide to leap, but somehow the Follower had got across. There it was on the other side: eyes gleaming with malice, daring him to jump.

"Oh, no," he panted, "I'm not that stupid!"

The Follower bared its brown teeth in a hiss and sped into the gloom, its claws clicking on the rocks.

Torak raced around the edge of the cleft to where the seaweed was drier and less treacherous. It occurred to him to wonder how a patch of dry seaweed had come to be in the middle of all this wet. . . .

Too late. The seaweed gave beneath him and he pitched into the Sea. Torak, you fool! A pitfall! The simplest trap of all!

Winded by the cold and covered in seaweed, he kicked to keep himself afloat as he sought a likely place to haul himself out. The swell was heavier than it had appeared from the rocks, but it should be easy enough, and the only harm done would be to his pride. The

Follower, of course, would be long gone.

Clawing the seaweed off his face, he reached for a handhold. The seaweed was tougher than it looked. He couldn't seem to get it off his face—or push his hands through it to reach the rock.

Because it isn't seaweed, he realized in surprise. It's rope made of kelp, knotted kelp, and this is a seal net. You've fallen into a seal net. Which, presumably, was exactly what the Follower had intended.

The swell threw him against the rocks, knocking the breath from his chest. Treading water was becoming difficult, as the net clung to his legs, hampering movement. It seemed to be tied to the rocks at the top, and weighed down with something, maybe a stone, because he had to work to keep his head and shoulders above the water.

How Bale will laugh about this! he thought bitterly. How they'll all laugh when they find me floundering in a net within arrowshot of camp!

If he'd had his knife, he could have cut himself free, but the Seals hadn't trusted him with weapons. He'd have to call for help, and endure the inevitable taunts.

"Help!" he shouted. "I'm over here! Somebody!"

The wind whistled across the bay. Terns screamed overhead. The Sea slapped noisily against the rocks.

Nobody came. Nobody could hear him.

Treading water was tiring. And strangely, the waves seemed to have risen: now they reached to just below his chin.

That was when the truth hit him, and he began to be frightened. He was trapped in a seal net, out of earshot of the camp, and the tide was coming in.

Fast.

TWENTY-TWO

The tide was creeping higher, and Torak had to fight to keep his chin above the waves.

The swell kept sucking him backward, then smashing him against the rocks. The Sea was pounding the breath out of him. Her salt smell was thick in his throat, her restless moaning filled his head. She had taken him, and she wasn't letting go.

He tried to close his mind to her; to think what to do. There had to be some kind of opening in the net. After all, he'd fallen into it, so there must be a way out. But somehow he couldn't find it.

The mesh was small—he couldn't force his fist

through—and the knots were hard as pebbles; a waste of time trying to unpick them with fingers grown numb. And the kelp was far too tough to rip apart with his hands, or bite through. "They've got to be strong to hold a full-grown seal," Detlan had told him at daymeal. "And they are."

If only he had his knife. . . . What else could he use?

Again he smacked against the rocks, scraping painfully over the limpets.

Limpets. They had sharp edges, didn't they? If he could prize one off, maybe . . .

The swell drew him back, then battered him once more. As he kicked his way to the surface, the Sea's endless laughter rippled through him.

Don't listen to her, he told himself. Listen to yourself, listen to the blood drumming in your ears—anything but her. . . .

Still kicking to stay above the waves, he pushed his thumb and two fingers through the meshing and grabbed the nearest limpet.

The creature clamped hard to the rock and refused to let go. Snarling, Torak clawed at its shell, but it stuck fast. It had become part of the rock.

Then he remembered the black-and-white bird he'd seen attacking a limpet on the shore. He'd spotted similar birds here on the Seals' island—Detlan called them oystercatchers. Torak remembered the way the bird had struck the limpet with its beak: abruptly, giving it no time to cling on.

He found another limpet and tried the same thing, striking a glancing blow with his fist. It worked. But the limpet slipped from his fingers and spiraled down, out of reach and through the net.

Again the Sea's vast laughter shuddered through him. *You cannot win,* she seemed to whisper. *Give up, give up!*

No! he shouted in his head. It's too soon!

The shout became a sob. Too *soon*. He had to find the cure, and make sure that the clans were safe. He had to see Wolf again, and Renn, and Fin-Kedinn. . . .

If that stone weren't dragging down the net, he'd have a chance.

The thought woke him like a slap in the face. If he could get free of that stone, the tide would become his friend: he could make the Sea work against herself, make her lift him and carry him onto the rocks.

So why are you wasting time with limpets? he thought frantically. Get under the water and deal with that rock!

He took a deep breath and dived.

It was frightening being in her world, in a swirling chaos of black water and murky seaweed. He couldn't find the rope that tied the rock to the net, couldn't even tell up from down.

He surfaced again, gulping air. The waves were lapping higher. Now he had to strain to keep his mouth above them. Salt burned his lips, his throat, his eyes. His legs were heavy, his thoughts fogging with cold.

"Help!" he yelled. "Somebody!" His cry ended in a gurgle that was horrible to hear.

The light was failing, and he couldn't see much: just the rock looming over him and a deep-blue sky pricked by faint stars that seemed to be sinking farther and farther away from him. . . .

Drowning. The worst death of all. To feel the Sea Mother squeezing the life out of you, wrenching your souls apart. And without Death Marks, they would never find one another. He would become a Sea demon, wandering forever, hating and craving all living things, striving to snuff them out. . . .

A wave washed over him, and he coughed seawater.

I am beyond pity or malice, the Sea Mother seemed to murmur in his ear, *beyond good and evil. I am stronger than the sun. I am eternal. I am the Sea.*

He was so tired. He couldn't keep treading water, he had to stop, just for a little while, to rest.

He sank, and the Sea Mother wrapped her arms about him—tight, tight, until his chest was bursting. . . .

A silver flicker in the darkness.

A fish, he thought hazily. A small one, maybe a capelin?

And now there were more of them, a whole shimmering shoal, come to watch this big creature dying in their midst.

Down he sank, and the silver darts divided and flowed about him like a sparkling river, as the Sea crushed him in her arms. . . .

A sickening jolt deep in his belly, as if his guts were being pulled loose. And now, quite suddenly, he was free of that crushing embrace; free of the cold and the darkness. He could no longer feel the net dragging him down, or the salt burning his throat. He couldn't even hear his own blood thumping in his head. He was light and nimble as a fish—and like a fish, he was neither cold nor warm, but part of the Sea.

And he could see so clearly! The murkiness was gone. The rocks, the floating weeds, the other capelin flowing about him—all were vivid and sharp, although strangely stretched at the edges. In some way that he didn't understand, he had *become* fish. He felt the tiny ripples in the water as each slender body flickered past; he felt the shoal's wary curiosity. He felt the stronger surges coming back from the rocks; and beneath them the vast sighs of the Mother.

Without warning, terror invaded the shoal. Panic coursed through them like lightning—and through Torak, too. Something was hunting them in the deep. Something huge . . .

What is it? asked Torak, fighting to master their terror, which had become his own. What is it that hunts us?

The shoal didn't answer. Instead it whipped around and fled for the deep Sea—fleeing the Hunter prowling beneath them—leaving Torak behind. Another sickening jolt inside him . . .

. . . and he was Torak again, watching the capelin vanish into the dark.

His chest was bursting, the blood roaring in his ears. No time to wonder what had just happened. He was drowning.

Blindly he kicked out, fighting the Sea Mother's lethal embrace—and the net fought him, holding him back.

At that moment, a column of white water sent him spinning sideways, and something big plunged in beside him. Powerful teeth savaged the net—tearing him *free*. . . .

Then hands were reaching down for him, trying to pull him out. They weren't strong enough—he was slipping back again, scraping his palms on limpets.

With his last shred of strength he gave a tremendous kick. It pushed him a little farther out of the water: enough for the hands to grab him and wrench him out.

The Sea Mother gave a sigh, and let him go.

Torak lay gasping like a landed fish. He felt the roughness of limpets against his cheek, and the grittiness of seaweed between his teeth. He'd never tasted anything so good.

"What were you *doing*?" whispered a voice that was oddly familiar.

He rolled onto his side, then onto his knees, and spewed up what felt like half the Sea. "D-drowning," he gasped.

"I could see that!" said the voice, managing to sound both angry and shaken. "But what were you *doing*? Why didn't you just climb out?"

Torak raised his head. "*Renn?* Is that you?"

"Sh! Someone might come! Can you stand? Come on! Follow me!"

Struggling to grasp what was happening, Torak staggered to his feet. He swayed, and would have toppled back into the water if Renn hadn't grabbed his wrist and dragged him toward the birch trees. "Through here," she whispered. "There's a bay where we won't be seen!"

Together they scrambled between huge tumbled boulders and straggly birch, emerging at last onto a little white beach shadowed by a looming hillside.

Torak sank to his knees in the sand. "How—did you find me?" he panted.

"It wasn't me," said Renn. "It was—"

A shadow bounded from behind a boulder and knocked Torak backward into the sand, covering his face in hot, rasping licks.

"It was Wolf," said Renn.

TWENTY-THREE

There was something fierce—almost desperate—
about the way they greeted each other. Wolf
whimpering and lashing his tail as he covered Torak's
face in kisses; Torak unnervingly like a wolf himself
as he licked Wolf's muzzle and buried his face in his
fur, murmuring in the low, fervent speech that Renn
couldn't understand.

She felt like an intruder. And she was deeply shaken
by what had just happened. She kept seeing the body
in the water: facedown, dark hair swirling. She'd
thought he was dead.

Her hands shook as she retrieved her quiver and

bow from where she'd hidden them behind a boulder, and shouldered her wovengrass bag of limpets. "Can you walk?" she said more abruptly than she'd intended.

Still on his knees with Wolf, Torak turned and gazed at her as if he had no idea who she was. With his bruised face and streaming hair he didn't look like her friend anymore. "I—I can't *believe* . . ." His voice was rough with unshed tears.

"Torak, we've got to get out of here! We're too close to the camp, someone might come!"

But she could see that he wasn't taking it in.

"Come *on!*" she said, pulling him to his feet.

The hillside was steep, and the deep moss and crowberry made it tough to climb, but to her relief he managed it. Wolf pranced about them, swinging his tail and leaping up to nuzzle Torak's face.

Just below the ridge, they had to stop for breath.

"How did you find me?" panted Torak, bent double with his hands on his knees.

"I was foraging on the shore," said Renn. "Suddenly Wolf gave that grunt he makes, and ran off." She paused. "Torak, what happened? Why couldn't you get onto the rocks?"

"I—was caught in a seal net."

"A *net?*"

"I tried to get out, but I couldn't. Wolf bit through it. He saved my life."

Renn thought about that: about the kind of love that had made Wolf brave the thing he feared the most. "He hates the Sea," she said. "I had a terrible time getting him into a skinboat."

"How did you manage?"

From inside her jerkin she drew out the thong on which hung the grouse-bone whistle.

Torak studied it. "So if I hadn't given it to you all those moons ago, you wouldn't have been able to bring him with you. And I would have drowned." He scratched Wolf's flank, and Wolf rubbed against him, wrinkling his muzzle in a grin.

Once again, Renn felt like an intruder. She realized that she knew nothing of what had happened to Torak since he'd left the Ravens. There was lots she had to tell him, too: about the sickness, and the tokoroth. "Come on," she said. "My camp's not far."

They crested the ridge, startling a pair of ravens who flew off with indignant caws. When Torak saw what lay before him, he cried out. "But there's a *forest*!"

Below them lay a steep-sided valley like an axe cut through the mountains, with a long, narrow lake at the bottom. On all sides the slopes were darkened by willow, rowan and ash.

"They're not very tall," said Renn, "but at least they're trees. The Seals don't seem to come inland, so hiding's been easy. But yesterday I found someone's tracks down by the lake. A man's or a boy's, I think."

"I miss the Forest so much," said Torak, gazing at the trees.

"Me too," said Renn. "I miss salmon, and the taste of reindeer. And the nights are so *light* here. You don't notice it in the Forest, but here . . . I can't sleep."

"Neither can I," murmured Torak.

"There's my camp," said Renn, leading him down to the hidden gully filled with ferns and meadowsweet and the frothy yellow flowers of bedstraw. A stream tumbled through, and in the east bank she'd dug herself a foxhole, with a firepit in front. A rowan tree spread its arms protectively overhead.

"You can dry off by the fire," she told him. "I'll cook the limpets. They won't take long."

Hanging up her quiver and bow, she knelt by the embers. They gave almost no smoke because she'd used ash, and peeled off the bark.

Before setting out, she'd placed a flat piece of slate over one end to heat up, and now she spat on it to check it was hot enough; it gave a satisfying sizzle. After rinsing the limpets in the stream, she set them on the slate to cook.

"What have you done for food?" asked Torak as he huddled by the fire, with Wolf leaning against him.

"Birds' eggs, mostly," said Renn. "A bit of hunting, but only small prey. There don't seem to be any elk or deer. There must be fish in the lake, but it's too exposed. That's why I went to the beach." She paused. "I'm all right, but I'm worried about Wolf. Those ravens led him to carrion, but it wasn't enough. And he won't go near seabirds, because he got spat at by a fulmar." She gave a slight smile. "He was so miserable. I had to find some soapwort and give him a wash. He hated that too." She stopped, aware that she was talking too much.

Torak was frowning at the fire. "Renn, I'm really glad you're here."

Renn looked at him. "Oh. Well, good."

The limpets were cooked. With her knife she knocked them off the slate and onto a large goosefoot leaf. After tucking a limpet in a fork of the rowan tree for the clan guardian, she divided the rest into three. She put a third in the grass a short distance away for Wolf, then showed Torak how to cut away the black, blistered guts to get at the chewy orange meat. He eyed the limpets thoughtfully, then started to eat.

He'd pulled off his jerkin and hung it to dry on the rowan, and she saw that he was thinner, and that there was a wound on his calf that had been quite badly sewn up, and needed the stitches taken out. She said so, and he told her he'd do it later; then he asked about the scab on her hand.

"It's a bite," she said, rubbing it against her thigh.

She didn't want to mention the tokoroth just yet.

Wolf had already finished his limpets, and was eyeing Torak's. Torak let him have them. Then he rested his chin on his knees. "What's it like in the Forest?" he said. "How bad has it got?"

"Bad," said Renn. She told him about the clans leaving, and the man in the Sea Eagles' camp.

Torak's frown deepened. "I dreamed about Wolf, you know. He was warning me. 'Shadow. Hunted.' I think that's what he was saying."

"Did he mean the sickness?" said Renn.

"I don't know. I'll ask him." Torak lowered his head and gave a soft grunt-whine—and instantly Wolf leaped up, ears pricked. Then his tail rose, and he licked the corner of Torak's mouth, whining a reply.

"What's he saying?" asked Renn uneasily.

"Same as before. 'Shadow. Hunted.' I wonder what it means."

Renn cleaned her knife in the ashes. "Is that why you left? Because he warned you in a dream?"

"What?" said Torak.

"Is that why you left without telling anyone? Without telling me." She couldn't keep the edge out of her voice.

"I left," he said steadily, "to find the cure. I didn't tell you because if you'd come with me you'd have been in danger."

Renn stared at him. "I was already in danger! We all were. Are! What could be worse than the sickness?"

He hesitated. "The Follower."

"What's that?"

"I don't know. It's small. Filthy. It's got claws."

"The tokoroth," Renn said in a low voice.

He sat up. "That's what the Forest Horses said. Is that what it's called?"

She nodded. "Saeunn told me after you left. That's why I came to find you. She says they're among the most feared creatures in the Forest."

"*They?*" said Torak. "You mean there's more than one?"

Again she nodded.

He considered that. "It crossed the Sea hidden in Asrif's skinboat—"

"It's *here?*" cried Renn. "Here on the island?"

"Like I said, it hid in Asrif's boat. And if one could do it—"

"—maybe others could too. They could have hidden in one of the Sea Eagles' canoes, or with the other clans."

They were silent, thinking about that.

"But are you *sure* it's here?" said Renn.

"Oh, yes," Torak said grimly. "I saw it. It set the trap that nearly got me drowned." He paused. "I was trying to find proof—a track or something—to show the Seals."

"To show the Seals? Why were you doing that?"

"They're helping me make the cure."

"They're *helping* you? I don't understand. They beat you up, they took you prisoner—"

"Then they let me go." He told her his story: about being followed through the Forest, and turned away from the Deep Forest; then being captured by the Seals, and talking his way out of punishment. "I'm sure the tokoroth is causing the sickness," he said, "but the odd thing is, it hasn't given it to me. It's as if it's— testing me. I can't work out why."

Renn was still trying to understand. "And you say you're *not* their prisoner?"

"I told you, the Seals are helping me make the cure. They even taught me skinboating. Well. They tried. We're leaving for the Eagle Heights tomorrow." He glanced east, where the light was growing. "I mean, today."

Renn reached for a stalk of goosefoot, and chewed. "This feels wrong. First they beat you up, and now they're *helping* you?"

"They need the cure too."

She was unconvinced. "This cure. I've heard of selik root, but never of its being used in Magecraft."

"So?" Torak said sharply. "Tenris knows what he's doing."

"Who's Tenris?"

"Their Mage. Renn, they've had the sickness before, and he cured them! He can do it again."

"Even if he can, what's to stop the Soul-Eaters sending more tokoroth?"

Torak stared at her. He got up and paced, then returned to the fire. "The tokoroth," he said. "What *are* they?"

Renn winced. Then she took a deep breath and told him everything Saeunn had told her.

As he listened, his face drained of color.

"Saeunn says they aren't children anymore," said Renn. "They're demon. Utterly demon."

"Like the bear that killed Fa," said Torak.

Wolf got up and went to lean against him; he scratched the furry flank. Then he moved closer to the embers and knelt down. "When I was in the net," he said, "something strange happened."

Renn waited, wondering what was coming next.

"I got a sick feeling. Deep inside. I've had it before, at the healing rite. It felt—as if I were being pulled loose." He swallowed. "This time, in the net, I felt as if I were the fish."

"*What?*" said Renn.

"I felt—I felt the shape of things in the water, like a fish would." He gazed into the fire. "Then something scared them. They felt a Hunter, somewhere in the deep water. And I felt it too, Renn. Just like a fish."

Renn was bewildered. "What fish? What are you talking about?"

Suddenly Wolf gave a grunt and trotted to the edge of the firelight, snuffing the air and standing with his tail extended. Even Renn knew that meant a possible threat.

She jumped up and reached for her bow.

Torak was already on his feet, pulling on his jerkin.

In the distance, a boy was calling Torak's name.

"It's Bale," said Torak. "I must go, or he'll get suspicious."

"Who's Bale?" said Renn.

"He's—Bale," said Torak unhelpfully. "He caught me in the Forest, but he—"

"And you want to go *back*?"

"Renn, I've got to. It's only three days till Midsummer."

"But—you don't have to go by Sea to reach the Heights! We can go overland, I'm sure of it! Tiu's mother was a Seal, he knows the island; I got him to draw it in the sand. We could set off right now. . . ."

Again that voice, calling for Torak.

"But you don't even trust them!" she cried.

"I trust—some of them," he said. "I think."

"What does that mean?"

"What I do know," he said, suddenly fierce, "is that my friends get hurt—or killed—when they're with me.

It happened to Oslak, and to the boar. You're better off staying here with Wolf."

"Torak, no, I—"

"Keep him with you, and don't let the Seals see either of you."

"So you're determined to go with them to the Heights."

"Renn, I've got to."

Her thoughts raced. "Then we'll follow overland. Me and Wolf. You might need help."

He met her eyes, saw that he couldn't dissuade her, and nodded once.

"Torak!" shouted Bale.

Swiftly, Torak went down on one knee and put his forehead against Wolf's, murmuring something Renn didn't understand. Wolf nosed his chin and whined.

Then Torak rose and started up the slope, heading back the way they'd come. "Stay hidden," he told Renn over his shoulder, "and watch out for tokoroth."

Uneasily, Renn glanced about her. She didn't want him to leave her here on this lonely hillside.

But he'd already gone, melting into the trees as silently as a wolf.

TWENTY-FOUR

"Torak!" shouted Bale. "Torak! Where are you?"

Torak raced down the hill toward the little white beach. He couldn't see Bale, but he could hear him pushing through the birch trees.

Stumbling from tiredness, Torak crunched onto the sand and leaned against a boulder to catch his breath. He felt bruised and stiff and anxious. It had been wonderful seeing Wolf and Renn—but it was also terrifying. What if something happened to them?

In the ghostly twilight, the beach glowed faintly. He made out his own erratic tracks where he'd staggered from the birch trees—and then, to his horror, the tracks of Wolf and Renn. If Bale saw them . . .

Among the birches he caught a glimmer of torch-light. Bale was coming. He'd better move fast.

He was about to run forward when two figures stepped from the trees, and Asrif said, "I told you he'd run away. He couldn't face the Heights, so he scuttled off to hide in the woods."

Torak drew back behind the boulder to listen.

"Maybe," said Bale, "or maybe he's in trouble." To Torak's surprise, he sounded worried. "I didn't see him get ashore."

"So?" said Asrif. "You don't have to look after him. I know you think you should because he's younger, but Bale, he's not your brother."

"I know that," snapped Bale. "I just should've made sure he got back. It's not safe on the water for a beginner, especially not now. If the Cormorants are right—"

"Let's hope they're not," said Asrif.

Torak stepped out from behind the boulder. "Right about what?" he called, walking toward them and scuffing the tracks as he went.

"What *happened* to you?" cried Bale. Like Asrif, he was holding a torch of twisted kelp dipped in seal oil. In the flickering light his face was drawn. "Where have you been?"

"Finding proof," said Torak. "Proof that I'm not a liar."

Bale's face closed. "Think of a better story. You've been gone most of the night."

"I got caught in a seal net."

"A seal net?" Asrif snorted. "Now we know you're lying. We never lay them this close to camp; there aren't any seals!"

"Maybe not," said Torak, "but that's what happened. I'll show you."

Praying that the tide hadn't carried it away, he led them through the birches and onto the main beach. Then he had an idea, and led them farther up the sand.

"I thought you said there was a net," said Bale.

"There is, but there's a track, too. I'll show you that first."

He was in luck. The tide hadn't reached as far as the tokoroth footprint, which was clearly visible in the torchlight.

Bale knelt over it. "What made this?"

Torak hesitated. "Something bad."

"I think I've found the net," shouted Asrif from the rocks. He hauled it out. "But why would anyone put it here?" he said as they ran down to him. "No seals come this close."

"They weren't after seals," said Torak. "They were after me."

Again Asrif snorted. "You're making that up!"

"No, I don't think he is," said Bale, kneeling to study the net. With his free hand he turned it over. "Whoever did this knew what they were doing."

"Why do you say that?" said Torak.

The older boy raised his head. "The way to set a seal net is to fix the upper part to a line that you attach to the rocks, leaving the lower part hanging free in the water. And you've got to make sure that only one of the upper corners is firmly tied to the rock, so that when the seal swims in, it pulls the other side free, and the net collapses around it."

"Well it worked," said Torak with feeling. Suddenly he was back in the water, feeling the slippery kelp clinging to his legs. . . .

"And look at this," said Bale, pointing to two rows of barbed bone hooks that were set like fangs on opposite edges of the net. "These make sure that when the net closes around the seal, it can't open again."

Torak nodded. "I wondered how I'd got in, but couldn't get out."

Bale stood up. "How *did* you get out?"

Again Torak hesitated. "A limpet shell. I cut myself free with a limpet shell."

Bale glanced from Torak to the ripped and tattered net, and raised his eyebrows.

Torak stared stubbornly back. He didn't like lying

to Bale, but he didn't trust him enough to tell him the truth. The only way to keep Wolf and Renn safe was to keep them hidden.

"It doesn't matter how I got out," he said. "What matters is whether you believe me. There's something bad on the island, and it's brought the sickness. We've got to get the cure."

Bale ran his thumb across his bottom lip. Then he said, "All right, I was wrong. I think you are telling the truth. Or part of it. But tell me this. Why did someone want to trap you? Why you? Who *are* you?"

Torak dodged the question. "I don't know what it wants any more than you do."

"Are you sure about that?" said Bale.

"Quite sure." He paused. "So what were you and Asrif talking about just now? You said something about the Cormorants."

Asrif and Bale exchanged glances.

Then Bale said, "Something happened today in the strait between our island and theirs. A party of Cormorants were fishing. They were attacked."

"Attacked?" said Torak.

"By a Hunter," said Bale.

"A lone one," said Asrif. "With a notched fin."

Torak thought of the black fins circling beneath a sky filled with seabirds; the towering fin with the notch in the tip. He thought of the terror of the capelin. . . .

"Do you know how rare it is," said Bale, "for a Hunter to leave its pack? Males leave to seek a mate, but that's only in winter. And from what the Cormorants told us, this one wasn't seeking a mate."

"Was anyone killed?" said Torak.

Bale shook his head. "It smashed three skinboats, then dived. They didn't see it again. Their Mage thinks it let them live because they weren't who it was looking for."

"Maybe it's after you, Forest boy," said Asrif.

"Why?" said Torak with more defiance than he felt. "Because I trailed some fishhooks in the Sea?"

"Leave him alone, Asrif," said Bale. He turned to Torak. "Tenris doesn't think it's that. He says it must be something worse." He peered at Torak. "You haven't done anything else we need to know about, have you?"

Torak shook his head.

"Or to put it another way," said Asrif, "are you sure you want to come with us to the Heights?"

"I'm sure," said Torak. But as he watched the dark waves sucking at the rocks, he wasn't sure at all. Maybe he'd done something wrong without even knowing it.

"If we haven't done anything wrong," said Bale, "we should be safe. We'll keep to the leads between the skerries and the coast; and to be certain, Tenris is making masking charms for the boats." He gestured to the camp. "Get something to eat. We're heading out soon."

He and Asrif made for the camp, and Torak followed a few paces behind. Once again he was back in the water, watching the capelin flee. He remembered Wolf's warning in the dream. *Shadow. Hunted.*

Hunted—or *Hunter?*

Was that what Wolf had been trying to say?

Long after Torak had gone, Renn sat by the fire, thinking over everything he'd told her. That dream of his. She wished she'd asked him more.

Renn knew about dreams, because her own sometimes came true. When she was little, that had frightened her, so to dispel her fear, Fin-Kedinn had asked Saeunn to teach her about them. The Raven Mage had shown her how to find the hidden meaning. "Dreams don't always mean what they seem to," she'd said. "You need to look at them sideways, as if you were searching for a dew trail."

Shadow. Hunted.

Did that mean the sickness? Or the tokoroth? Or perhaps neither; perhaps it meant the Hunter that Torak had mentioned.

The thought made her shiver. On the journey across the Sea, the Sea Eagles had been wary, having heard from the Kelp Clan that there was a lone Hunter roaming the Sea: an angry one. She should have told Torak, but there'd been so little time. . . .

Wind stirred the rowan branches, and her hand crept to the hilt of her knife. It was a warm, blustery night, and the trees were moaning. Here and there she glimpsed a crouching boulder. Or maybe a tokoroth . . .

She sprang to her feet. It was no use staying here, scaring herself. It was at least a daywalk to the western tip of the island and the Eagle Heights; she should break camp now, and get a head start on the skinboats.

Feeling better for making a decision, she stamped out the fire and began gathering her things.

When she raised her head, she was startled to see that Wolf was already waiting for her on the trail. He had known what she was going to do almost before she'd known it herself.

This had happened a few times before; it was what Torak called "the wolf sense," and usually Renn found it intriguing. Tonight she found it unnerving. It reminded her that there were some things about Wolf that would always remain hidden. And here, on this windy hillside haunted by tokoroth, that was not a comforting thought.

Shouldering her pack, she set off along a narrow hare trail that delved into gullies and gave the best cover. Wolf trotted before her, pausing now and then to catch the scents. His tail was relaxed and his hackles down, so Renn's fears began to ebb, and she let her mind drift.

It felt as if I were being pulled loose, Torak had said. *I felt as if I were the fish.*

That troubled her almost more than the tokoroth. And it had troubled Torak, too.

Suddenly she stopped. *I felt as if I were the fish.* That had nudged something in her memory—something just out of reach.

She knew it was connected to the sickness, but when she tried to grasp it, it sank beneath the surface. . . .

Uff!

Wolf's warning dragged her back to the present.

He was standing motionless, gazing down at the lake.

Renn dropped to the ground and crawled behind a juniper bush.

There. Sliding through the water. A skinboat.

The light was too poor to make out who was in it. All Renn could see was that it was a man—or maybe a boy—with the long fair hair of the Sea clans. He was paddling silently east, in the direction of the Seal camp. Or almost silently. Now and then she heard the click of his paddle against the side of the boat.

Something in the turn of his head indicated stealth, and even though she was forty paces above him, Renn held her breath as she watched him reach the end of the lake and step into the shallows.

She knew that the lake drained into a stream which tumbled through a ravine and down into the Bay of Seals. The ravine was too steep and the stream too fast for anyone to pass through it—so what would the skinboater do now? The only means of reaching the bay was the way Tiu had shown her, by the little white beach.

She watched as the skinboater carried his craft ashore and hid it in a clump of birch. Then he disappeared into the trees—in the direction of the little white beach. Which meant that he was either a Seal, or someone who knew the island well.

Renn sucked in her cheeks, wondering what to do. She wanted to go after him and find out who he was and what he'd been doing; but she also needed to get a head start on Torak, or she'd never reach the Heights in time.

The thought of the Heights decided her. She didn't trust the Seals one bit; she couldn't let Torak go there alone. She would head west. And maybe when the light improved, she could pick up the skinboater's trail, and find out what he'd been doing.

As she stood up, she saw that Wolf had left her, in the noiseless way that wolves do. No doubt he'd simply gone off on one of his hunts, but she wished he'd stayed.

Treading as quietly as she could, and placing one hand on her clan-creature skin for protection, she started west.

Wolf was worried. As he loped toward the Den of the pale-pelted taillesses, he hardly smelled the voles scurrying on the other side of the Still Wet, or the female crashing through the brush. He would catch up with her once he'd made sure that his pack-brother was all right—and found something to eat.

The female had been generous with her kills, though a haunch of hare was nothing; he could happily have eaten a whole roe buck. But in this strange, light land where no wolf had run before, there weren't any roe buck. Or horses. Or elk. And the fish-birds were best left alone, because if you got too close, they spat.

Settling into the lope and trying to ignore the hunger gnawing his belly, Wolf raced up to the ridge, where the smells wafting from the valley were many and fascinating—then down the other side, past his friends the ravens, and on toward the Great Wet. The crunchy white ground scratched his pads, and the stink of the salt-grass made him sneeze, but Tall Tailless's scent was strong, and Wolf followed it easily to the Den.

Keeping to the shadows, he pricked his ears and

snuffed the air. Tall Tailless was too far off to see, but Wolf smelled and heard him well enough—although of course his pack-brother and the other taillesses didn't even know he was there.

Taking long, deep sniffs, he sorted the different smells. Then he shook himself in frustration. Taillesses were so *complicated*. One of the pale-pelted ones spoke as a friend, but hid a terrible hunger. And Tall Tailless himself didn't say all that he felt, not even to his own pack-brother.

As Wolf stood uncertainly, a distant howling reached him—so far away that he could hardly hear it. In its feeling it was like a wolf, but not in the sound. Between the howls came many hard snapping noises, and high, swift squeaks.

Wolf had heard this howling before: once on that terrible journey in the floating hides; then again, the previous Light. It came from under the Great Wet. It came from the big black fish who hunted in packs, like wolves.

Wolf knew that the howling he could hear now was coming from the lone blackfish who had left its pack and was roaming the Great Wet alone, bitten by anger and sadness. Wolf dropped his ears in fear, and flicked his tail between his legs. He knew that against this blackfish he was as helpless as a tiny blind cub.

Tall Tailless, of course, was not helpless—but the strange thing was, he didn't know it.

Wolf had been astonished when he'd sensed this in his pack-brother as they'd sat together by the Bright Beast-That-Bites-Hot.

Tall Tailless didn't know what he was.

TWENTY-FIVE

"I told Bale you won't be taking any gear in your boat," said Tenris as he helped Torak carry his craft down to the water. "You'll need all your strength just to keep up." He cast Torak a worried glance. "You look tired. Didn't you sleep?"

Torak shook his head. He wanted to tell the Seal Mage about the net and the tokoroth, but there was no time. Already the others were loading their boats.

It was a hot day, and the Sea was deceptively smooth. But Torak kept thinking of the terror of the capelin; of black fins slicing the waves.

Tenris guessed his thoughts. "I've put a masking

charm on your hull. The Hunter won't even know you're there."

"I wish you were coming," said Torak.

Tenris smiled. "So do I." With his good hand he touched Torak's shoulder. "Be careful." Then he walked off up the beach.

Detlan approached, holding out a gutskin parka. "You'll need this," he said.

"Thanks," said Torak. The gutskin felt stiff as he pulled it on over his jerkin, and it chafed his throat and wrists. But it would keep him dry.

"And tuck this inside your jerkin," said Detlan, handing him a small roll of dried whale meat. "But *don't* eat it."

"What's it for?" said Torak.

"Always carry food on a Sea journey," said Detlan, his brow creasing. "Then if you go down, you don't go empty-handed."

Torak stared at the whale meat, then tucked it in his jerkin.

On the beach, those Seals who hadn't yet left for the Cormorant island were waiting to see them off.

Detlan's little sister was trying not to cry. She was old enough to remember the last time the sickness had struck, and now, in her terror that her family would be taken, she was making a nuisance of herself by checking everyone's hands for sores.

Asrif's mother was subdued as she patted her son's chest, and told him for the tenth time to be careful.

Bale's father pressed something small into his son's hand. Bale murmured his thanks. His father's smile lit up his blue eyes.

Torak felt a pang, seeing them together. Then he thought of Wolf and Renn, and he didn't feel so bad.

"Is that an amulet?" he asked Bale when the older boy came over to check his skinboat.

Bale nodded. "A rib from the first seal I ever caught. Fa's wound it with cormorant gullet, so if there's a storm, it'll help pull me to shore." He glanced at Torak. "What amulet do you carry?"

"I don't," said Torak. "But when I was in the Forest I had my father's knife and my mother's medicine horn."

Bale looked thoughtful. Then he ran up the beach to the shelters, returning moments later with a slender rawhide bundle. "Your amulets," he said. "Tenris says you can have them back."

Torak unfolded the bundle. Inside were the blue slate knife, his medicine pouch, and the antler-tine horn. "Thanks," he muttered. But Bale had turned away, and didn't hear him.

Without ceremony they got under way. At first Torak had his hands full merely keeping his balance, but as they rounded the headland, he risked a glance over his shoulder. Tenris stood beneath the jawbone arch, watching them go. That gave Torak a twinge of unease. For a moment it looked as if the Seal Mage were being swallowed.

Heading west, they made good progress, accompanied by herring gulls and guillemots. A light breeze sprang up, shivering the surface of the Sea like the wrinkles on an old woman's face.

"She's at peace," said Detlan, bringing his boat near Torak's.

Torak was unconvinced. Despite Tenris's masking charm, he couldn't stop scanning the water for tall black fins. Every time a fish darted beneath him or a gull's shadow slid across his bow, he jumped. Notched Fin could be anywhere. It could be under his skinboat right now.

All morning they paddled, as the sun beat down from a cloudless sky, and the coast slipped past. Torak surprised himself by keeping up, but soon the rhythm of the paddles sent him into a daze.

He was gazing blearily over the side when, almost directly beneath him, he saw a small dark shape rising—growing rapidly bigger.

He snapped awake, his skinboat rocking dangerously. He tried to shout a warning, but it stuck in his throat.

A sleek gray head broke the surface beside his paddle, and shook the droplets from its whiskers. Then the seal yawned—baring lots of very sharp teeth—and gazed up at him with mild, curious eyes.

Torak blew out a long, shaky breath.

The seal blew out too, opening its nostrils wide. Its smooth gray fur was dotted with dark rings, which explained why it was so friendly; it knew it wouldn't be hunted.

Bale had seen it too. He was grinning as he brought his boat about. "The guardian! Now I know we'll be all right!"

The seal floated lazily on its back with its tail flippers curled over its belly, watching him go by. Then, with a soft *oof*, it shut its nostrils, and disappeared beneath the waves.

Maybe because of the guardian, they saw no sign of Notched Fin, and made such good speed that in the midafternoon they put in at a little bay to rest.

The tide was out, and the sand was webbed with seaweed and the three-toed tracks of oystercatchers. Bale and Asrif built a fire, then went to refill their waterskins, while Detlan showed Torak how to catch shellworms. Soon they had a pile of the long brown shells, which they baked in the embers. Torak thought the shellworms tasted slightly better than they had the first time. He must be getting used to them.

With the shellworms they ate the crunchy stems of

a sea plant that Asrif had gathered. It tasted like salty green ice, and Torak only ate it because the others did; more to his liking were the baked marshmallow roots that oozed a gluey sweetness. Nobody spoke while they ate, and it struck Torak as odd that he should feel almost at ease with the same boys who'd hunted him only four days before.

The afternoon passed, and as they paddled west, Torak's arms and thighs began to ache. More than once he nodded off, jolting awake just when his paddle was about to slip from his hands. But still the Seals kept going, their fair hair streaming behind them.

He'd given up hope of ever stopping when he heard the distant din of seabirds. Narrowing his eyes against the glare, he saw a rock face rising sheer from the Sea toward a peak shaped like a Hunter's fin. At the very top he could just make out a few dark specks slowly circling.

Eagles, he thought.

"And you're really going up there?" said Torak, craning his neck at the Heights.

"I've done it before," said Asrif with a shrug. But his face had gone the color of wet sand.

"Once," muttered Bale, "you did it once. And never all the way to the eyries."

They were standing right beneath the Heights, on a

narrow stretch of rocks that followed the line of the cliffs, then reached out into the Sea like a claw. It was on this claw that they'd left the skinboats—so that, as Bale said, "if he falls, he won't damage the boats."

The Eagle Heights were the tallest cliffs Torak had ever seen. Scarred by the frosts of many winters, their gaunt flanks were the dark red of raw whale meat, and spattered with bird droppings. The stink caught at his throat; the din made his head throb.

And if he'd thought the cliffs at the Bay of Seals were crowded, this was far worse. You couldn't slip a feather between the cormorants huddled on the lowest rocks; farther up, hordes of guillemots jostled for space, while kittiwakes and herring gulls squabbled above them. The highest crags of all held the huge, shapeless eyries of the eagles.

"Some of those eyries are hundreds of winters old," murmured Bale, "and some of the eagles are over fifty." Despite the noise he spoke softly, and Torak understood why. It wasn't just the eagles they had to watch out for. The Heights themselves were awake, and would shrug off an unwanted intruder. At his feet lay fragments of shattered stone, which meant only one thing. Rockfalls.

And yet according to Bale, the Seals did sometimes climb the Heights, if other prey was scarce, and they couldn't get enough eggs closer to camp. That explained the short stone pegs jutting at intervals from the rock all the way to the lowest eyrie, dizzyingly high above.

That was their target; but Torak couldn't see any plants growing around it, let alone the selik root Tenris had described. "Small, about a hand high, with purple-gray leaves, and hooked roots, like the talons of an eagle."

Torak's neck was getting sore, and he rubbed it. "Who put in the climbing pegs?" he asked.

"My grandfather's grandfather," said Bale. "Although we have to replace them when the cliffs move."

"And we don't usually go as far as the eyries," said Asrif.

"And it's a bad time to be trying it," said Detlan. "They've got nestlings. They'll think Asrif's after them."

"Let's hope they've got the wisdom to know that he's not," said Bale. From a pouch at his belt he took a withered gray-green stalk which he broke into four. "Here." He handed out the pieces.

Detlan and Bale chewed theirs, but Torak eyed his suspiciously. "What is it?"

"Cliffwort," said Bale with his mouth full. "Takes away giddiness."

"I thought only Asrif was going up."

"He is," said Bale. "But you can get just as giddy looking up as you can looking down."

The stalk was bitter, but almost immediately Torak's head cleared.

He felt spare and useless as he watched Deltan help Asrif put on the heavy kelp-rope harness, and check the big wooden hook at its back; Bale slinging the coil of rope over his shoulder, and testing the hook at its end.

"What can I do?" he asked.

Asrif flashed him a grin that was more of a grimace. "Catch me if I fall."

"Just keep out of the way," muttered Bale.

Torak ground his teeth. They wouldn't even let him help.

Stifling his frustration, he watched Bale draw back his arm and throw the rope. The hook floated high, then dropped neatly over a peg about ten paces up. Asrif caught the hook and fixed it to the one at his back, and Detlan took the other end of the rope and pulled it taut. Asrif began to climb, finding cracks and climbing pegs with his hands and feet, while Detlan braced himself to take his weight if he fell.

When he neared the peg over which the rope had been flung, he found a ledge beside it and balanced on his toes, clinging to the rock face with one hand while he unhooked the rope from his harness and tossed it down. It hit the ground with a thump—Torak had to jump smartly back—and Bale cast it again, this time over a higher peg, taking care to avoid knocking Asrif off. Asrif needed good balance to catch the swinging hook and attach it to his harness.

As he climbed higher, seabirds lifted off the cliff and fluttered indignantly about him. A couple of times, he slipped and came off the rock face. Only the harness—and Detlan's muscle—stopped him plunging to his death.

While Detlan and Bale sweated at the rope, Torak stood by, hating his helplessness. Asrif made his way precariously up the cliff. For the last few lengths—which were out of Bale's reach—he cast the rope himself, choosing pegs that were close enough to allow him to do so without losing his balance. By now he was nearing the eyrie.

As Torak watched, shading his eyes with his palm, he saw a dark, hunched shape lift off a crag. It had the enormous, blunt-fingered wings of an eagle; and it was spiraling slowly down toward Asrif.

A solitary eagle circled the peak. Renn thought of Torak on the other side, and quickened her pace.

Although the sun was getting low, it was still hot on the trail, and the breeze wafting from the lake did little to cool her. She'd been walking since well before dawn. Wolf had returned soon after, to her great relief; but he'd been keen to head west, and it had been a struggle to keep up with him. Even now he was racing ahead—although always running back for her.

She wondered if he knew where Torak was, or if he'd picked up the trail of the skinboater she'd seen on the lake. She had found no trace of him, except for a second skinboat hidden under some brush at the edge of the lake. The boat had been empty. A spare, maybe. But that told her nothing about what the skinboater had been doing in this part of the island.

"These days, the Seals don't go inland," Tiu had told her. "They used to, but they've become much stricter about keeping Forest and Sea apart."

"Doesn't anyone live on the west coast?" Renn had asked.

Tiu had shaken his head. "It belongs to the eagles. You can see their home from far away: a great red peak shaped like a Hunter's fin."

Renn had first glimpsed the peak at midday. Now, as she left the lake behind her, she stood directly beneath it.

From this side it was unscaleable: a treacherous scree slope on which not even crowberry could gain a hold. To her left, though, among some straggly rowan trees, there might be a way around its southern foot, and down to the Sea. She would need that if she was to find Torak.

But to her surprise, Wolf wasn't interested in that way. Instead he went north, disappearing into a birch thicket, then bursting out again, keen for her to follow. He didn't seem worried; simply excited. She decided to go after him.

Pushing through the thicket, she found herself climbing a rocky slope that soon had her breathless and scratched. It was a relief to come out on a windy ridge high above a beach of glittering black sand. To the north the beach came to an abrupt end where a cliff had fallen into the Sea, leaving a tumbled mass of boulders. In the midst of these, screaming flocks of birds squabbled over something large and dead.

Carrion, thought Renn, watching Wolf race down the slope to the beach. No wonder he's excited. Now he'll have enough to eat.

She'd come this far, so she decided to see what it was.

The wind changed, and she caught the stench of rottenness. As she reached the bottom and crunched through the charcoal-colored sand, she saw Wolf at the other end of the beach, scattering the birds. Crows and gulls dived at him, but he fended them off with a few good snaps. The wiser ravens settled on the rocks to wait their turn.

Then she saw that someone else had been here before her. Beside Wolf's tracks were a man's. Walking, not running. Whatever the skinboater had been doing here, he'd taken his time.

As she drew nearer, the carrion stink grew so strong that she had to breathe through her mouth. In the glare of the sun she couldn't see much of whatever had died among the boulders. Just a big, humped shape splashed with bird droppings; and Wolf tearing hungrily at the dark-red flesh.

At her approach he moved around to the other side, to put more distance between them. That should have told her to give him more eating space, but what she saw made her forget about that. Oh no, she thought. It can't be.

Wolf raised his head and growled at her, then gave an uncertain whine and wagged his tail. He was telling her that he liked her, but she was getting too close to his meat.

She stumbled backward. She'd seen enough.

The young Hunter had been trapped in a kelp net, and killed with an axe. Then its carcass had been left for the birds. Only its teeth had been hacked out.

Feeling sick, Renn sank to her knees in the sand,

staring at the small black fin covered in peck marks. Why would anyone do such a thing?

Then she remembered the Kelp Clan's warning about the lone Hunter.

No wonder it's angry, she thought.

TWENTY-SIX

On the Heights, Asrif was in trouble.

He'd reached a ledge just beneath the eyrie, but the back of his harness had caught on a rock, and he couldn't unsnag it.

"He could cut himself free," said Detlan, craning his neck.

"Then what does he do for a harness?" said Bale.

Torak said, "If he's really caught, then—"

"—then he can't get down," snapped Bale. "Yes, we've already thought of that."

"What I mean," said Torak, "is I could go up and help him."

"*What?*" said Detlan and Bale together.

"Those other pegs, a bit to the side? If I could reach them—"

"*If,*" said Bale.

Torak looked at him. "You've got a spare harness and a spare coil of rope; and I'm lighter than Asrif. I saw how he did it."

Bale was staring at him as if he'd never seen him before. "You would do this?"

"We need that root," Torak said simply. "Besides," he added, "what else are we going to do?"

The first ten paces were easy. The harness crossed loosely over Torak's shoulders and around his waist, with the big wooden hook at the back linking to the hook at the end of the rope. A quick check reassured him that both hooks were well made, of good hard spruce.

With Detlan holding Asrif's rope, Bale held Torak's while he climbed to the first ledge.

"Don't look down," Bale warned him. "And don't look too far up, either."

Torak forgot that almost at once. As he waited to catch the hook after Bale tossed it over the next peg, he caught a glimpse of Asrif, impossibly high above; and above Asrif, a raft of branches jutting from a cleft. The eyrie. But where were the eagles?

At the second attempt he caught the hook, and after an awkward struggle, managed to link it to the one between his shoulder blades. Then, when he felt the tug on the rope that told him Bale was ready, he began to climb.

The pegs were sturdy, but too widely spaced for him, and twice he slipped, and the harness snapped taut, checking his fall.

The heat on the rock face was intense. Before starting, he'd taken off the gutskin parka, but even so, he quickly broke out in a sweat. Every ledge and cranny was smeared with bird slime. The stink stung his eyes, and soon his hands and feet were gray and slippery.

Throwing the rope was a lot trickier than it had appeared when Asrif did it, but he managed it after several attempts. It reassured him to feel his father's knife bumping against his thigh, and the weight of his medicine pouch at his belt, with his mother's medicine horn inside.

Here and there he passed incongruous tufts of pink clover shivering in the breeze. A guillemot chick twisted its scrawny neck to watch him. Most birds fled at his coming, but some tried to chase him away. Kittiwakes fluttered screaming about him. As he climbed past a ledge crowded with fulmar chicks, he narrowly avoided a faceful of foul-smelling spit.

Just when he was beginning to wonder if he would ever get there, he heaved himself onto a ledge that brought him level with Asrif.

The Seal boy was a little over an arm's length away, on his hands and knees with his back to Torak, his shoulder strap hopelessly snagged on a jagged tongue of rock. No wonder he hadn't been able to free himself.

Asrif glanced awkwardly over his shoulder. "Good to see you, Forest boy," he said, trying for a grin that didn't work. His face was red, although whether from exhaustion or humiliation, Torak couldn't tell.

"I think I can unhook you," said Torak. He began edging sideways along a narrow crack that led from his ledge to Asrif's.

"Watch out for the eagles," warned Asrif.

Torak risked a glance up—and nearly fell off the cliff in shock. Directly above him, the eyrie blotted out the sky. A huge tangle of lichen-crusted branches, it was easily as big as a Raven's shelter. From deep inside he heard a faint *chink chink* of nestlings. But of their parents he could see no sign.

"Where are they?" he murmured.

"Circling higher up," said Asrif. "I think they know I'm stuck. It won't be the same for you."

Torak swallowed, and glanced back to the ledge he'd just left. His rope was securely looped over the final peg, a short way above it. If he missed his footing, that should stop him falling too far. If, of course, the rope didn't break, or his harness didn't snap, or the peg didn't crack . . .

If, if, if, he told himself impatiently. Get on with it.

He moved farther along the crack. But even straining as far as he could, he couldn't reach Asrif's harness.

He tried to get closer—but his rope held him back. He tugged at it—the signal for Bale to feed him more slack—but nothing happened.

"He can't give you any more," said Asrif. "There's none left."

Torak glanced down—a dizzying drop to the upturned faces far below—and saw Bale shaking his head.

He thought for a moment. Then he wriggled out of his harness, and let it swing free from the final peg. Now there would be nothing to hold him if he fell.

"What are you *doing*?" whispered Asrif in horror.

"Try to keep the birds off me," said Torak as he edged closer.

Again he reached out for Asrif's harness—and this time his fingers brushed it.

A shadow slid across the rock—and he ducked as a herring gull flew at him with a strident *kyow*. Asrif shouted and threw a stone. He missed, and the gull flew away, spattering them both. Foul white slime clogged Torak's hair and leaked down his face, narrowly missing one eye. He spat out the worst and tried again.

This time he grabbed Asrif's shoulder strap. His fingers were slippery with bird slime, and he couldn't pull the harness off the snag. "Move back a bit," he gasped, "let it slacken."

Asrif shuffled back.

With a jerk that nearly took him with it, Torak yanked the harness free of the rock.

Asrif was still on hands and knees, openmouthed with shock. He turned and met Torak's eyes. "Thanks," he muttered.

Torak gave a curt nod. "The root. Did you get the root?"

Asrif shook his head.

"*What?*"

"I couldn't reach." His face puckered with shame. "I chose the wrong pegs, climbed myself to a dead end. Should've taken your route instead."

Torak risked another glance up, and saw that a short way to his right, a deep, slanting crack zigzagged up toward the nether part of the eyrie. At its top, in the very shadow of the eyrie, nestled a clump of glossy, dark-purple leaves. Selik root.

He thought about going back to the ledge he'd just come from, and putting on his harness. But there was no more slack in the rope; it wouldn't allow him to reach the eyrie. He would have to do without.

"I should be able to make it," he said, with more confidence than he felt.

His arms and legs trembled with strain as he sought handholds and hoisted himself up the crack. He was hot and tired, and the stink of bird slime was making him sick.

Beneath his foot, the crack gave. Just in time he climbed farther up—and watched part of the rim disintegrate, the fragments rolling and bouncing before shattering on the boulders, dangerously close to Detlan and Bale.

It occurred to him that he should have shouted a warning, but it was too late now. Besides, shouting would displease the cliff, which seemed to be waxing impatient with these interlopers on its flank.

He edged farther up the crack toward the selik root.

"Look out!" whispered Asrif below him.

A menacing *klek klek* echoed off the cliff—then a shadow sped toward him—and he looked around to see an eagle coming straight at him, its vicious talons reaching for his face. He needed both hands to cling on, he couldn't even shield his head, could only flatten himself against the rock. He caught a fleeting glimpse of fierce golden eyes and a sharp black tongue—heard the hiss of wings wider than a skinboat. . . .

A stone struck the eagle on the breast, and it wheeled away with a screech.

Torak glanced down at Asrif, who'd found another pebble and was fitting it to his slingshot.

Torak couldn't see where the eagle had gone. Maybe it had been frightened off, but he didn't think so. More likely it was circling for another attack.

Above him, the cleft widened and became much easier to climb. When he reached the top, he found to his relief that it was deep enough to allow him to go down on his right knee, and by pressing himself against the sun-hot rock, reach down with his left and unsheath his knife.

The sky darkened. More wing beats—more hammer-like alarm calls—this time from *two* eagles: the mated pair fighting to protect their nestlings.

"I'm not after your young!" cried Torak, forgetting to lower his voice as he brandished his knife.

Not surprisingly, the eagles didn't listen. As he reached for a clump of the selik root and dug at it with his knife, he expected at any moment to be wrenched off the cliff.

Several well-aimed strikes from Asrif warded them back, but the eagles kept coming. The cliffs rang with their calls.

"Hurry *up*!" called Asrif.

Torak thought that too obvious to need a reply.

The selik root had taken hold in a sunbaked "earth" of rotten wood and eagle pellets, and it didn't want to let go. Sweat poured down Torak's sides as he chipped away at the base of the plant with Fa's blue slate knife. The rim of the cleft on which he knelt was crumbly, and as he worked, more fragments broke off and bounced into nothingness. Desperately he grasped a clump of selik root by the stems, and rocked it loose.

"Hurry!" cried Asrif. "I'm running out of stones!"

At last the plant came free. The root was small, no bigger than his forefinger: a pale, mottled green. For a moment Torak stared at it, unable to believe that so insignificant a thing could deliver the clans from the sickness.

"I've got it," he called to Asrif. Tucking the root inside his jerkin and resheathing his knife, he started back down the cleft toward the ledge where his harness waited.

Beneath his foot, the rim cracked—and gave. He flung himself back, clutching at rock. *"Look out!"* he yelled, as a sheet of rock almost as big as he was broke off and hurtled down the cliff—taking his harness with it.

Torak clung to the rock face, watching in disbelief as the harness tangled with the rock—narrowly missed Asrif—and floated almost lazily down, striking the boulders with a distant thump a few paces from Detlan and Bale.

The noise of the seabirds fell away. All Torak could hear was his own breath, and the trickle of pebbles.

Above him the eagles spiraled higher. They knew that he would trouble their nestlings no more.

Below him, Asrif raised his head and met his eyes.

Both knew what this meant, but neither wanted to say it. Torak now had no way off the cliff—except to attempt the long climb down without a harness, which would almost certainly kill him.

Asrif licked his lips. "Climb down to my ledge," he said.

Torak thought about that, and shook his head. "No room," he said.

"There might be. We could share my harness."

"It'd never take the two of us. We'd both be killed."

Asrif did not reply. He knew Torak was right.

"You take the root," Torak said abruptly.

Asrif opened his mouth to protest, but Torak talked over him. "It makes sense—you know it does. You can get down from there. You can take it to Tenris, he can make the cure. For everyone."

He sounded very sure, but his heart was fluttering like a fledgling. Part of him could not believe what he was saying.

Leaning down as far as he could, he lowered his

arm, then let fall the root. Asrif caught it and tucked it inside his jerkin. "What will you do?" he said.

Torak felt surprisingly clearheaded as he thought over his choices. Maybe that was the cliffwort; or maybe he simply hadn't taken in what was happening.

The stretch of rocks where Bale and Detlan stood was directly beneath him. It was narrow, and behind it lay the Sea. If he jumped, he might hit that instead.

"You could *try* climbing down," said Asrif, his face young and scared.

"With you below me?" said Torak. "And what about Detlan and Bale? If I fell, I might kill you all."

Asrif swallowed. "But what else—"

"Watch your head," said Torak, and launched himself off the cliff.

TWENTY-SEVEN

Torak was falling through glowing green water—
through glowing green light—and he wasn't
scared at all, just hugely relieved that he hadn't hit the
rocks.

After the heat of the cliffs, the water was so cold it
was a kick in the chest, but he hardly felt it, because
now he was falling into a Forest.

Golden, sun-dappled kelp shimmered and swayed
to the rhythms of the Sea. Its roots were lost in darkness, and through its undulating fronds the silver
capelin sped like swallows.

And here through the kelp came the guardian,

shooting toward him with one thrust of her flippers, then rolling over to gaze at him upside down. With her big round eyes and bubble-beaded whiskers, she was so friendly and inquisitive that he wanted to laugh out loud.

The swell carried him sideways into colder water— and suddenly a sharp pain stabbed his gut. No time to wonder what was happening—no time to be afraid. Besides, the pain was fleeting, it had already gone. And now he wasn't cold anymore, he was wonderfully *warm*, and weightless, and so at home in this beautiful, soft green world that he didn't ever want to leave.

And yet—he had to have air.

Reluctantly he kicked toward the surface. Up he spiraled, shooting through the water in a stream of silver bubbles. But when he put out his head, the world above the waves was so jagged and harsh that he shut his nostrils tight and flipped over again, back into the beautiful green light. Down he dived, faster than he'd ever thought possible, back into the kelp.

Something was floating down there in the kelp. Curious, he swam closer to take a look.

It was a boy: limp, unconscious, the current rolling him to and fro as the kelp entwined him. Torak wondered if Asrif had fallen in, or maybe Detlan or Bale. But the long, waving hair was darker than that of the Seal boys—and as it parted, he glimpsed a thin face with staring gray eyes; and on both cheekbones, the blue-black tattoos of the Wolf Clan.

With a surge of terror he realized that he was looking at himself.

His thoughts teemed like frightened fishes. What's happening? Am I dead? Is that why the guardian has come, to take me on the Death Journey?

Then he came to his senses. Don't be stupid, Torak, this guardian's a seal, and you're Wolf Clan! Your guardian would be a *wolf*!

But if I'm not dead, he thought as he stared in horrified fascination at the floating boy, *then what's happening?*

He dived closer toward himself, then came to a sudden halt by spreading his front flippers to push back the water.

His flippers?

And they were *his* flippers, there was no doubt about it. He could open and close them like hands—and as he did so, he saw their short gray fur waving gently in the water.

He rolled over and swam upside down, and found to his astonishment that he could see far down into the dark, to where purple starfish made their prickly way across the bottom. He could hear the tiny, hard biting sounds of fish nibbling kelp; the brittle clink of crabs feeling their way over rocks.

But most of all, he could *feel* through his whiskers. His whiskers were so keen that they could pick up the rippling tracks of the smallest fish as it darted through the water. The Sea was webbed and crisscrossed with thousands of invisible fish trails. And he felt, too, the strong, slow tremors that the kelp sent back through the water; and the waves echoing off the rocks. He hung upside down, trying to make sense of this bewilderment of trails.

Then—faint and far away, he heard singing.

Long, eerie shrieks; a furious hailstorm of clicks. A song of anger and loss, coming to him from the open Sea.

A shudder ran through him from the tips of his whiskers to the end of his stubby tail. And now he felt the huge disturbance in the water as the creature came closer at incredible speed. . . .

His mind flooded with dreadful certainty.

The Hunter is coming.

Another sickening jolt—another sharp pain in his gut—and suddenly he was Torak. He was bitterly cold and desperate for air, and he couldn't see much at all—he was too far down—but out of the corner of his eye he saw a flash of silver flippers as the guardian fled for the shelter of the deep.

The Hunter is coming!

With all his might, Torak kicked for the surface. His limbs were dream-heavy and he moved with infuriating slowness, but at last he broke free of the waves.

Gasping, coughing, he got a choppy view of limpet-crusted boulders—and saw with enormous relief that the current had carried him close to the claw of rock that jutted from the cliffs. Desperately he struck out for it. Maybe he could reach it before the Hunter . . .

Glancing over his shoulder, he saw that Asrif had managed to get down off the cliffs, and was jumping up and down, shouting frantically. Then, to Torak's horror, he saw Bale and Detlan setting out in their skinboats—setting out to rescue him. Didn't they know that they were far more at risk than he? He at least had a chance of reaching the claw—but in their boats, they would be utterly exposed to the wrath of the Hunter.

"*No!*" he yelled. "Get back! *Get out of the water!*"

They couldn't hear. Or did they think he was calling for help?

Swimming as fast as he could, he yelled again. "Get out of the water! The Hunter's coming! *The Hunter's coming!*"

This time Bale heard him—but instead of turning his skinboat about, he paddled faster toward Torak, shaking his head in puzzlement. And Torak saw with consternation that the Sea around him was treacherously calm, with not a black fin in sight. Bale didn't understand the warning—*because he couldn't see the Hunter.* He didn't know it was coming.

"Get back!" yelled Torak again. "The Hunter is coming!"

Now Bale understood—and plunged in his paddle and brought his skinboat about, shouting at Detlan to do the same. "Back! Back!"

The waves threw Torak against the claw, and he grabbed seaweed and hauled himself out—just as a loud, throaty *kwoosh!* erupted behind him, and a shower of spray shot high into the air.

As he collapsed on the rocks, he caught a fleeting glimpse of a great black back arching out of the water— then a towering, notched fin. He was so close that he saw the wave curling back from its edge; and as the huge blunt head powered past him, he met the dark, unknowable eye of the Hunter. Then it was gone, sweeping past him, making straight for the skinboats.

They had heeded his warning too late. Bale was nearly at the rocks, where Asrif was reaching out to him and yelling encouragement—but Detlan was farther behind, and Notched Fin was gaining on him.

Torak scrambled to his feet and ran toward them, leaping over skinboats, slipping on seaweed. But the Hunter was many times faster than him, and he watched in horror as it closed in on Detlan—swerved, and slammed its enormous tail, catching the stern of the skinboat and sending it flying.

Detlan landed with a scream on the rocks, then slid

back into the water. Asrif and Bale ran to his aid as the black fin raced toward him—then, at the last moment, twisted around and disappeared beneath the waves.

Asrif and Bale pulled Detlan's limp body from the water and laid him on the rocks.

Breathless and shaken, Torak scanned the Sea—but saw nothing. Only white foam rocking on the waves where the Hunter had been, moments before.

Then, far in the distance, he saw a black fin heading out to Sea. Whatever—whoever—Notched Fin was seeking, it hadn't found them here. Torak turned and ran toward the others.

Asrif was on his knees, wrenching out the plug of a waterskin with his teeth. Bale was shaking the contents of a medicine pouch onto the rocks. Detlan lay with his eyes closed. His face was frighteningly pale, his lips blue with shock; but as Torak got nearer, he saw to his relief that the Seal boy was breathing.

Bale shot Torak a glance. "You all right?" he said.

Torak nodded. Then to Asrif, "Do you still have the root?"

Asrif touched his jerkin, but didn't speak.

Detlan's skinboat was shattered, and so was his leg. Torak could see the white gleam of shinbone poking through bloody flesh.

"Why me?" gasped Detlan. "Why was it after me?"

Bale put his hand on his friend's shoulder. "I don't

think it was," he said. "If it had been, you'd be dead by now."

"The Cormorants were right about one thing, though," muttered Asrif, putting the waterskin to Detlan's lips. "It's after someone."

"But who?" said Bale.

Then he turned to Torak, and asked the question that Torak was already asking himself. "And how in the name of the Sea Mother did you know it was coming?"

TWENTY-EIGHT

Renn thought Torak looked pale as he knelt by the injured boy.

Hiding among the boulders thirty paces away, she trilled her signal: the song of a redstart. She'd chosen a redstart because they are Forest birds, so he'd be sure to notice.

He didn't. That astonished her. For Torak not to notice something like that—he must be shaken indeed.

It was a hot, sticky night, with the breathless feel that comes before a storm, and she'd been sweating by the time she'd found her way through the rowans and boulders at the foot of the cliffs. She'd arrived just after the Hunter had attacked.

Neither Torak nor the Seal boys seemed to know *why* it had attacked; but she did. She could still smell the carrion stink, still hear Wolf's famished champing. He'd been so intent on his food that when she'd left the beach, he'd hardly glanced up.

As the sun sank lower and the blue midsummer glow descended, she waited among the boulders, desperate to tell Torak about the slaughtered Hunter—but almost as desperate not to be seen by the Seals.

Then another Seal arrived in a skinboat: a man in a gutskin parka with a terribly burned face, who took charge of everything. The short, slight Seal boy drew something from inside his jerkin, and the man put it carefully in a little pouch at his neck; Renn guessed it must be the selik root. Then, using pieces of the wrecked skinboat, the man splinted the wounded boy's leg, while giving orders to the others.

Renn was surprised at how Torak's face lit up when the burned man came; and she felt a small stab of jealousy when the man told him to fetch wood for a fire, and he instantly obeyed.

"Is it all right if it's from ordinary trees instead of driftwood?" he asked, his voice carrying over the rocks.

The burned man nodded, and Torak started moving across the rocks.

Renn forgot her jealousy. Maybe he'd heard her signal after all.

She watched him stoop for a stick of driftwood, then wander down to the Sea; then turn and start toward the boulders.

"Where are you?" he said softly.

"The rowan trees," she whispered. "Up here—no, farther along."

When he got within reach, she grabbed his jerkin and pulled him behind a spur, which cut them off from the others. "At last!" she breathed. "I've been waiting and waiting—"

"Where's Wolf?" he said abruptly.

"In the next bay, feeding. That's what I—"

"You'd better gather some wood too," he muttered. "I can't go back empty-handed."

"What? Oh. Yes, of course." Close up, she saw that he was still pale, and not meeting her eyes. "Torak, are you all right?"

He shook his head. "What about you?"

She brushed that aside. "Listen. I know why the Hunter attacked." She told him about the murdered young one and the tracks of the fair-haired skinboater. "No wonder it's angry," she said. "That young one must have been its kin, and the skinboater trapped it and cut out its teeth, then left it to rot."

"But—why would anyone do that?" said Torak.

"I don't know, but it's got to be some kind of spell. Although who would dare do anything that evil. To break clan law—to kill a *Hunter* . . ."

"Revenge," murmured Torak to himself. "Yes, that would be it." He sounded sad as well as angry.

Renn was puzzled. "Who did?"

His face contracted as if in pain. "When I was in the water. It was so . . . I don't—I can't—"

"Torak, don't you see what this means?" she broke in. "The skinboater who did this—*he was a Seal!*"

"What? What are you saying?"

"Something is terribly, terribly wrong—*and the Seals are part of it!* Who knows, maybe they're even causing the sickness! Maybe that's why he needed the teeth!"

Torak took a step back from her. In disbelief he shook his head.

"Haven't you ever wondered," she went on, "why none of them has fallen sick, and yet you've been on the island for days, and so has the tokoroth?"

"That doesn't mean anything," he whispered.

"Then why did they send only boys to fetch the root? If they really thought they were threatened, why not send men?"

"Because Asrif is the best at climbing, and—"

"And you believe that?"

Torak hesitated, then shook himself. "Ever since they knew about the sickness, the Seals have been trying to *help*."

"Torak—"

He turned on her. "Tenris kept me off the Rock! Asrif defended me from the eagles! Detlan and Bale were coming to *rescue* me when the Hunter attacked! Bale lost his *brother* to the sickness three summers ago!"

"Why are you so keen to defend them?"

"Why are you so keen to condemn them?"

"Because the skinboater had fair hair! Because his tracks show that he was the one who murdered the Hunter!"

"But almost everyone in the Sea clans has fair hair! Besides, you said yourself that you heard his paddle click against his skinboat! If you knew anything about Seals, you'd know they never *make* any noise! The man you saw could have been anyone. A Cormorant, or one of your friends the Sea Eagles—"

"But not one of your friends the Seals," Renn said bitterly.

"They're not my friends," he retorted. "They're my kin."

She flinched.

Stonily he took the firewood she'd gathered and added it to his own. "I've got to go back," he said without looking at her.

Renn was horrified. "Haven't you been listening?"

"Renn, it's nearly Midsummer. We've only got a day to reach the camp."

"By *Sea*? With a storm coming, and a vengeful Hunter—"

"Tenris has a masking charm, and he says—"

"And Tenris is never wrong."

Torak did not reply.

"If I'm right about this," said Renn, "you're going back into danger, and putting the clans at risk— because you won't listen."

Torak turned on his heel and left.

It was much later, and on the cliffs, the seabirds were agitated. Many were leaving their roosts to fly inland. There was a storm on its way.

Torak had woken after a brief, unrefreshing sleep. Soon he would set off with Tenris and Bale. The plan was to leave Asrif and Detlan here, so that the three of them could return to camp at speed; with luck they would reach it before the bad weather hit, and in time for Midsummer night and the preparation of the cure.

On the other side of the fire, Detlan slept deeply, thanks to Tenris's sleeping potion, Asrif and Bale through sheer exhaustion. Tenris sat by the fire, smoking his crab-claw pipe.

Blearily, Torak rubbed his face. He was tired, but he

knew he wouldn't get any more sleep. The fight with
Renn had left him churned up inside. They'd had
quarrels before, but never one this bitter. He felt cut off
from her—and not only because of what had been said
between them, but because of what had happened in
the water.

He had been a seal. He had heard things, felt things
that only a seal could. But he had also been Torak. . . .

Tenris tapped his pipe on a stone, making him
jump.

A corner of the Mage's mouth lifted in a slight smile;
Torak tried to smile back. Tenris had arrived without
warning, saying simply that he'd "felt he was needed."
Torak hadn't been able to say just how glad he was.
Now he watched the Mage frown as he refilled his
pipe, holding it in his twisted hand, while with his good
one he tamped in another wad of aromatic leaves.

"Bale told me what happened out there in the
water," he said. Lighting the pipe with a glowing
brand, he took a few puffs, narrowing his eyes against
the smoke. "Why don't you tell me the rest? How did
you know the Hunter was coming?"

Torak hesitated. "I can't explain. I don't understand
it."

Tenris raised an eyebrow. "But you know more than
you told Bale. Maybe I can help."

Torak put his chin on his knees and stared into the

fiery valleys of the embers. "The seals," he murmured. "They feel it in their whiskers; the sounds coming through the water."

From the corner of his eye, he saw Tenris tense.

"I was with the guardian," Torak went on. "She heard—no, she *felt*—the voice of the Hunter—from very far away." He swallowed. "That's how I knew it was coming."

When Tenris still said nothing, Torak raised his head.

The Seal Mage sat with his pipe forgotten in his hand. His face was open and aghast.

"What does it mean?" whispered Torak.

The pipe slipped from the motionless fingers and rolled into the fire. Tenris made no move to retrieve it. Lurching to his feet, he staggered to the water's edge, and stood with his back to Torak. He stayed there for a long time. When he returned to the fire, he looked older, but also strangely excited. "Tell me everything," he said.

Torak took a deep breath—and did.

It was a relief to tell someone. He hadn't realized what a burden it had been, keeping it to himself. But the intensity in the Mage's face was frightening.

When he'd finished, there was silence between them.

Tenris ran his good hand shakily over his beard.

"Has this happened before?"

"I—think so."

"You *think* so?" Tenris spoke with unusual sharpness. "What do you mean?"

"I—I fell in a seal net. There were some capelin. . . . But only for a moment."

"For a moment? How long?"

"A few heartbeats, I don't know."

The gray eyes pierced his: as if trying to see into his souls.

"What—what is it?" faltered Torak. "What's wrong with me?"

Tenris did not reply at once. Then he said, "Nothing is—wrong with you." He glanced at the others to make sure they were still sleeping, then moved closer to Torak. "It is—" He broke off, shaking his head.

"It's what? Tell me!"

Tenris sighed. "Ah, how to explain?" Picking up a stick, he probed the fire, sending sparks shooting skyward. "Everything in the world," he said at last, "has a spirit. Hunter, prey, river, tree. Not all of them can talk, but all can hear and think. You know this, of course."

Torak nodded, wondering what was coming next.

"The three souls of every creature—the souls that make the spirit—these are rooted in the body." Again he probed the embers. "Maybe the name-soul might slip out from time to time, if you're ill, or dreaming; but it rarely goes far, and it soon comes back." He cast aside the stick and put out his hands to the fire, as if to draw something out of the flames. "But once in every thousand winters, a creature is born who is—different."

Despite the heat, Torak began to feel cold.

"This creature's souls," Tenris went on, "can leave its body—leave it for much longer than any Mage ever achieves when he is curing the sick. This creature's souls can travel farther." He paused. "They can enter the bodies of others. And when that happens, this creature sees, and hears, and feels, just as the body into which it has strayed—and yet remains himself." His fists came to rest on his knees, and he turned and met Torak's horrified gaze. *"This creature,"* he whispered, *"is a spirit walker."*

Torak couldn't breathe. "No," he said.

The gray gaze never wavered.

"No!" said Torak. "It doesn't make sense! If the souls leave, then the body is dead! I would have been dead; that's what death is!"

Tenris gave him a look full of pity and understanding. "But Torak. In spirit walking, not all the souls *do* leave the body. The Nanuak—the world-soul—always remains. It never leaves, not till the moment of death. It is only the name-soul and the clan-soul that walk."

Torak had begun to shake. He'd never even heard

of spirit walking. He didn't want to know anything about it.

Tenris put his good hand on his shoulder and gave him a little shake. "You're right to be frightened. Spirit walking is the deepest of mysteries. All we know about it has been passed down from Mage to Mage; garbled, half understood." Again he paused, as if wondering how much more Torak could take. "What we do know is that even for the spirit walker, it is very hard, and very dangerous."

And it hurts, thought Torak, remembering the sickness and the pain. It had felt as if something deep inside him were being torn loose. . . .

Then a thought occurred to him that gave him hope. "But this can't be right!" he said eagerly. "I'm not a spirit walker; I've got proof! In the Forest, I was treed by a boar. He nearly got me, and I was terrified—and *it didn't happen!* I didn't get the sick feeling, or the pain, and I never for one instant knew what he was feeling!"

The Seal Mage was shaking his head. "Torak, Torak, that is not how it is. Think! You know enough about Magecraft to be aware that even for ordinary Mages, when they wish to cure the sick, they need help to free their own souls. There are many ways of doing this. A trance. A soul-loosening potion. Sometimes simply going without food, or holding your breath. It is the same for the spirit walker. Being merely afraid, as you were of that boar, would not have been enough to loosen your souls."

Torak thought back to the other times when it had happened. At the healing rite, there had been Saeunn's soul-loosening smoke. In the seal net, he'd been close to drowning. With the guardian, too, he'd been drowning. It was beginning to make a terrible kind of sense.

"Besides," said Tenris, and Torak was surprised to see that his half smile was back, "you were lucky you *didn't* spirit walk inside that boar. His souls would have been too strong for yours. You might have been trapped in there for good."

Torak got to his feet, stumbled to the edge of the rocks, and stood there shivering. He didn't want to be different. And yet—wasn't this why his father had kept him separate from the clans? Why he'd said as he lay dying, *There's so much I haven't told you?*

"This is a curse," he said, his teeth chattering. "I don't want to be different. It's a curse!"

"No!" Tenris came to stand beside him. "Not a curse, but a *gift*! You may not think so now, but in time, you will see this!"

"No," said Torak. "No."

"*Listen* to me," said the Seal Mage, his beautiful voice shaking with emotion. "What you did so easily—without even trying—is something the cleverest Mages strive their whole lives to achieve! Why, once I knew a Mage—a good one—who tried for six winters on end. Six winters of trances and potions and fasting. Then finally, for a few heartbeats—he succeeded. And he counted himself the luckiest of men!"

"I don't want it," said Torak. "I never—"

"But Torak, this is the very *purpose* of Magecraft!" The handsome, ruined face was alight with fervor. "We do not learn Magecraft merely to trick fools with colored fire! We do it to delve deeper! To know the hearts of others!" He caught his breath. "*Think* what you could do if you learned to use this! You could discover such secrets! You could know the speech of hunters and prey. You could gain such power. . . ."

"But I don't want it!" cried Torak—and on the other side of the fire, Bale stirred in his sleep.

"I don't want it," said Torak more quietly. He had never felt so frightened and confused. All his life, he had been Torak. Now Tenris was telling him he was someone else.

He stared out across the cold, heaving Sea. He longed for Wolf, so that he could tell him all about it. But how would he ever get Wolf to understand? He had no idea how to describe spirit walking in wolf talk. And that seemed to him to be the very worst of it: that in this he would be cut off from Wolf.

"What should I do now?" he said to the cold Sea.

Again Tenris put a hand on his shoulder. "You should do what we planned to do," he said calmly. "I will waken Bale, and we will make ready to leave. We will take the selik root back to camp. And on Midsummer's night—this coming night—we will take it up to the Crag, and you will help me make the cure. That is what we shall do."

His voice was as steady as an oak standing firm in a gale, and Torak took strength from it. "Yes," he said. "Yes. This doesn't change what I have to do. Does it, Tenris?" He turned and looked up into the Mage's face.

"No," said Tenris, "it doesn't change anything."

TWENTY-NINE

At last the hunger had been chased back into its
Den, and Wolf was free to seek the female and
Tall Tailless.

But while he'd been gulping down delicious soft
chunks of rotting blackfish, the dark had come. Not the
true Dark, but the dark that covers the Up when the
Thunderer is angry. And this time it wasn't after Wolf.
The taillesses were the ones in danger.

Over the hot black earth he raced, then up the slope
and down again, to the boulders where the female had
waited for his pack-brother. He smelled that Tall
Tailless had been here too, and that he had fought with

the female. *Fought!* Wolf could not believe what he was smelling! The snarling, the baring of teeth.

Swiftly he found the Bright Beast-That-Bites-Hot, with the two pale-pelted half-growns sleeping beside it. Then to his horror he smelled that his pack-brother had gone out on the Great Wet, in one of the floating hides.

Mewing in distress, Wolf scrambled back up the boulders after the scent of the female. Ah, she was clever. She'd returned to the Still Wet, where there was less danger from the Thunderer, and there she'd dragged out a floating hide. She'd headed into the wind, so Wolf easily caught her scent. Now he knew what to do. He must follow her. She too was seeking Tall Tailless.

A roar from the Up. The wind began to howl through the valley, and the Wet came pouring down. Trees bent, fish-birds were tossed about like leaves. And still Wolf loped, flying over the rocks and the angry little Wets crashing down from the peaks.

As he ran, another scent hit him, and he skittered to a halt. Raising his muzzle, he took deep sniffs to make sure.

His claws tightened. His fur stood on end.

He smelled *demon*.

"Take my hand!" shouted Tenris, leaning perilously over the side of his skinboat and reaching for Torak.

Torak fought to keep his head above the waves, and strained to grasp the outstretched hand. He caught it—but another wall of water engulfed him, dragging him under.

Over and over, he rolled in the crushing darkness. He couldn't see, couldn't breathe.

The Sea threw him above the waves, playing with him. His gutskin parka helped him stay afloat, and he bobbed up and down, gulping air.

Tenris was gone. Bale was gone. The sky was black as basalt. Crackling flares of lightning revealed nothing but raging Sea.

"Tenris!" he yelled. "Bale!" The storm whipped his voice away.

Through the murk he glimpsed his overturned skinboat tossing about on the waves. He swam for it—the Sea dashed it against him—and he grabbed it with both hands. *"Tenris!"* he shouted.

But the Mage was gone.

Suddenly the skinboat gave a terrific jolt, and he was thrown against a rock. Winded, he reached for it with one hand, clutching the skinboat with the other. The Sea sucked at the boat, pulling him off the rock. He had a heartbeat to decide what to do.

He let go of the skinboat and hauled himself onto the rock. The boat was carried away into the gloom.

Shivering, storm-battered, he clung on.

He didn't know where he was. If he'd been thrown onto the shore, he had a chance. If not—if this was an isolated skerry somewhere in the Sea—he was in trouble.

A groping search of his haven soon told him that the rock was no bigger than a Seal's shelter, and surrounded by nothing but waves.

Panic gripped him.

Bale was gone. Tenris was gone. He was stranded on a rock in the middle of the Sea.

The storm blew over as abruptly as it had arisen.

By the time Renn reached the eastern end of the lake and laid down her paddle, the water was lapping the rocks, and scarcely stirring the reeds in the shallows.

She didn't want to think of how it must have been for Torak on the open Sea. *Why* hadn't he listened to her and come overland, instead of going with the Mage and the tall Seal boy?

Wearily she dragged her borrowed skinboat ashore, lifted out her pack and her sleeping-sack, then hid them behind a boulder. She didn't know what she would find at the Seal camp, but she doubted that she'd need anything but her quiver and bow.

Straightening up, she noticed that the sky wasn't clear, as it should be after a storm. Dirty white clouds were pouring down from the peaks, and tongues of mist were seeping toward her across the lake. Mist after a storm. She'd never seen that before.

At a run she started up the slope, making for the little white beach on the other side. She crested the ridge—and gasped. The Sea had disappeared behind a yellow wall of sea mist that was rolling menacingly toward her.

This shouldn't *be*, she told herself. This *can't* be.

Then she remembered that it was Midsummer night. And on Midsummer night, anything is possible.

Exhausted, wet and scared, she half stumbled, half slid down the tussocky slope, and fell to her knees in the coarse white sand.

Anything is possible. . . .

Maybe it's even possible that the Seal Mage is right: that Torak really is a spirit walker.

Back at the Heights as she'd crouched among the boulders, she'd flatly rejected what she'd heard the Mage telling Torak. It couldn't be true. It had to be some kind of trick.

But all through the long, hard journey on the lake, she'd been turning it over in her mind, and now she knew that it *was* true.

Torak was a spirit walker.

A spirit walker.

She had heard of such creatures, but only in the

stories of long ago that Fin-Kedinn sometimes told on winter's nights: how Raven learned to hold on to the wind, how the First Tree came, and the first clans, and the first—spirit walker.

Now, as she crouched shivering on the little white beach, she sensed that in some way she didn't understand, Torak the spirit walker lay at the heart of everything. The tokoroth—the sickness—the cure. If only she could see the pattern.

Torak clung to the rock. He was cold, wet and hungry, and although the storm had passed with startling suddenness, he was trapped in the fog, with no idea where he was. The fog could take days to lift. He didn't have days.

Then he remembered the little roll of dried whale meat that Detlan had given him before they'd set off. It was smelly and salt-stained, and if he ate it, he'd have nothing for the Sea Mother. He ate it anyway.

The meat made him feel a bit better. Then another thought occurred to him that heartened him some more. He didn't have the selik root. Tenris did—and maybe Tenris had made it back to land; maybe the clans still had a chance. . . .

A wave slapped into him, nearly knocking him off the rock.

Concentrate, he told himself. You've got to get off

this rock and back to land.

He didn't have many choices. Sooner or later, he would have to swim for it. But he was exhausted, and he knew he wouldn't last long in the water. He'd need help to stay afloat.

The skinboat was gone, and so was his paddle. All he had were his clothes and Fa's knife, and his mother's medicine horn, safe in its pouch. It contained a small amount of earthblood: just enough for Death Marks. He wasn't ready for that yet.

More waves buffeted the rock. He crawled higher, drawing the gutskin parka closer about him.

The gutskin parka.

He remembered the way it had buoyed him up in the storm. He remembered the Seal children splashing in the shallows, their beginners' boats steadied by a cross pole with an inflated gutskin sack at either end.

Yanking the parka over his head, he cut off the laces at the neck and used them to tie one wrist shut, and also the neck, and the waist. Then he put his mouth to the remaining wrist, and blew.

Blowing made him giddy, but after a sickeningly long time, he had a slightly squashy air sack that floated when he tried it on the water. If he lashed it to his belt, it might help him stay afloat—or at least stop him sinking if he got too weak to swim.

Around him the Sea swirled and the fog billowed. Somewhere out there lay the Seal island. But which way?

All he could see was black water. No seabirds, no drifting seaweed; no silvery currents to indicate a headland. He couldn't see the sun, had no sense of the direction he should take. For all he knew, he might be making straight for the open Sea.

Far away, a wolf howled.

Torak caught his breath.

There it was again. A long howl, followed by several short, sharp barks. *Where are you?* called Wolf.

Torak put his hands to his lips and howled a reply. *I'm here!* Again the answer—faint but clear, piercing the fog—floating to him across the Sea.

Again Torak howled. *Call to me, pack-brother! Call!*

Hunger, fatigue, cold—all were forgotten. He wasn't even scared of Notched Fin anymore, because now Wolf was with him, showing him the way back. His guide would not let him down.

The water was freezing, but he didn't give himself time to think. With the air sack lashed to his back, he slid off the rock and struck out through the fog and the whale-haunted Sea.

Alone in the fog on the little white beach, Renn heard wolf howls, and froze.

It sounded like—yes! Wolf! And Torak! She'd know his howl anywhere! That had to mean that he was all right!

He would be making for the Seal camp. That made her feel a bit braver about heading there too.

The fog was so thick that she couldn't see two paces in front. With her hands before her like a blind girl, she blundered through the birch trees and the boulders toward the Bay of Seals.

The trees ended. She still couldn't see. No camp. No Sea. No sounds except—somewhere nearby—the rush of wavelets on shingle. The howling had ceased.

She left the trees and stumbled toward where she hoped the Seal camp lay.

A scrape and a muffled gasp somewhere close. The sound of a skinboat being set down. Then—before she could draw back—a tall figure loomed out of the mist and ran straight into her.

With shouts of alarm they leaped apart.

"Who are you?" cried the boy.

"Where's Torak?" cried Renn.

Both were openmouthed and staring with fright.

Renn recognized the tall Seal boy who'd set out with Torak from the Heights.

"Who *are* you?" he said, his eyes narrowing.

"I'm Renn," she said with more assurance than she felt. "Where's Torak? What have you done with him?"

His glance flicked to her bow, then back to her face. His shoulders slumped. "The storm," he muttered. "We got separated. I—I saw his skinboat go over."

"What do you mean?" she said.

He rubbed his eyes, and she saw how tired he was. "Tenris tried to reach him. So did I. We couldn't. . . . Tenris is still out looking for him." He seemed genuinely distraught, and if he hadn't been a Seal, Renn would have felt sorry for him. "I heard strange howls," he said. "I've never heard anything like it."

She was tempted to tell him, but she hardened her heart. He was not to be trusted; let him go on thinking Torak was lost. She would not believe it. She'd heard Torak howling with Wolf; that had to mean they were safe.

Another skinboat slid out of the mist, and a man got out and lifted it onto the beach. It was the Seal Mage.

Full of concern, he ran to the Seal boy—saw Renn—recoiled in surprise—then turned back to the boy. "I couldn't find him," he said. Like the boy, he seemed devastated, and Renn began to wonder if she'd misjudged the Seals.

"And who is this?" said the Seal Mage, turning to her. His expression was kind, his voice as quiet and strong as the Sea on a sunny day. But something about him put Renn on her guard.

"I'm Renn," she said. "I'm from the Raven Clan."

"And what are you doing here, Renn from the Raven Clan?" he asked.

"I'm—looking for Torak." She hadn't meant to say it. But his voice compelled obedience.

"So are we," he said, looking grim. "Come. We'll go up to the camp and decide what to do."

As he walked, he pulled his gutskin parka over his head, and Renn saw for the first time his magnificent Mage's belt, and heard the soft clink of its puffin-beak fringe.

She stopped.

That sound sent ripples through her memory. It was the same sound she'd heard as she watched the skin-boater gliding over the lake.

Sea mist settled clammily on her skin. Her heart began to race. The pattern was coming together before her eyes. The tokoroth. The sickness. The Soul-Eaters . . .

The Seal Mage turned, and asked her what was wrong.

Blood thudded in her skull as she stared up into his handsome, terribly scarred face. She thought, *There is a Soul-Eater among the Seals. There is a Soul-Eater among the Seals, and his name is Tenris. And he is after Torak— Torak the spirit walker.*

"You've gone very pale," said Tenris in his beautiful, gentle voice.

"I'm—I just need to find Torak," she said.

"So do I," he said, and a corner of his mouth lifted in a smile. It was a smile full of warmth, but as Renn met his calm gray gaze, she knew with a clutch of terror that he'd seen the knowledge in her face. He knew that she knew.

"Come," he said, reaching out and taking her icy fingers in his. "Let's go and get something to eat."

Then he saw the scab on her hand, and his face contracted in pity. "Oh, my poor child, what's this?"

Before she could reply, he turned to the Seal boy. "Look, Bale. The poor little thing has the sickness."

Bale stared at her hand; then his own crept to his clan-creature skin.

"No I don't," protested Renn, trying to pull her hand from the strong, steady grip. "It's not the sickness, it's a—"

"You mustn't worry anymore," said the Seal Mage, taking both her hands in his. "From now on, I will look after you."

THIRTY

Torak was woken by Wolf licking his nose.

He was too tired to open his eyes. Instead he snuggled closer, pressing his face into soft wolf fur. He felt wonderfully warm and safe—and it was so *quiet*. No seabirds. No wind. Just the sighing of the Sea and the beat of Wolf's heart against his own.

Lick, lick, lick.

Hazily he remembered finding his way ashore. Wolf knocking him backward into the sand, and keeping him there with a frenzy of snuffle-licks. Then curling up together and slipping down into sleep . . .

The licking turned to grooming-nibbles. Then a sharp, impatient nudge under his chin. *Wake up!*

He opened his eyes.

Crunchy sand under his cheek; Wolf's whiskers tickling his eyelids. Beyond that—nothing. The fog was so thick that he couldn't tell Sea from sky.

How long had he been asleep?

The cure.

He jerked upright, heart pounding. Where was he? Where was Tenris? It was Midsummer night—had they missed their chance? The fog blotted out the sun. He couldn't tell.

He got to his feet—and the blood soughed in his ears. He was stiff and sore all over. Thirst burned his throat.

Somewhere not far off, he heard a trickling sound. He stumbled through the fog, and splashed into a shallow stream choked with weeds. He knelt and gulped handfuls of gritty water.

Wolf trotted over to him, his paws making no noise on the sand. Still on his knees, Torak nuzzled his scruff and said a heartfelt *thank you.*

Wolf swung his tail and licked the corner of Torak's mouth. *My pack-brother.*

Feeling slightly better, Torak stood up and looked about. He still couldn't see two paces ahead, but this sand was familiar. White, coarsely crushed seashells. Maybe he was closer to the Seal camp than he'd dared hope. . . .

To his right he heard the lapping of the Sea. He staggered across the beach—and suddenly birch trees and tumbled boulders loomed out of the mist. He ran toward them.

Behind him Wolf gave a low, shuddering growl.

Torak spun around.

Wolf's head was down, his lips peeled back in a snarl.

Whipping out his knife, Torak dropped to the ground and spoke in an urgent grunt-whine: *What is it?*

More growls. The fur on Wolf's hackles stood on end.

Torak felt the hairs on his own neck prickling. And yet—he couldn't see anything amiss. Up ahead, the birch trees were utterly still.

I have to go on, he told Wolf.

Again Wolf growled, warning him back.

Never before had Torak ignored his warnings, and it felt wrong to do so now. But he had to find Tenris. *I have to go on*, he said again. *Please. Come with me!*

To his dismay, Wolf backed away, growling.

Full of misgiving, Torak rose and entered the trees without him.

He was halfway through when a strong hand

gripped his arm. "*There* you are!" cried Tenris. "Thank the Sea Mother you're safe!"

Torak glanced back over his shoulder—but Wolf was gone.

"We thought you'd drowned!" said Tenris, pulling him through the remaining trees.

"You frightened me," said Torak.

"Sorry," said Tenris. "Come, let's go! Time's short, we've got to get up to the Crag."

"You still have the selik root?" said Torak as they ran across the beach.

"Yes, of course!"

"And Bale? Did he make it ashore?"

"Yes, he's fine, he's guarding—he's fine."

Torak stopped. "Guarding who?"

Tenris face became grave. "She's sick, Torak. We had to lock her up."

"Who?" said Torak. "Who's sick?"

"It doesn't matter," said Tenris. "Come, we're wasting time."

"Who is it?" Torak insisted. But a part of him already knew.

"Torak—"

"It's Renn, isn't it? Tenris, please. I need to see her."

Tenris sighed. "It'll have to be quick." At a run he led Torak through the deserted Seal camp and out to the cave at the end of the bay, where the man who'd killed the whale had spent his lonely vigil. "We put her where we kept them before," he said as they drew near.

The cave mouth was all but sealed by a massive door of whale bone and seal hide, and Bale stood on guard with a harpoon. When he saw Torak, his face lit up. Torak pushed past him without a word.

Through a gap between the door and the cave wall, he saw Renn pacing up and down. It was too dark to see her properly, but he made out her disheveled hair and furious expression; and the sore on the back of her hand. A cold weight sank inside him like a stone.

When she saw him, her face cleared. "*Torak!* Oh, thank the Spirit! Now get me out of here!"

"Renn—I can't," he said. "You're sick."

Her mouth fell open. "But—you don't believe them. Of course I'm not sick!"

Behind him, Tenris put his hand on his shoulder. "They all say that," he murmured under his breath. "But don't worry. Bale will look after her. And I've made sure she'll not go hungry."

When she saw the Mage, Renn shrank back. "Get away from me!" Then to Torak, "I'm not sick!"

"Tenris is right," said Bale, gripping the harpoon so hard that his knuckles were white. "My brother was just the same."

"Renn," said Torak, putting both hands on the seal-hide door. "I'll bring you the cure, I promise. You will get—"

"I don't need the cure!" she spat. "Why don't you believe me?" She pointed at Tenris. "It's him! *He's the Soul-Eater!*"

"In the end, they suspect everyone," said Bale.

"Why won't you believe me?" cried Renn. "Tell him to show you his mark! Make him show you his tattoo! He's a Soul-Eater!"

Tenris touched Torak's arm. "Torak, we have to go—or it'll be too late for her or anyone else."

"No—Torak—don't go!" shouted Renn. "He'll kill you! *Torak!*" She threw herself against the door.

Bale braced it with his shoulder. "Go," he told Torak. "I'll make sure she comes to no harm."

"You will get better!" called Torak. "I promise! You will get better!"

"Torak!" she screamed. *"Come back!"*

With her cries ringing in his ears, Torak followed Tenris into the fog.

"Quickly," muttered the Seal Mage. "The turn of the sun is close, I can feel it."

With Renn's cries fading behind them, they started up the trail. Soon all Torak could hear was his own breathing and the sound of water trickling over the rocks. He felt oppressed by a choking sense of wrongness. In the space of a few heartbeats, he'd ignored warnings from both Wolf and Renn.

A clatter of claws behind him.

He swung around. *Wolf?*

He couldn't see anything in the swirling whiteness—except Tenris up ahead, disappearing into the fog. "Tenris!" he called. "Wait for me!"

More clattering claws—then a small humped figure scuttled across the trail. Not Wolf. The tokoroth.

Torak raced forward. "Tenris! *Look out!* The tokoroth!"

Pain exploded in his head, and the rocks rushed up to meet him.

Torak woke with a start.

His head was throbbing, his shoulders ached. Someone had taken off his jerkin and laid him on a cold stone slab. Someone had tied his wrists together, pulled his arms above his head, and hooked them over a horn of rock. The binding was tight—he couldn't wriggle out—although if he could push himself up with his heels, he might be able to unhook his wrists and . . .

Someone gripped his ankles, holding him back. Someone with sharp claws and a knife. When he tried to kick free, they pressed its point against his calf.

Mist swirled about him, tinged blue with wood-smoke. He heard the crackle of a fire, and caught the tang of juniper. He couldn't hear the Sea. He must be high up on the cliffs.

At his feet, two demon eyes glared at him from a face tattooed with leaves.

Fear settled on him like a second skin. He was on the Crag, laid out on the altar rock, guarded by the tokoroth.

Then a second tokoroth emerged from the smoke. A girl with matted hair falling to her knees, and stick-limbs covered in bruises. Her fingernails and toenails were yellow, and filed to long, pointed claws.

In silence she leaned over him, and his skin crawled as her greasy locks brushed his belly. Her bony fingers drew his father's knife from the sheath at his belt.

"What do you want?" he whispered.

In silence she raised the knife in both hands.

"What do you *want?*"

In silence she laid the cold slate knife on his chest.

A soft clinking in the mist—and both tokoroth cowered on the ground.

A figure loomed out of the mist. With every step, the puffin beaks clinked at his belt.

Torak felt as if he were falling from a great height. All the kindness, the gentleness . . . all a lie. Wolf had been right. Renn had been right. And he had been wrong, wrong, wrong.

The Seal Mage had taken off his jerkin to reveal a lean, muscled body that was horribly burned down the whole of the left side. His arms were smeared with wood ash, obscuring his clan-tattoos. His face was an ashen mask—as if, thought Torak with a sick sense of dread—he were already mourning someone dead. He wore no amulet, except for a twist of something red and shrunken on a thong at his neck, and his naked chest was unmarked, save for a stark black tattoo over the heart. A three-pronged fork for snaring souls. The mark of the Soul-Eater.

"You," said Torak. "A Soul-Eater."

"One of the seven, Torak." His voice was the only thing that hadn't changed. Still beautiful; still as calm and powerful as the Sea on a sunlit day. "But with your help," he said quietly, "I shall rise above the others. I shall become the greatest of them all."

Slowly Torak shook his head. "I won't help you do that."

Tenris smiled. "You don't have a choice." Turning his head, he barked a command at the tokoroth, his voice suddenly harsh and cruel.

The boy raced to fetch a heavy basket almost as big as himself, while the girl scurried to the neck of the Crag. Torak saw that she was building a wall of driftwood across it, cutting them off from the trail.

The boy tokoroth hadn't finished the bindings around his ankles. So if he could keep Tenris talking, maybe he could work his feet free. And maybe if he howled for Wolf. . . .

But what then? Tenris had a spear and a harpoon lying ready by the fire, and both tokoroth had knives at their belts. Three against one. Against such odds, what could even Wolf achieve? "Your friends can't help you," said Tenris as if he'd read his thoughts. "One of them is guarding the other. There's a kind of beauty in that, don't you think?" From the basket he took out several pale, cone-shaped objects and began laying them out around the altar rock. This time he didn't seem to care about treading on the silver lines polished in the stone.

Torak had to keep him talking, to give himself time to think. "The sickness," he said. "You were the one who sent it."

"I didn't *send* it," said Tenris, standing back to study his work. "I *created* it. My tokoroth have the demon skill for creeping into shelters. And I . . . well, I'm very good at poisons."

"But—*why?*"

"That's the interesting part," said Tenris, resuming his task. "When I began three summers ago, I had no idea how I'd use it; I simply knew that I needed a weapon." He shook his head. "Sometimes not even I can tell all that the future holds."

Torak felt sick. "So Bale's little brother . . ."

Tenris shrugged. "I just wanted to know if it worked."

"And this summer. The clans. *Why?*"

The Seal Mage raised his head, and his gray eyes glittered. "To smoke you out. To find out what you can do."

So Fin-Kedinn had been right, after all.

"And it worked," said Tenris, "although not in the way I expected. You see, I didn't know who you were. All I knew was that there was someone in the Forest with power. I thought that whoever it was would perform some great feat of Magecraft to rid his people of the sickness." His lip curled. "Instead what did you do? You came to me—*me!* Begging me to make the cure! Oh, it was meant to be!"

"And the cure," said Torak. "Was that a trick too?"

Tenris snorted. From the pouch at his belt he took the selik root and tossed it on the fire. "There is no cure," he said. "I made it up."

The flames flared a deep, throbbing purple. The two tokoroth drew closer and gazed at it in fascination.

Tenris eyed them with contempt. "Sometimes being a Mage is almost too easy. All it takes is a little colored fire." He gave the girl a savage kick that sent her flying. Hissing, she scuttled back to her woodpile.

To Torak's dismay, the boy rushed back to the bindings at his ankles. He kicked out sharply. The boy tokoroth jabbed his calf with the knife to make him hold still.

"So now that you've smoked me out," he said to Tenris, "what next?"

Tenris gazed down at him, and his face contracted with pain and longing. "When I found out what you could do, I could not believe it. That a *boy* should have such power. Power to tame hunters and trammel prey. Power to rule the clans . . ." He shook his head. "What a waste."

Then he leaned closer, and Torak smelled the bitterness of ash. "Soon," he murmured, "that power will be *mine*. I will take it for myself, and become the spirit walker. *I* will be the greatest Mage who ever lived. . . ."

"How?" Torak said hoarsely. "What are you going to do?"

"Midsummer," breathed the Seal Mage. "The most potent night for Magecraft—and it's your birthnight! Oh, it is perfect! All the signs point to this, all telling me to do it!"

Gently he put out his hand and pushed back a lock of hair from Torak's forehead. "Do you remember what I told you about Midsummer night? That it's all about change?"

Torak tried to swallow, but his mouth was dry.

"Tree into leaf," murmured the Seal Mage, "boy into man." He leaned down, and his breath heated Torak's cheek as he whispered in his ear. *I'm going to eat your heart.*"

THIRTY-ONE

Wolf had done what no wolf should ever do. He had abandoned his pack-brother.

He had been so astonished when Tall Tailless ignored his warnings—so astonished and so *cross*—that he had deserted him.

So while Tall Tailless went off alone to the Den of the pale-pelts, Wolf loped up the ridge and down to the Still Wet, where he snapped at the reeds in his anger, and chewed up a hunk of dead wood, until at last all the crossness had been spat out.

And now as he stood in the Wet to drink, he thought of the time when he'd been a lonely cub, and his pack-brother had found him. Tall Tailless had shared his kills, and given him the crunchy hooves to play with. When Wolf's pads had been hurting from the trail, Tall Tailless had carried him in his forepaws for many, many lopes.

A wolf does not abandon his pack-brother.

Wolf gave an anguished yelp, and raced back toward the Den. He loped over the ridge and down again; wove soundlessly between the birch trees and out onto the pebbles.

He couldn't see the Den, as it had been swallowed by the breath of the Great Wet—but he could smell it. And he could hear the female padding up and down in the smaller Den in the mountain. She was angry, worried, and scared, and the pale-pelted tailless was growling at her; Wolf didn't know why. But apart from them, the Den was empty.

In fact, it was *too* still. He smelled the lemmings cowering in their burrows. He heard the fish-birds on the cliffs hiding their beaks under their wings. All were waiting. Frightened to move.

Wolf raised his muzzle to catch the smells. He smelled much fish, and the left-behind scents of many taillesses; he smelled the fat, friendly fish-dogs who swim in the Great Wet, and sometimes lumber up onto the rocks. And he smelled the other smell, too: the demon stink.

The stink grew stronger as he padded forward, and his hackles rose. When he was a cub, that stink had frightened him. Now it awakened a strange hunger: deeper than the blood-urge, stronger even than the Pull of the Mountain. . . .

But where was Tall Tailless? With all the smells whirling in the windless air, Wolf couldn't catch the one scent he longed to find.

And now the female and the pale-pelt were snarling at each other—and as Wolf ran toward them, he saw that the pale-pelt was carrying meat for the female in his forepaws: *meat that stank of demon!*

Wolf sensed that the female was hungry, and wanted to eat. He had to stop her! But what if she ignored his warning, just as Tall Tailless had done? What if she didn't even understand what he was telling her?

Wolf lowered his head and crept forward, placing each paw with silent care. He had an idea. There was one thing the female always understood.

A snarl.

"I'm not hungry!" snarled Renn as the Seal boy set the bowl on the ground. "And for the last time, *I'm not sick!*"

"Just eat," said the boy. Backing out of the cave, he dragged the seal hide across the cave mouth, leaving a gap a couple of hands wide for air.

Renn didn't like the Seal boy, but she wished he hadn't gone. It was frightening being in here on her own. She could feel the suffering of the sick from three summers ago; the walls were dank with their despair.

But *you're* not sick, she reminded herself. You're just tired and hungry, and worried about Torak.

She decided to try again with the Seal boy. "Do you know *why* the Hunter attacked?" she called out.

Silence.

"Because your Mage killed one of its young. I found the carcass. He trapped it in a seal net—the kind only your clan makes—and he took nothing but its teeth. Does that sound like something a good man would do?"

No reply.

She clenched her jaw. "I know it was him," she said. "I heard his belt clink as he rowed across the lake."

Still no answer, but she could tell that he was listening. She could hear him breathing on the other side of the door.

"The teeth of a Hunter?" she went on. "Only a Mage would have any use for those." She paused. "If I'm right, and he made the sickness—then he killed your brother."

For a moment there was a stunned silence. "How do you know about my brother?"

"Oh, I know many things," said Renn. "He killed

your brother," she said again. "I know what it's like to lose a brother. I lost mine not long ago."

"Be quiet," said the Seal boy.

"Think back," said Renn, "to just before your brother fell sick. Tenris had been up on that cliff top, hadn't he? Doing Magecraft."

"So?" came the reply. "He's the Mage, that's what he does."

"He did Magecraft, and then your brother got sick."

It was a guess, but a good one. She heard a sharp intake of breath.

"He did it to bring the prey," whispered the Seal boy. "He did Magecraft to bring the prey. . . ."

"That's what he told you," said Renn.

She heard the crunch of sand as he walked up and down. "No more talk," he said abruptly. But there was doubt in his voice.

"You know I'm right," she said.

"*I said no more talk!*" he shouted.

"Why won't you *listen!*" Renn shouted back.

The seal hide shuddered, and she knew that he'd punched it.

After that, neither of them spoke.

The smell of meat filled the cave. Renn hesitated— then went over to examine the bowl. Smoked whale meat with juniper berries. It smelled *really* good. But if she ate it, the Seal boy would think she was giving in.

She put the bowl down. Paced the cave. Went back and picked it up.

She was just about to try a piece when the Seal boy gave a cry, and in through the gap leaped Wolf—leaped straight at her—sending her flying, sending the meat spattering against the wall—flattening her beneath him. He was snarling, his black lips drawn back from his big white fangs. She tried to scream, but his forepaws were heavy on her chest. What was *wrong* with him?

"Wolf!" she gasped. "Wolf—it's me!"

"I'm coming!" yelled the Seal boy, wrenching aside the hide and leaping in with his harpoon.

With astonishing speed, Wolf sprang off Renn and twisted around to face him.

"*No!*" screamed Renn. "Don't hurt him! He must be sick—or—something!"

The Seal boy ignored her, and jabbed at Wolf with his harpoon.

Wolf sprang sideways, snapping at the shaft.

Renn saw her chance to escape—the cave mouth was wide open—but what about Wolf?

He was dodging the harpoon with ease.

She picked herself up and fled.

Behind her she heard another yell from the Seal boy—more in outrage than in pain—and glanced back to see Wolf leap from the cave and disappear.

Too shaken to make sense of it, she turned and raced off into the fog.

It was thicker than ever. She had no idea where she was; no idea how to find Torak.

She tripped over a pile of driftwood, then blundered into a rack full of whale meat. A shelter loomed out of the whiteness, and she clapped her hand to her mouth to keep from screaming. At any moment she dreaded to see the Seal boy leaping out at her—or the tokoroth—or the Soul-Eater.

Suddenly to the north, fire flared high in the sky.

She stopped.

Torak had said that the cure would be made in a rite on a cliff top. Although "the cure" had to be a Soul-Eater trap.

She set off at a run toward the fire.

A noise behind her. She ducked. Too late. A hand grabbed her arm and yanked her back.

On the Crag, no trace remained of Tenris the kindly Seal Mage. That mask had been burned away, leaving nothing but ashes and bitterness.

Muttering spells under his breath, the Soul-Eater squatted by the altar rock, painting signs on Torak's chest. His brush was a bundle of seal's whiskers bound to the shinbone of an eagle; his paint was a dark, stinking sludge. Torak guessed it was the blood of the murdered Hunter; that the pale objects set in a ring around him were its teeth.

A scratching at his ankles told him that the boy tokoroth was back, to finish tightening the bindings. Torak kicked out hard, knowing his only hope lay in wriggling free when the time was right.

"Hold still," snapped Tenris. He'd been chewing on a foul-smelling paste that had stained the whites of his eyes yellow, and turned his tongue black. He didn't look like a man anymore.

Out of the corner of his vision, Torak caught a furtive movement.

There—beyond the wall of driftwood the girl tokoroth was building, and soaking in seal oil. *Wolf.*

Torak's heart tightened with dread. Three against one. If Wolf tried to help him, he'd get himself killed.

"*Uff!*" called Torak, warning him back. "*Uff! Uff!!*"

Wolf pricked his ears, but did not retreat. He'd found a gap in the wall where the girl tokoroth hadn't yet piled the driftwood high. But it was right on the edge of the cliff.

Go back! Torak tried to tell him silently. *You can't help me!*

Fortunately, neither Tenris nor the tokoroth had spotted Wolf. All three were staring at Torak. "*What* did you say?" Tenris scowled.

Torak thought quickly. Jerking his head at the ring

of teeth around him, he said, "Those teeth—they're the Hunter's, aren't they? What are they for?"

Tenris regarded him narrowly. "Spells," he said, dipping his brush in the blood. "When you showed me your father's knife, I suspected that you were the one. But I had to make sure."

"And for that a Hunter had to die?"

"What do I care? They can't hurt me." With his twisted claw he touched the amulet at his throat. "A masking charm."

Torak thought of Detlan, clenching his teeth in agony as Bale tended his shattered leg. If he lived, he would be a cripple. And all because Tenris had needed "to make sure."

Wolf was nosing his way through the gap, perilously close to the edge.

Quickly Torak spoke to Tenris. "You said you thought I was 'the one.' What did you mean?"

The ruined face darkened. "The one who destroyed the bear."

Torak tensed. "The bear."

"*I* created it," Tenris said between his teeth. "*I* caught the demon. *I* trapped it in the body of the bear. You destroyed it."

For a moment, Torak forgot about Wolf. "You're lying. Whoever made the bear was crippled. A crippled wanderer."

Tenris put back his head and laughed. Still laughing, he rose to his feet and circled the fire, limping piteously. "Easy, isn't it? Although I confess I did get very bored."

Tenris had created the bear—the bear that killed Fa. . . .

Torak thought of the clearing where he and his father had camped on that final night. Fa's face, laughing at the joke Torak had made. Fa's face as he lay dying . . .

"What's this?" sneered Tenris. "Tears?"

"You killed him," whispered Torak. "You killed Fa. . . ."

At that moment the boy tokoroth touched his ankle. Torak lashed out savagely. *"You killed Fa!"* he screamed, fighting his bonds with all the rage and grief inside him. The rawhide held firm.

Just then, Wolf hurtled out of the mist and leaped at Tenris. The Seal Mage snatched up his harpoon—the tokoroth scuttled like spiders, drawing knives, seizing firebrands and lashing out at the attacker.

"Wolf!" shouted Torak, struggling to push himself off the horn of rock, but held back by the bindings around his ankles. *"Uff! Uff! Uff!"*

Tenris lunged with the harpoon.

Wolf gave a great twisting leap—and the vicious barbs pierced empty fog.

Tenris barked a command, and the girl tokoroth set her firebrand to the driftwood wall. Flames shot up, licking at the sky. The tokoroth lashed out at Wolf with their torches—and he shrank back against the burning wall, snarling, cornered.

Just when Torak thought he was finished, Wolf spun around and scrambled over the last section of driftwood that had yet to catch light—pursued by the tokoroth with their flaming torches. The fire roared higher. The gap closed. The neck of the Crag was cut off by the blaze.

Tenris threw down his harpoon and turned to Torak. "He's gone," he said. "Not even a wolf could get past that now."

"Nor can your tokoroth," said Torak. Both tokoroth were gone, clattering off down the mountain after Wolf.

Tenris shrugged. "I don't need them anymore," he said as he took up the knife that lay on Torak's chest. "I can manage this part on my own."

Torak's heart was pounding. Wolf was gone. The wall of flames cut him off from all hope of rescue. He might be able to work his feet out of the bindings—he might even be able to push his wrists over the horn and roll off the altar—but what then? He was trapped on a cliff top, pitted against a grown man with a knife and a harpoon, who meant to kill him and eat his heart.

But there was one thing he had to find out first.

"Why did you do it?" he said as he stared up into the yellow eyes of the Soul-Eater. "Why did you kill my father?"

Tenris shook his head in wonder. "Ah, you're just like him! Always wanting to know *why*. Why, why, why."

He circled the altar rock, fingers flexing on the knife, mouth twisting as he tasted bitter memories. "He betrayed me," he said. "He was weak. Worthless. And yet he thought that he could—"

"He wasn't worthless," said Torak.

"What do you know?" snarled Tenris.

"He was my father," said Torak.

Tenris stood over him and bared his blackened teeth. "He was my brother."

THIRTY-TWO

Renn craned her neck to see what was happening on the cliff, but the mist was too thick, the overhang too deep. Only when the Soul-Eater moved right to the edge did she glimpse him: dark and sticklike against the flames.

"He's got a knife," she said.

"It's too far up," said the Seal boy beside her. "We'd never get there in time."

"But we can't just—"

"Look at that fire—it's right across the Neck! What are you going to do? Fly?"

Renn shot him a suspicious glance. Despite his

professed change of heart, she still didn't trust him. But as she opened her mouth to protest, a wolf howled.

"What *is* that?" said the Seal boy.

"It's Wolf," said Renn. She cupped her ear to listen. "Oh, this is bad, he's somewhere in the west! *Why?* Why isn't he up there helping Torak? If not even Wolf can reach him . . . " She thought quickly. "You're right," she told the Seal boy. "We can't get up there in time. Fetch my bow."

His jaw dropped. "I won't let you shoot him! Whatever he's done—"

"How else do we save Torak?"

"But he's still our Mage!"

"Bale," said Renn urgently, "I don't want to kill him any more than you do, but we have to do something!"

Just then the Soul-Eater moved away from the edge, and disappeared. With a cry Renn ran backward, desperate to catch sight of him again.

"The overhang's too deep," said Bale. "Quick. The skinboat."

"What?" cried Renn.

Bale seized her wrist and dragged her after him. "You can't see the altar rock from the land—only from the Sea!"

Down they raced toward the water. Bale ducked into a shelter, then came out again, and tossed Renn her quiver and bow. Grabbing his skinboat from a rack, he slid it into the shallows, practically threw her into the prow end, then vaulted in after her and snatched up his paddle. Renn had to grip the sides with both hands as they moved off faster than she would have thought possible.

A wind was getting up: an east wind from the Forest. As Renn turned to face the cliff, the fog blew apart to reveal the Soul-Eater—holding a knife high above his head, like an offering. At his feet lay a figure. It wasn't moving.

"I can see them!" shouted Renn.

With astonishing skill, Bale brought his craft about. Renn lurched and would have fallen overboard if he hadn't taken hold of her jerkin and yanked her back.

Her hands shook as she whipped out an arrow and nocked it to her bow. Despite Bale's best efforts, the skinboat rocked in the swell. She'd never be able to stand, she'd have to shoot from kneeling.

On the cliff, Torak still wasn't moving. A terrible fear seized her that they were too late.

"We're too far out," muttered Bale. "No one could make that shot."

Setting her teeth, Renn forced herself to ignore him—to think only of the target, as Fin-Kedinn had taught her.

Staring hard at the target, she took aim.

🐾 🐾 🐾

The arrow came arching out of the sky, and thudded deep into Tenris's palm. With a howl he fell to his knees, and the knife clattered away across the rock.

Torak seized his chance and wriggled out of the bindings around his ankles, then used his heels to launch himself forward. His arms felt heavy and bloodless, but he managed to hook his wrists over the horn—and rolled off the altar.

On the opposite side, Tenris was still on his knees, clutching his wounded hand. Rising to his feet, he staggered away from the cliff edge—out of range of further arrows.

Torak struggled to stand, and circled out of reach. His shoulders were burning, his wrists throbbing from the bindings. They were on opposite sides of the altar; the edge of the cliff was directly behind him.

With a hiss, Tenris grasped the arrow and wrenched it from his palm. Sweat coursed down his face, scouring rivulets through the ash to reveal the scorched red flesh beneath. "Give up, Torak," he panted. "It's over!"

More wolf howls. *The demons are gone!* called Wolf.

"He's far away," said Tenris, snatching up his harpoon. "He can't help you anymore."

"He's helped enough," said Torak.

Tenris snorted. "You're on your own now, Torak. Your friends can't try another shot at me, or they'd risk hitting you."

Torak did not reply. He needed all his strength just to stay standing.

"Give up, Torak," urged that beautiful, powerful voice. "You've done well, but it's time to pass your power to one who knows how to use it."

Torak glanced over his shoulder. The east wind was strengthening, blowing away the fog. A shaft of silver light was pouring down onto the Sea.

"I'll make it quick," said Tenris. "I promise."

Far below him, Torak saw the restless, shimmering Sea. He felt the wind from the Forest on his face; he thought of Wolf and Renn and Fin-Kedinn, and of all the clans he'd never even met. If he let Tenris take his power—if he let the Soul-Eater become the spirit walker—then none of them would ever be safe.

"You have no choice," murmured the Soul-Eater. "You know that."

Torak squared his shoulders, and met that intense gray gaze.

Too late, Tenris realized what he meant to do—and his eyes widened in disbelief.

"There's always a choice," said Torak, and walked backward off the cliff.

THIRTY-THREE

Down, down he fell—into the splintered Sea—into the golden forest of kelp—down into darkness.

Down he sank, kicking feebly at the water with what remained of his strength. It wasn't enough. His wrists were bound so tight that he couldn't slip free; his sodden leggings were dragging him down. He would never reach the surface.

But he had known that when he stepped off the cliff. He had known that this time there would be no friendly guardian; no Wolf leaping in to save him. This time there was only Torak and the hungry Sea. This time he was going to die.

He turned his face for a last look at the light—and saw, impossibly far above, a figure darkening the sun. It was swimming toward him, swimming faster than an eel. Hope kindled. Was it Wolf? Renn? Bale?

Tenris seized him by the hair and yanked him upward.

Torak struggled and kicked, but the Soul-Eater was too strong. With both hands, Torak grabbed the kelp around him—jerking Tenris backward in a flurry of silver bubbles. Furiously they fought till their lungs were bursting, till the water flooded scarlet with blood from the Soul-Eater's wound.

The Seal Mage wrenched Torak's hands free of the kelp, and they rose again—locked together like vipers as they spiraled up toward the light.

Together they burst from the Sea.

"So you'd rather kill yourself, would you?" gasped Tenris. "How noble! But I won't give you the chance!" Still gripping Torak by the hair, he struck out for the shore, swimming one armed, but powering through the water with swift, sure strokes.

Torak tried to bite his hand—but Tenris lashed out with his free arm, landing him a savage blow on the temple.

Stunned, Torak went under. As he surfaced, he heard a deafening *kwshsh!*—and saw an enormous black fin slicing toward them.

Terror turned his limbs to water.

Tenris hadn't seen the Hunter; he was bent on reaching the shore. Torak had an instant in which to act. . . .

With one final burst of strength, he twisted around and lunged at the Soul-Eater, ripping the masking charm from his throat.

Tenris grunted in surprise, and lost his grip on Torak. Torak kicked with all his might, and swam out of reach.

Tenris turned to catch him—and saw the Hunter. His hand flew to his throat to grasp the masking charm, and clawed naked skin. He saw the charm in Torak's hand—he strained to grab it. Torak dodged and hurled the masking charm across the waves. Tenris gave a shout of rage and plunged after it—but it had sunk.

Now they were both at the mercy of the Hunter, with no help in sight.

Torak saw Notched Fin bearing down upon them, shooting spray high into the air. At the edge of his vision he glimpsed a skinboat racing toward them—but it would never reach them in time. . . .

And now Sea, sky, skinboat—were blotted out by the Hunter. Through the green water Torak saw the great blunt head looming closer . . .

At the last moment the Hunter swerved, showering him with spray as it made for Tenris.

A sudden stillness came over the Soul-Eater's ruined features as he watched his doom slicing toward him.

In the final heartbeat he turned his head and met Torak's eyes. "Ask Fin-Kedinn about your father!" he shouted. "Make him tell you the truth—"

Then he was lost in a flurry of silver water.

Torak heard one terrible scream, abruptly cut off— as the great jaws dragged the Soul-Eater down into the deep.

THIRTY-FOUR

The fire on the Crag was burning low, and gray smoke was rising into the sky as the skinboat reached the shore.

Bale hoisted his craft on his head and went to put it on the rack, leaving Renn and Torak in the shallows. Neither spoke as they trudged up the beach to the nearest shelter.

Renn wiped the spray off her bow and hung it from a rafter, then went inside to rummage for food.

Torak took driftwood from a pile and started waking up a fire. He felt shaky and cold, but at least the Sea had washed the markings from his chest. Inside his head, however, the marks would not so easily be washed away.

He wanted to tell Renn everything: about what had happened on the Crag; about being a spirit walker. But it was still too raw. Instead he said, "I'm sorry. I really thought you were sick. You looked sick."

Renn set a bowl on the ground, and sat down. "Well," she said, "I thought you were dead. Seems we were both wrong." She pushed the bowl toward him. "I found some whale meat. No juniper berries, I'm afraid, but it tastes all right without."

Both of them looked at the bowl, but neither made a move to eat.

Then Torak said, "Renn. There is no cure. What he said about the selik root. He made it up."

Renn clasped her arms about her knees and frowned.

"Did you hear what I said?" said Torak. *"There is no cure."*

Suddenly Renn stopped frowning and straightened up. She stared at Torak, then at the meat. "The juniper berries," she said.

"What?" said Torak.

"When I was in the cave. Bale gave me some food, and Wolf leaped at me, and knocked it over. I thought he'd gone mad. But he was—Torak, he was *saving* me! Warning me off the juniper berries!"

She sprang to her feet and started to pace. "That's how the Seal Mage caused the sickness! He sent the tokoroth to poison the juniper berries! And then the juniper berries went into the salmon cakes, and people got sick." She stopped. "That's why Wolf stopped me eating the food, because it was poisoned. And—that's why I *didn't* get sick before, even though I was eating salmon cakes, because I'd stolen Saeunn's, which were left over from last summer—"

"—and that's why I didn't get sick either," put in Torak. "Because I didn't take any with me."

They stared at each other.

"So if everyone gets rid of their juniper berries," said Renn, "*and* their salmon cakes—"

"Maybe they'll get better—"

"Maybe we won't *need* a cure."

This was the answer. Torak could feel it. It had the kind of elegance that would have appealed to Tenris.

How he must have laughed as he watched them striving to find a cure that didn't exist! How clever he must have felt! How powerful.

And yet even now, Torak couldn't hate him. Tenris had been his bone kin. Torak had *liked* him. He'd wanted Tenris to like him back.

Bowing his head to his knees, he tried to shut out the pain. But that handsome, ruined face was still before him; that voice still rang in his ears. *Ask Fin-Kedinn about your father! Make him tell you the truth!*

What truth? What had he meant?

At that moment, Bale ran up. "Come quickly!" he panted.

He led them to the south end of the bay and across the stream to the foot of the waterfall.

The tokoroth lay on the rocks where they had fallen. Spray misted their grimy faces and their broken stick-limbs.

Craning his neck, Torak gazed at the mountainside, and wondered what had made them scramble up there. Then he remembered Wolf's howls. *The demons are gone!*

"What *are* they?" whispered Bale.

"Tokoroth," said Renn in a low voice.

Bale gasped. "I thought those were only in stories. I thought—"

The girl tokoroth moaned, and a spasm convulsed her scrawny frame.

"She's still alive," said Torak. He felt a twinge of pity. They looked so young. No more than eight or nine summers.

"They're killers," Bale said grimly. Drawing his knife, he moved forward.

Wolf appeared from behind a boulder, warning him back with a growl.

Bale froze. "What . . ."

Torak went down on one knee, and Wolf trotted over to him, snuffle-grunting and nuzzling his cheek. Torak glanced at Renn. "He says he chased the demons away."

"Where?" said Renn. "Where did they go?"

Torak met Wolf's eyes for a moment, then shook his head. "I'm not going to ask. They're gone. Let that be enough."

Bale was staring at him in amazement. "You can talk to it?"

"Him," said Torak. "Wolf is a him."

"So that's a wolf," said Bale. Placing one hand on his heart, he bowed. "Beautiful."

Again the tokoroth stirred.

Renn ran to kneel beside them. Her face became grave. "Not long now," she said. Then to Torak, "Your medicine horn. Do you have any earthblood?"

Torak handed it to her; but Bale looked troubled. "What are you doing?"

"Death Marks," said Renn.

"They don't deserve them!" cried Bale.

Renn turned on him. "They were children once! Their souls are still in there, deep inside! They'll need help to get free—"

"They're killers," said Bale, unmoved.

"Let her do it," said Torak. "She knows about things like this."

As they watched, Renn made the red ochre into a paste with water, then daubed the Death Marks on both tokoroth: forehead, heart, heels.

Wolf came to sit beside her, whining softly and sweeping the grass with his tail. There was a light in his golden eyes. Torak wondered what he could see.

Renn's face became distant, and she began to murmur under her breath. Torak felt a flicker of unease. He guessed she was summoning the child souls from deep within; calling them out from their hiding place.

Suddenly the boy tokoroth clenched his fists. The girl tokoroth twitched, then opened her eyes.

A tear rolled down Renn's cheek. "Go in peace," she whispered. "You're free now. Free . . ."

The boy tokoroth shuddered, then lay still. The girl gave a long, rattling sigh that ended in—silence.

A breeze stirred the suncups. Wolf turned his head, as if to follow the passing of something swift.

"They're gone," said Renn.

🐾 🐾 🐾

Next day the Seals returned from the Cormorants' island, and Torak, Renn and Bale spent a long time talking with the Clan Leader.

Surprisingly, Islinn was not as crushed by the news of his Mage's death as they had expected. In fact, the knowledge that he must now take charge seemed to imbue him with fresh vigor. He looked visibly younger as he dispatched his fleetest messengers to the Forest to warn the clans against the poison, and others to fetch Asrif and Detlan home. The bodies of the tokoroth were placed in a skinboat, taken out of sight of land, and given to the Sea Mother.

When all was done, Islinn ordered everyone out of his shelter, except for Torak. "I'm sending Bale with you tomorrow," he said. "He will make sure that you get back safely."

"Thank you, Leader," Torak said tonelessly.

The Leader studied him. "You are wrong to blame yourself. He tricked me too. And I have lived a good many more summers than you."

Torak did not reply.

"You grieve for him," stated the old man.

Torak was surprised that he should have perceived that. "He was kind to me," he said. "I mean—before the end. Was it all a lie?"

The Seal Clan Leader regarded him with eyes that had witnessed every kind of wickedness and folly. "I doubt if even he knew the answer to that." He paused. "Go back to the Forest, Torak. It's where you belong. But if you ever need a home, you have one here."

Torak put his fists over his heart to show his thanks, but he didn't think he would ever take up Islinn's offer. For him this island was too full of ghosts.

They left the following morning. Wolf went in Torak's skinboat, and Renn in Bale's. It was a brilliantly sunny day, with a brisk west wind to speed them on their way. As they left the Bay of Seals, Torak looked back one last time. Smoke rose above the humped shelters, and children splashed in the shallows. Rowan trees and birches lapped the feet of the mountains, where white seabirds wheeled.

He knew that he didn't belong in this precarious, rocky world that was forever at the mercy of the Sea. But in its way it was rich and beautiful, and at last he understood why Bale loved it so much.

Then his gaze traveled higher, and he saw the Crag, and his spirits plunged. He hadn't been able to bring himself to return. Bale had gone up alone, and found Fa's knife, and brought it to him without a word.

They made good speed, with nothing but puffins and sea-eagles for company. Once in the distance,

Torak thought he saw a tall, notched fin that followed them for a while. When he blinked, it was gone.

It was late in the day when Wolf gave a low bark, then stood up in the prow with his ears forward, wagging his tail. Soon afterward, Bale shouted something that Torak didn't catch, and Renn grinned and raised high her bow.

Then Torak turned and saw the Forest rising above the waves.

It was night by the time they reached the shore, although the huge amber sun still hung low over the Sea.

Swiftly Torak changed into his old buckskin jerkin and leggings, and bundled up his seal-hide clothes. It felt good to have his clan-creature skin back, as well as his pack and bow and sleeping-sack. But as he helped Bale stow the borrowed clothes in his skinboat, he wondered when—or if—he would see the Seal boy again.

Bale had decided to head off at once. He was silent as they went down to the shallows, and Torak could see that he was thinking about the last time he and his friends had been on this beach, and the rough handling they'd meted out to the stranger from the Forest.

Torak said, "I'll see you again, Bale. Someday I'll show you the Forest."

Bale glanced at the tall pines fringing the beach. "A few days ago, I wouldn't have thought that possible. But I suppose—I never thought I'd see a wolf in a skinboat. So—"

"—so why not a Seal in a forest?" said Torak with a smile.

Bale grinned. "Why not indeed, kinsman?" Then with a nod to Renn and Wolf, he was back in his skinboat and heading off into the west, his fair hair flying behind him, and the Sea around him turning to gold in the sun.

That night, Torak and Renn built a real Forest shelter of living birch saplings in a glade filled with green ferns and the deep pink flowers of willowherb. They had a real Forest meal of stewed goosefoot leaves and baked hawkbit roots, with some early raspberries that Torak found by the bog where he'd decoyed Detlan and Asrif. "And not a juniper berry in sight," said Renn with a sigh of satisfaction.

Afterward they sat by the fire, smelling the tang of pine smoke and listening to the full-throated warbling of the Forest birds. For the first time in days, they were in half darkness beneath whispering trees. They could even see a few pale stars between the branches.

Wolf trotted off on one of his nightly hunts, and Renn gave a huge yawn. "Do you realize," she said, "it'll soon be the Cloudberry Moon? I like cloudberries."

Torak did not reply. He couldn't put it off any longer. Ever since Bale had left, he'd been working up the courage to tell Renn about who—what—he was.

"Renn," he said, frowning at the fire. "There's something I've got to tell you."

"What," said Renn, rolling out her sleeping-sack.

He took a breath. "When we were at the Eagle Heights, the Seal Mage told me something. Something about—me."

Renn stopped what she was doing. "You're a spirit walker," she said quietly.

He stared at her. "How long have you known?"

"Since he told you." She picked at a loose stitch on her leggings. "That night after we had the fight, I was worried, so I followed you. I heard everything."

He thought about that. Then he said, "Do you mind?"

"What do you mean?"

"About—what I am."

To his surprise, she grinned. "Torak, you're a *who*, not a *what*! You're still a person."

There was silence for a while. Then Renn said, "When I found out, I wasn't really that surprised. I've always known you were different."

Torak tried to smile, but couldn't manage it.

"Don't be sad," she said. "After all, maybe it's why you can talk to Wolf."

"What do you mean?"

"Well it's always bothered me," she said, renewing her attack on the stitching. "You were just a baby when your father put you in the wolf den; much too small to learn person talk, let alone wolf talk. So how come you did?" She put her head on one side. "Maybe your souls slipped into one of the wolves, or something. Don't you think?"

Torak chewed his lower lip. "I never thought of that."

Wolf came back from his hunt, his muzzle tinged with red. He wiped it off on the ferns, and sniffed the fire, then padded over to Torak and nosed his chin.

"Do you think he knows?" said Renn.

"About me?" said Torak, scratching behind Wolf's ears. "How could he? And I couldn't begin to say it in wolf talk."

Renn wriggled into her sleeping-sack and curled up. "But he's still your friend," she said.

Torak nodded. Somehow that didn't make him feel any less cut off.

Again Renn yawned. "Get some sleep, Torak."

Torak got into his sleeping-sack, and lay on his back. He was tired, but he didn't think he would sleep.

Wolf slumped against him with a *humph*, and was

soon twitching in his dreams.

Torak lay wide-eyed, staring at the fire.

Much later, Renn said, "Torak? Are you awake?"

"Yes," he said.

"At the end, when you were both in the water, the Seal Mage shouted something. What was it?"

Torak had been hoping she wouldn't ask. "I can't tell you," he said. "At least, not yet. First I've got to talk to Fin-Kedinn."

THIRTY-FIVE

"Tell me the truth," Torak said to Fin-Kedinn seven days later.

It had taken him and Renn four days to reach the Raven camp, making their way through a Forest where the sickness was slowly ebbing, and the smell of burning juniper berries hung heavy in the air. Islinn's messengers had done their work swiftly. It was made easier by the fact that Fin-Kedinn had persuaded the Open Forest Clans to stay together, and help one another through the sickness. Many of the afflicted were now recovering. But the Ravens had lost five of their people.

For two days after they rejoined the clan, Torak couldn't get Fin-Kedinn alone. The Raven Leader was busy tending his clan, and making sure that every last hunting party in the Forest had been warned about the juniper berries.

But on the seventh day, things began to return to normal. Some of the Ravens went hunting, while others stayed by the river to spear trout. Renn sat with Saeunn, explaining how she'd freed the hidden souls of the tokoroth. Wolf, who had no liking for dogs, disappeared into the Forest.

Torak found the Raven Leader preparing lime bark on the banks of a stream that fed into the Widewater. It was a hot day, but the trees cast a cool green shade. The sweetness of late summer blossom filled the air, and the branches hummed with bees.

"So you want the truth," said Fin-Kedinn, testing the edge of his axe with his thumb. "About what?"

"Everything," said Torak, seething with a frustration that had been building for days. "Why didn't you *tell* me?"

With one stroke Fin-Kedinn cut a sucker from the base of a lime tree, and started peeling off the bark. "What should I have told you?" he said.

"That I'm a spirit walker! That the Seal Mage was my father's brother! That the sickness was my fault!"

Fin-Kedinn stiffened. "Don't ever say that."

"He sent the sickness because of *me*," said Torak. "Because of *me* he killed Oslak and the others. It's my fault!"

"No!" The blue eyes blazed. "You did nothing wrong! You cannot be blamed for the evil that man did. He was the one, Torak. Remember that."

For a moment they faced each other, and the air crackled between them. Then the Raven Leader tossed the bark on a pile at his feet. "And you're wrong. I did not know that you're a spirit walker, not till Renn told me last night. None of us knew."

Torak frowned. "But—I thought Fa must have told Saeunn. When I was little, at the clan meet by the Sea."

Fin-Kedinn shook his head. "He told her he'd put you in a wolf den when you were a baby; and that you might someday be the one to vanquish the Soul-Eaters. He didn't say why."

"Why would he keep that from her?"

"Who knows? He'd been a hunted man for a long time. He'd grown wary."

Wary toward his own son, too, thought Torak. That was the worst of it: that sometimes he was angry with Fa. For not telling him . . .

"He did what he thought was best," said Fin-Kedinn. "He didn't want your boyhood darkened by destiny."

Torak threw himself down on the bank and began pulling up grass. "You knew them both, didn't you? My father and his brother."

Fin-Kedinn did not reply.

"Tell me about them. *Please.*"

The Raven Leader stroked his beard and sighed. "I first met them twenty-eight summers ago," he said. "I was eleven, your father was nine. Wolf Clan, like his father. His brother—who was my age—was Seal Clan, like their mother. We spent five moons together, fostered with the Wolf Clan."

"With the Wolf Clan?" Torak said, surprised. "But I've never even seen them, so how—"

"They weren't always as elusive as they are now. Times change. People grow mistrustful." With a length of withe he tied the pile of bark into a bundle. "The three of us became friends," he went on. "I lived for hunting; but with the others it was always Magecraft. Your father was eager to learn the ways of trees, hunters, prey. His brother . . . " He gave the knot a sharp tug. "His brother wanted only to control. To dominate."

Hoisting the bundle on his shoulder, he stepped down into the stream and set it to soak beneath a stone. "Ten winters came and went, and we stayed good friends. The eleventh winter changed all that." Water swirled around his calves as he bent to retrieve another bundle which had been soaking for days. "Your father was named the Wolf Mage," he said, tossing it on the bank. "His brother—although the older and some said the more skilled—was not named the Seal Mage." He shook his head. "It was a bitter blow. None of us knew how bitter until it was too late. He left his clan, and wandered alone."

"Where did he go?" asked Torak.

Sadness shadowed Fin-Kedinn's face. "I don't know. I never saw him again. But six summers later, I heard from your father that his brother had reappeared. Joined a group of Mages called the Healers."

"But—he wasn't a Mage," said Torak.

Fin-Kedinn's mouth curled. "He was persuasive. You of all people should know that." Climbing back onto the bank, he knelt by the bundle. "I told you once how the Healers became the Soul-Eaters. How they brought terror to the Forest." He paused. "Then came the great fire that broke them. Some were terribly wounded. All were scattered, in hiding."

"He was burned," murmured Torak. "On his face and down his side."

"What none of us knew," said Fin-Kedinn, "was that he'd found his way back to his clan. All we knew was that the Seals had become—separate. Ceased their dealings with the Open Forest, traded only with the Sea clans. And they had a new Mage."

Torak tossed the grass into the stream, and watched it sucked under by the current. He thought of Tenris, dragged down into the deep. He said, "He was after me because I'm a spirit walker. Because he wanted that power." He stared into the water. "The other Soul-Eaters will want it too."

Fin-Kedinn hesitated. "They may not know about you yet. Maybe the Seal Mage acted alone."

"And maybe he didn't," said Torak. "Maybe he had help."

Suddenly the Forest seemed to close in around him. The buzzing of the bees became strangely menacing. In his mind, Torak saw again the yellow eyes of Tenris the Seal Mage. He thought of the other Soul-Eaters—the faceless ones whose names he didn't know, but who were out there somewhere. Waiting.

He said, "They'll find out what I can do. They'll come after me."

The Raven Leader nodded. "You could make them more powerful than they ever dreamed. Or you could destroy them utterly."

Torak met his eyes. "Is that why you've never offered to foster me? Because I'm dangerous?"

Something flickered in the blue gaze. "I must look

to the safety of the clan, Torak. You could help us defeat them. Or you could be our ruin."

"But I would never harm the Ravens!" cried Torak, leaping to his feet.

"You don't know that!" Fin-Kedinn said fiercely. "You don't know what you will become. None of us does!"

"But—"

"Evil exists in us all, Torak. Some fight it. Some feed it. That's how it's always been."

With a cry, Torak turned away.

Fin-Kedinn made no move to comfort him. Instead he cut open the bundle, chose a strip of bark, and began peeling off the bast.

Torak felt giddy and frightened. He felt as if he stood at the edge of a cliff, about to jump off into the unknown.

Mustering his courage, he asked the question that had been eating away at him ever since Tenris had met his end. "Last winter, when you told me about the Soul-Eaters, you said there were seven. But you only described five."

The Raven Leader's strong hands stilled.

"The Seal Mage was the sixth," said Torak. "I need to know about the seventh." His fists clenched. "My father had a scar on his chest. Here." He touched his breastbone. "That made it hard when I—when I put the Death Marks on him." He tried to swallow. "Something the Seal Mage said made me think that—the seventh Soul-Eater . . ."

Fin-Kedinn rubbed a hand over his face. Then he laid the lime bast in the grass.

"My father," said Torak. "It was my father."

A gust of wind shivered the branches, hazing the air with drifting sweetness. The trees were trying to soften the blow. "No," said Torak, sinking to his knees. *"No."*

He read his answer in the Raven Leader's eyes.

After a while, Fin-Kedinn came and sat beside him. "Do you remember," he said, "when I told you that in the beginning they were not evil? Your father believed that. That's why he joined them. To heal the sick, to chase away demons." His gaze became distant and full of pain. "Your mother never believed it. She knew. But by the time he saw the truth, it was too late." He spread his hands. "He tried to leave. They wouldn't let him."

"Is that why they killed him?" said Torak.

Slowly the Raven Leader nodded.

Torak sat with his head bowed to his knees, shaken by dry, wrenching sobs. Fin-Kedinn sat beside him: not touching, not speaking, but steadying by his presence alone.

At last the Raven Leader rose to his feet. "I'm going back to camp now. You stay here. Peel the rest of this bundle. Wash the bast in the stream. Hang it up to dry."

Torak nodded, too numb to speak.

"Tomorrow," said Fin-Kedinn, "I'll teach you how to make rope."

Torak had run till he could run no farther, but his thoughts would not be stilled. Fa had been a Soul-Eater. Fa, his own Fa . . .

There was a tightness in his chest that made it hard to breathe. A storm of rage and grief and fear.

He came to a halt by a boisterous stream that tumbled over big, mossy boulders. A squirrel shot up a sycamore tree. An otter stopped eating a trout and fled into the ferns.

Torak knelt to drink, and his name-soul stared back at him. Torak of the Wolf Clan. Torak the spirit walker.

With a cry he snatched a clump of yellow suncups and tore them to pieces. He didn't belong with the Ravens. He didn't belong anywhere. . . .

After a while, the otter came back for its half-eaten trout and settled down to finish its meal. In the sycamore, the squirrel started nibbling bark to get at the sweet, sticky tree-blood.

Torak sat with his back against the trunk, watching them—and some of his tumult eased. They didn't care that his father had been a Soul-Eater. They didn't care that he was a spirit walker. As long as he left them in peace, they were content for him to remain.

He placed his palm on the tree's rough bark, and felt its power coursing through him. The power of the Forest.

Deep within him, he felt a stirring of resolve. *This* was where he belonged: here in the Forest. Through all the bad things that had happened, the Forest had given him strength. Strength to defeat the bear. Strength to survive Tenris and the Sea Mother. Strength to face his destiny. And maybe Fa's spirit—wherever it was— knew that, and was proud.

Above him the sycamore stirred in the breeze: spreading wide its arms, watching over him. Torak raised his head and stared at the glowing green leaves. With the help of the Forest, he would face his destiny. He would do whatever lay in his power to vanquish the Soul-Eaters.

"I will do this," he said out loud. "I *will* do this."

Wolf found his pack-brother sitting by the little Fast Wet, tearing up shiny gray petals in his forepaws.

Wolf splashed into the wet to cool his pads, then ate some of the flowers to be companionable. He wagged his tail. Tall Tailless did not smile back. Wolf smelled his sadness and was puzzled.

Wolf was feeling *very* happy. His confusion was

gone. He knew what he was for. When he'd been a cub, he'd helped Tall Tailless fight the demon bear. Then on the island of the fish-birds, he'd chased the demons out of the half-grown taillesses. *This* was what he was for: to help Tall Tailless fight demons.

It meant never returning to his pack on the Mountain, but Wolf didn't mind too much, because he would be with his pack-brother. If only Tall Tailless wasn't so sad.

To make him feel better, Wolf leaned against him, and rubbed his scent into his pelt.

Tall Tailless turned to him and said, *Do you know what I am?*

Wolf was surprised. *My pack-brother.*

But do you know what creature I am? What I can do?

Yes, I know, Wolf replied a little impatiently. He'd always known.

To his surprise, Tall Tailless stared at him hard—which was scarcely polite. Then he began to smile. *You know?* he said.

Wolf wagged his tail.

He decided they'd had enough talk, and went down on his forepaws, barking and asking Tall Tailless to play. When his pack-brother still didn't move, Wolf pounced.

His pack-brother gave a startled yowl and toppled backward onto the bank. Wolf nose-nudged him in the flanks. His pack-brother grabbed Wolf's scruff and play-bit him on the ear.

Soon they were rolling about in the grass, and Tall Tailless was making the odd, breathless yip-and-yowl that was his way of laughing.

SPIRIT WALKER

is the second book in the

CHRONICLES OF ANCIENT DARKNESS

series, which tells the story of Torak's adventures in the Forest and beyond, and of his quest to vanquish the Soul-Eaters. *Wolf Brother* is the first book. The third book, *Soul Eater*, will be published in 2007.

Find out more about
Chronicles of Ancient Darkness
at www.chroniclesofancientdarkness.com.

Visit Michelle Paver's website at
www.michellepaver.com and meet other
readers of *Spirit Walker* at the official
worldwide fan site, www.torak.info.

AUTHOR'S NOTE

Torak's world is the world of six thousand years ago: a time after the Ice Age and before farming, when the whole of northwest Europe was covered by Forest.

The people in Torak's time looked just like you or me, but their way of life was very different. They didn't have writing, metals or the wheel, but they didn't need them. They were superb survivors. They knew all about the animals, trees, plants and rocks of the Forest. When they wanted something, they knew where to find it, or how to make it.

They lived in small clans, and many of them moved around a lot—some staying in camp for only a few days, like Torak of the Wolf Clan; others staying for a whole moon or a season, like the Raven and Boar Clans; while others stayed put all year round, like the Seal Clan. And in case you're wondering, the Ravens and the Boars have moved a bit since the events in *Wolf Brother*, as you'll see from the slightly amended map.

When I was researching *Spirit Walker*, I spent time in the Lofoten Islands of northwest Norway, and also in Greenland. I studied the traditional ways of life of the Sami and Inuit peoples, and learned about their ways of building boats, hunting seals and making clothes.

The inspiration for the Crag came from a visit to the ancient rock carvings of the Dyreberget at Leiknes in northwest Norway.

The inspiration for the Hunters came from swimming with

wild killer whales in Tysfjord, north Norway. I couldn't have written about Torak's experiences in the water without having been there, too; and like Torak, I found that swimming in the sea with killer whales altered forever my perception of these amazing creatures.

I want to thank the people at the Polaria in Trømsø, Norway, for helping me understand what it's like to be a seal; the people of western Greenland for their hospitality, openness and good humor; the UK Wolf Conservation Trust for some unforgettable times with some wonderful wolves; the people of Tysfjord for helping me get close to killer whales and white-tailed eagles; and Mr. Derrick Coyle, the Yeoman Raven Master of the Tower of London, for sharing his extensive knowledge of some very special ravens. Lastly, as always, I want to thank my agent, Peter Cox, and my editor, Fiona Kennedy, for their unfailing enthusiasm and support.

MICHELLE PAVER
LONDON, 2005